ALSO BY BRANDI BRADLEY

Mothers of the Missing Mermaid

PRETTY GIRLS GET AWAY WITH MURDER

BRANDI BRADLEY

RUMOR MILL PRESS, LLC. rumormillpress.com

First published in the United States of America

by Rumor Mill Press, LLC, 2023

Book cover design by Greg Stark

ISBN: 979-8-9872612-2-4

eBook ISBN: 979-8-9872612-3-1

brandibradley.com

PRETTY GIRLS GET AWAY WITH MURDER

CHAPTER 1

THE DAY AFTER THE MURDER

A trio of uniformed police officers gathered around one of the remaining desktop computers in the bullpen of the Pleasant Springs Police Department.

One of them held a tiny basketball in his clasped hands — the type that insurance companies used to toss into the crowds at the high school home games. The officer who sat at the desk ran through the grainy black and white security footage of a house in Silver Maple Estates.

The camera was fish-eyed so as to make sure it captured all the angles. The officer clicked the right direction arrow on the bottom of the screen and quickly jetted through the inactivity. The prime vantage of the camera was a frosty lawn across the street: a small, brick and stone, ranch-style home. The driveway led around to the side of the residence.

The clock in the bottom corner of the video ticks away the hours in military time. The sun dims. At 1715 a black Chevy Tahoe pulls into the drive. The garage door raises and a man exits the vehicle. He's medium height, a little over 200 lbs., brown hair, mid-20s. A motion-activated light flickers from inside the garage, where he soon disappears.

The Tahoe backs out of the drive and the garage door closes.

"What's the mileage on those?" one of the officers asked.

"The Tahoe? About 18 in town."

"Can it haul?"

"It's alright. My wife has one."

Hours tick by on the recording. The house remains still. Lights flicker on and off. No movements outside of the house.

Around 0200 hours, a trio of young men enter the frame. They sway as if inebriated. One wears a ballcap with ΘΔN stitched onto the crown. The others wear sweatshirts over button-up shirts and trousers, possibly Vintage Vines or knock-offs. They carry a golf umbrella, warding off the sleet that had come on that night. The one with the hat pauses long enough to relieve himself on the lawn of the owners of the camera.

"Are those the boys y'all picked up?"

"Not them. We picked up a whole different crew that stripped down to their underwear at Hardee's."

The kid zips up and the boys walk out of frame. A crowd of youths meander down the street. Girls huddle under umbrellas in pairs or packs, staggering in their heels or chunky boots. Most of the party-goers drop or toss bottles onto the lawns.

"That whole neighborhood's going to be happy when the Nu house moves over to the College Greek Suites."

The clock ticked by. The street now empty. The light changes indicating the sun rising. Cars, trucks, and SUVs drive past the camera, including from the home where the camera had been perched. The owner of the camera backs out of the driveway and pulls away. A woman enters the frame in pajamas and a heavy overcoat. She removes the bottles and cans from the yard, dropping the cans in the garbage can and hauling it to the edge of her drive.

The clock ticks on.

A man enters the frame walking a golden retriever. The garage door they were watching remains closed.

At 0930, the Chevy Tahoe returns. Again, it pauses, but this time the garage door doesn't lift. Eventually, a young woman climbs from the car. Her winter wrap drags along the ground as she exits the SUV. She march to the garage and lifts it open.

"There she is…" Detective Lindy D'Arnaud walks closer to the desk, guiding one of the other officers out of the way so she can peer closer at the screen. He circles her and stands shoulder to shoulder with another uniformed officer out of the way.

Two minutes tick by on the clock.

The woman on the camera bolts back out of the door, something dark smeared on her blouse, the wrap flying behind her like wings. She drops to her knees on the lawn. Her head lifts in a terrified, soundless scream. She falls forward on her hands and knees. The woman who they'd seen cleaning the yard runs over, crouching by the woman.

The officer paused the playback.

"Did you see anyone come in or leave?" Lindy asked the group of officers.

One responded, "Could they have been waiting inside to ambush him?"

Another officer countered, "When did they leave?"

"And she didn't follow him in when she dropped him off?"

"Nope," one checked the file on the desk. "TOD is right around 10 pm."

The officer rewound the footage to 2200 hours. Again they watched the youths crowd the streets and the cars lurch past the camera. The crowd of party-goers march down the street in clusters or pairs. The officer squinted at the video of the house, past the rabble, and paused it. He clicked it back fifteen seconds then played it again. Clicked it back fifteen seconds and played.

"You see that?" Lindy pointed at the corner of the garage.

The officer at the desk clicked fifteen seconds back again and paused it. "What's that, you think?"

"I don't know. Maybe someone was cutting through the backyard?"

On the screen where the officer paused, he pointed at a dark blotch in the corner that could have been a shadow.

CHAPTER 2
THE MORNING AFTER THE MURDER

Lindy took a shortcut through the Walmart parking lot to avoid the light on 12th Street. She rounded the garden center and shot out the back parking lot, passing the eighteen-wheelers that dropped off deliveries that morning.

It was a gray, crisp morning. Last night they'd gotten a layer of ice, delaying the opening of schools and government buildings. Ahead she could see a salt truck coming in her direction. She waved as it passed.

She'd forgotten her gloves when she left the house that morning. Gripping the steering wheel of her Crown Victoria, her hands looked purple and shriveled. She rubbed her right hand against her black trousers and grabbed the small tube of lotion from the cup holder. She steered with her knee and applied the lotion to her hands.

She passed the ΘΔN fraternity house when she turned into Silver Maple Estates, a newly developed subdivision. The esteemed members of the board of regents, at Southwest Kentucky University had promised the homeowners association of Silver Maple Estates that the ΘΔN house would be relocated to an on-campus residential suite before all the units were sold. They were right about that part. The development had only sold half of its units before the Great Recession stalled the project. Development ended, leaving many concrete slabs in their place. The ΘΔΝ on-campus residential suite awaited its new tenants, but the Alumni association of the ΘΔΝ national office dug in their heels and stalled the relocation with negotiations and litigation in an attempt to get the house listed on the historical registry. After years of litigation, the fraternity lost, and the boys were expected to vacate the house and relocate to the Greek Suites before the beginning of the spring semester in a month.

The lawn of the fraternity house was trashed. Cans, kegs, bottles, clothes, someone even hauled a toilet onto the lawn and smashed it. Everything in the yard was coated in a thin layer of ice. "Goddamned animals," Lindy muttered as she drove past.

Lindy could see her partner's SUV parked behind the cruisers in front of the house. CSI was also on the scene. The uniformed officer strung police tape around the perimeter. She saw a pair of techs entering the domicile wearing matching white jumpsuits. Uniformed cops interviewed neighbors standing outside in pajama pants and coats. Lindy parked behind one of the cruisers. She zipped her keys in the pocket of her fleece jacket and stepped onto the scene.

She spotted Boggs. He was crouched on the lawn speaking with a young woman resting in the grass, wrapped in a blanket. The young woman stared off into the middle distance, droopy-eyed and dazed. The grass crunched under Lindy's boots when she walked across it. Boggs stood when Lindy approached and met her at the sidewalk.

"Morning."

"Is she the one who discovered the body?"

"Yeah." Boggs folded his notebook and slid it into the

pocket of his heavy hunting jacket. He wore a black toboggan hat and nice thick gloves. "I was about to have someone drive her to the station. She said that she entered the premises to wake the victim for work and discovered him in the shower, covered in blood."

"Is she the girlfriend?"

He shook his head. "Said they're just good friends."

Lindy made a disbelieving noise. "Right. What's her name?"

"Jenna."

The woman's body heat had melted the icy grass into a circular perimeter around her. Her microfiber tunic looked dry, including the splotch of dried blood across the front. Her black cotton leggings were soaked from the moisture on the ground. Her fake leather boots bunched around the ankles, scuffed on the back of the right heel from excessive driving. She looked professional but she was not stylish. Lindy speculated that Jenna was a sales associate. The blanket draped around Jenna wasn't a department-issued blanket, but a black wrap with a white accent stripe woven into the material. It was the same one Lindy's sister-in-law wore to Thanksgiving a few weeks ago. On Jenna's, the white stripe was now crusted with dried blood.

They would need to take her clothes for evidence. Survivors of violent crimes endure multiple unspoken traumas.

The sun was starting to break through the overcast sky. The frozen grass glimmered and reflected glares of light into Lindy's eyes. She felt her pocket for her sunglasses but came up empty. She squinted. "Hey, Jenna. I'm Detective Lindy D'Arnaud. Detective Boggs is my partner. We should get you some dry clothes."

Jenna shook her head.

"Okay. Well, if it's okay with you, we're going to take you to the station. You can warm up there and we can talk some more. Would that be okay?"

"I need to call my boyfriend."

"We can do that. We'll tell him to bring you some dry clothes."

"What about my truck? I have the Tahoe–," she pointed over her shoulder at the black SUV in the drive.

"We can have it brought to you."

When Jenna stood, Lindy realized how tall she was. Even slouched, she was an inch taller than Lindy, who was average height for a woman in the academy. Lindy's grandma would have called Jenna "stout."

Lindy offered, "Here, lean on me, girl," but Jenna refused.

Instead, she wrapped herself tighter in the wrap. "Where's my purse?"

"Someone will bring that, too." Lindy handed Jenna over to a pair of uniformed officers and instructed them to make Jenna comfortable at the station. She watched as Jenna climbed into a department SUV.

Boggs said, "Probably the worst day of that girl's life."

Together Lindy and Boggs walked up the driveway. The house was like all the others in the subdivision. The off-white aluminum siding had a brick entryway that most likely no one used. Through a garage window, Lindy could see Jenna's truck was parked behind the victim's black SUV. Two black Chevy Tahoes. Twins.

On the steps, Lindy asked, "Have you seen it, yet?"

"Not yet. CSI was on the scene before I even got the call."

"How did that happen?"

"Hanson's wife keeps their scanner on her bedside table next to a picture of their kid."

When Lindy got the call that morning, she was frantic to grab her phone before it could wake the snoozing baby on April's side of the bed. It had been a rough night because of a sudden ear infection. Sleep was precious in their house, and Lindy would put one between the eyes of anyone who tried to steal that sleep from her. The last damn thing she would do was place a scanner by the bed.

"Do you know the vic? Is he a cousin or someone you went to elementary school with?" Detective Ian Boggs was born and bred in Pleasant Springs. His family had owned tobacco fields that were transitioned into corn fields, which were eventually sold to a corporation who harvested it to make syrup. Everyone in town was a friend, went to his church, went hunting with him, was a cousin of a cousin, or went on beer runs with him back when the county was dry. It helped that people kept him in the loop. The downside was in instances like this one when they were called out to a murder. He'd had to excuse himself from cases in the past because of conflicts of interest.

"Not this time. The vic's name is Ethan Moll. He has family out around LBL in Lake City. They're on their way."

Inside the glass security door, an officer pointed them down the hallway. On the left, a black leather sectional occupied most of the living room space, looking more like a bed than a couch. Video game consoles and controllers had been discarded on the floor in front of an enormous TV. The floors were dark walnut hardwood. On the right, the art on the walls was primarily black and white photography of old tobacco barns, rusted trucks, and horses in pastures. No photos of people. Only iconography. Kentucky things. A tech was walking down the hall holding a laptop computer.

Down the hall, they could turn left into the eat-in kitchen or right down another hall to the bedrooms. The kitchen was clean but not well organized. Evidence of a person who expected someone to follow behind them and place things back for them. Several blue and white University of Kentucky mugs sat on the counter. No matter what college anyone attended, Kentucky kids wore the University of Kentucky or University of Louisville logos and colors as if they did attend those schools. Lack of professional sports teams throws allegiances toward the college teams.

Everything about the place read: family-style home on the outside, bachelor pad on the inside.

The body had been discovered in the master shower. He had been stabbed multiple times. Blood pooled in the drain. The CSI techs were taking photos and placing tape at the blood splatter spots. Lindy nodded at the tech and slid her hands into the pockets on her jacket, nicking a cuticle on her keys.

"Don't touch anything." Hanson barked from behind them. He wore his white jumpsuit and booties with the confidence of a man who wore Wranglers and boots when off duty. He was a possessive man. Until he was done, this house belonged to him.

"My hands are literally in my pockets." Lindy turned and showed Hanson how well contained she was.

"Keep it that way." He pushed past her into the bathroom.

The victim was lying face up and splayed on the floor of the walk-in shower. Someone had turned off the rain shower head, but water and blood pooled under him. He was muscular, with long legs and a short torso. He had thick, dark hair, the water making it look black. Devoid of blood, his skin had turned blue.

"He was young," she said loudly from the bathroom.

Possibly to Boggs. Maybe Hanson. Whoever was listening. She estimated that the vic was in his late-20s.

"He was fit." Boggs stepped closer and leaned over the body. Hanson cleared his throat and Boggs moved out of the way.

Crouching close to the body, Hanson pointed at the wounds. "They loved him," Hanson said.

"How's that?" Lindy asked.

"Not a scratch on the face. One stab in the back. He probably turned and then stab, stab, stab."

"Doesn't look like much of a struggle," Boggs said. "The shampoo and conditioner are all still in the caddy. Nothing broken or askew in the bedroom."

"The floor looks chalky over here. Like someone tried to clean it up." Lindy leaned close. "Not bleach, though. Some kind of abrasive cleaner. Comet?"

"We're testing it," Hansen said. "But I'm thinking Soft Scrub. The clean-up looks half-hearted at best."

"Maybe they used what was here." Boggs opened the cabinet under the sink with the toe of his boot. Rolls of toilet paper, body wash, and an old bottle of Soft Scrub. Hanson peeked into the cabinet then left the bathroom.

Lindy held out a plastic evidence bag to Boggs, who tipped the bottle inside.

"So this crime wasn't planned," she speculated.

"Or wasn't planned well," Boggs said.

They stepped over the mess to exit the room and review the rest of the house.

Back at the station house, Lindy went to the break room and poured herself another cup of coffee. She also purchased a Honeybun from the vending machine, watching her singles be slowly consumed by the machine. Leaning next to it, she took a moment to eat.

Boggs entered the room and spotted her hiding. "What are you doing?"

"Trying to eat in goddamned peace." She shoved the last bite of bun in her mouth.

"Shame-eating is just sad."

"Not shame-eating, just not telling April eating … shut up. Go buy me some McDonald's?"

"You can go get your own damn McDonald's. And we don't have time. We have to interview the witness." He gestured for her to follow him. They exited the room together and Boggs led her down the hall. "What does April think of how you eat?"

"Don't say anything to April about it." Lindy stifled a burp. She was no longer a young woman and shotgunning an old honeybun from the machine was a bad choice. "We're on Weight Watchers."

"April might be on Weight Watchers. You're on–"

"That joke you're about to make, I am not here for it."

They walked across the bullpen of the department. Multiple phones rang, like school children singing rounds of "Row, Row, Row Your Boat." Uniformed officers busied themselves around the room. A narcotics detective in street clothes exited one of the interrogation rooms. A pair of uniforms escorted two stumbling young men still wearing last night's clothes. One of them wore a **ΘΔN** shirt and the other a T-shirt stained with vomit. They barked complaints at the officers as they were marched to the desk where a pack of young men – what could be speculated was their fraternity's bail out crew – and one dad in a blue and white University of Kentucky hooded sweatshirt waited for their release. The dad looked mortified when he was handed the kid in the ΘΔN shirt. The bail out crew patted the vomit-stained boy on the back, telling him he was going to be okay, as if he had just served 5-10 for a crime he didn't commit.

Lindy opened the door of the interrogation room where Jenna held the hand of a young man. He was pretty put together for someone who was wearing sweatpants. He looked a little too polished for a tech career but a little too plain for sales. He was at least six inches shorter than Jenna, which explained why she carried herself with a slight curve in her spine.

The young man clutched his phone with his free hand. When it lit up, he turned it to see the notification, then turned it back facedown on his knee, which was gently bouncing like he needed more caffeine or had too much already. His eyes were red and swollen like Jenna's.

When Lindy approached, she held her hand out for him to shake it. He stood, dropping Jenna's hand, but still clutching the phone. "Hello. I'm Ross." His grip was firm and practiced. "Ethan was my old roommate and Jenna—"

"He's my boyfriend," she interrupted.

"Fiancé," he corrected.

"Yes. Right," Jenna muttered. "Fiancé. You're my fiancé. He's my fiancé." Jenna was there but not there. She'd changed from her blood-stained clothes and now wore a pair of scrub pants and a Pleasant Springs Police Department T-shirt. She stared ahead of her, not looking at her forgotten fiancé or either of the officers.

Ross sat back down next to Jenna and resumed holding her hand. A hand that was missing an engagement ring.

Lindy placed a folder on the table and leaned against the wall. Boggs sat across from the couple with a legal pad and a pen. Boggs had one of those welcoming faces. He was local, familiar and was good at talking to people. Lindy was still the outsider in this town and often came across as brusque.

Boggs explained to the couple, "Now, I want to make sure y'all know that we record all the meetings in this room. And the reason we do that is it helps us with conversation recall, okay?"

"Have you been recording this whole time?" Ross looked around the room for the camera mounted in the corner of the room.

"Yeah," Lindy said. Civilians were always surprised when they realized cops record all interviews.

Boggs reached across the table and laid his palm in the space where Jenna's eye naturally fell. "Jenna, can I get you another water or—?"

"Were both of you close friends with Ethan?" Lindy cut in. She didn't have the patience to make sure the person being interviewed was comfortable. Someone had died. It wasn't a tea party.

"Yes," Jenna said. "Since college."

Ross added, "Going on ten years."

"Did you all work together, too?"

Both shook their heads. Ross said. "I do freelance marketing. Right now, I'm running the social media account for Ellen Hawk Realty, and Jenna is a local rep for Pfizer. Ethan was the Digital Marketing Recruiter for Integrated Business Solutions."

"What's Integrated Business Solutions?"

"It's a networking group for small businesses and entrepreneurs," Jenna answered. "He consulted on their digital marketing strategies and coordinated the networking events. He also acted as a liaison for Integrated Business Solutions' investments."

"Investments?" Boggs asked. "Is it like a hedge fund?"

"No," she said it as if they hadn't been listening to her. "It's a networking group."

Boggs made a note on his legal pad. "What were you doing at Ethan's house this morning?"

"I was taking him to work. His truck had been acting up, and he'd asked me yesterday to follow him to the dealership mechanic to drop it off."

"He gets his car serviced at the dealership?" Boggs asked.

Jenna shrugged.

Lindy asked, "Why don't you take us through what happened this morning again?"

Jenna sat up in her chair. "I drove to Ethan's house and texted him. He didn't reply, but sometimes he was like that. I have a remote to his garage. He always leaves the door to the garage unlocked. I walked into the house and called his name, but he didn't respond. So I walked back toward his room, but he wasn't there either. I could hear the water on, so I called again. He should have heard me. I knew something was wrong, like the whole thing seemed wrong. He didn't shower in the mornings. And if he did, he would have the TV playing in the background. I walked into the bathroom and I found him."

Her voice broke on the word "found." She began to cry again and everyone took a moment, waiting for it to pass and for her to pull herself back together. Ross squeezed Jenna's hand and Boggs nudged the bottle of water on the table nearer to her. Jenna took a breath. "There was just blood everywhere, and water, and I don't know what happened next. I was outside, and the neighbor lady was screaming to get my attention. She was the one who called 911."

"You didn't realize anything was wrong until you went into the house?"

"No."

Ross sucked snot up his nose, then made a noise that could have been a stifled sob. "That was Ethan. He always made everyone wait. Jenna had to drag him out of the house all the time."

"You picked him up a lot?"

"Ethan didn't like to drive. I did. It was our thing." Jenna pulled Ross closer to her.

"Do you know if Ethan was into anything dangerous? Gambling? Drugs?"

Jenna said, "No. Ethan didn't do drugs."

Everyone always said that. It didn't mean he didn't. Most people tried to justify it: doesn't everyone smoke a little … do a little blow … run up to the casino in Metropolis and hit the slots on the way to the buffet? No matter how close you think you are, people will always surprise you with how little you actually know them.

Ross removed his phone from the table and placed it in his pocket.

"What about old girlfriends?"

"There's Gabbi," Jenna said. "But he hasn't seen her in months."

"Who's Gabbi?" Lindy asked.

"This girl who was all wrong for him," Jenna said. "I believe she was stalking him."

"Why do you say that?" Lindy asked.

"Because she didn't live here but she was always in town, like even after they'd broken up. I ran into her at Kohl's one day and she said this weird thing about how I didn't understand their relationship. She was so weird."

"She wasn't weird," Ross said.

"Why are you always defending her, Ross? She was weird. She was in one of those cults!"

"She was in a cult?" Boggs asked.

Ross shook his head but Jenna pushed. "Yes. She was in one of those internet guru cults. What was her name?" Jenna gestured to Ross. "Remember. She was always quoting her and trying to attend all her conferences and workshops. Celestia … Celestial? But that's not it."

Ross shrugged like he had no idea what she was talking about.

Jenna continued. "Gabbi was always talking about vibes and her tarot cards, and she wore those chunky prayer beads."

"Gabbi didn't do this," Ross said.

"Why would you say that?" Lindy asked.

Ross said, "Because she didn't live-stream it."

"That's not funny." Jenna lifted her head and gazed up at the ceiling. "I swear to God, Ross." Her eyes were glossy with tears.

After they finished the interview, Lindy sat at her desk across from Boggs, who typed their initial report. She read through the notifications on her phone. One was a missed call from April.

"What do you think?" Lindy hit the button to return the call.

"That we don't know enough, yet."

April answered on the first ring. "Are you okay?" which was what Lindy always asked when she returned her wife's calls. Lindy always assumed the worst. She knew too much.

"I'm fine. I got a call today from Jeff, and he wants to come see us. I wanted to tell him yes, but I wanted to check with you first."

Jeff was April's best friend from college and their sperm donor. Since April had the baby, Jeff called or texted April several times a day and had already come to town to visit three times now – Ella was only 14 months old. When they suggested the idea of him being a sperm donor, they said he could be as involved or not involved as he wanted. He chose to be involved.

"Sure. If he wants to come visit that's fine."

"Wouldn't it be great if he could stay until Christmas? He'd get to see Ella open all her gifts."

"Great, babe, I gotta get back to —"

"Sure, sure. We can talk about it tonight. Love you."

"You, too."

Boggs continued to type and ignored her, which Lindy appreciated.

JENNA

I never liked her.

She was one of those girls who were way too invested in their appearance. You know those girls. They spend all day at the gym and all night watching reality shows and make-up tutorials. They take mirror selfies in their bathroom and post them on their Instagram accounts with stupid captions like "Felt cute … Might delete later." What do they call it? Thirst trap. That's it. She was a walking thirst trap, wanting men to want her.

It's just so obvious.

I have had to watch girls – women – try to trap Ethan into dates, relationships, and commitments, thinking he'll marry them – that he'll turn them into a *Real Housewife*.

I mean, he was a catch. He came from a good family. He had a good job. He was handsome. But he couldn't take care of them. He needed to be taken care of. He needed a personal assistant, not a housewife.

We took care of him. Me and Ross.

That's why I was there that morning. Something was wrong with his truck, so who does he call? Me. It's been like that ever since he was running socials for that stupid fraternity —*the Nus*—and he needed my notes from class so he wouldn't flunk out. I helped him study; he got me the invite for all the parties. Not that I ever went to the parties. All those Nu bros were so obnoxious and the girls … well, the girls were all like Gabbi: too tight clothes, too big lips, too low-cut tops.

The first time I met her was at O'Charley's. We often met up at O'Charley's on Sundays for brunch. I knew he'd been dating someone. He was being evasive and always driving into Tillman for some reason or another. I'd go to his place, and he'd be texting someone the whole time. Finally, he gave me a name—Gabbi.

Ross and I got to brunch first. We always arrived everywhere first because Ethan was notoriously late. We grabbed a table and the hostess plopped menus in front of us. I ordered a Diet Coke and Ross asked for a Bloody Mary. She said, "Remember, that our brunch drink specials do not begin for another 30 minutes in accordance with the city ordinances."

"Yeah, we're aware," Ross told her. "Can you go ahead and put in for that Bloody Mary now, so we can get it right when it hits noon?"

"Sure thing, hon," I thought the waitress was going to lean in and boop Ross on the nose. Waitresses always flirted with Ross. If they realized I was the one paying the tab, maybe I'd be the one to get a boop on the nose. Not that I wanted it.

"And the little blueberry muffins," I added before she completely disappeared. Since the city modified its ordinance prohibiting alcohol sales, many restaurants popped up boasting bottomless brunches. The Baptist crowd turned a blind eye to bottomless mimosas if it meant the town could have restaurants like O'Charley's, Applebees, and Buffalo Wild Wings. The tag team of college students and drink

specials meant the restaurant had taken a loss on complimentary muffins—broke college students ordered the cup of
loaded potato soup, stuffed themselves with muffins, and got
tanked on Bloody Marys, mimosas, brunch beer, and more.
The rumor was all the restaurants were cutting corners to keep
out the moochers and the brunch skunks. Apparently,
O'Charley's was withholding their blueberry muffins until
after they knew how much money they would make on the
table. It wasn't a horrible policy, but I wasn't a college kid. I
was a grown-ass woman who wanted muffins.

We'd skipped church that morning. We'd stayed out late
seeing Ross's brother's Christian rock band perform at a
megachurch recreation center in Tillman the night before, and
they didn't make it all the way home until well after 2 am.
Ross was the band's public relations representative, so he took
photos and posted them on the band's Instagram page during
their performances. I sometimes helped. I can sometimes
round up hyper teens in glow necklaces for group photos on
my way to the bathroom. Last night I wasn't in the mood and
told Ross that if I had to sit through one more performance of
the band's most-streamed song, "Higher is Your Love", I was
going to cancel the wedding.

The wedding that I can't even announce on my social
media pages because he still hasn't given me a ring.

I'd worn my lilac shawl that day. They keep all the restaurants so cold in the spring and summer. I remember draping
it around me while we waited. Somehow even in a tunic and
leggings, I still need to wrap myself to stay warm. Ross is not
broad shouldered, so he can't really offer me his hoodie to
keep me warm. He's not that kind of guy anyway. He
scrolled through his social media apps while we waited,
responding to every comment or notification on his bro's
Instagram page. I often have to remind him that I am a live

person sitting at the table with him. But today, I just studied the menu.

I removed my phone from my tote bag, checking to see if Ethan had texted back, and then placed it on the tabletop. No messages from Ethan yet. He had texted earlier that he was on his way, but I knew better. *On my way* meant he was getting out of bed. *Leaving now* meant he was about to step into the shower. *In the car* meant he was putting on his shoes.

The waitress appeared with the drinks, but no muffins. I asked for them again. "Sure. I'll bring them right out. Are you ready to order?"

"We're waiting for the rest of our party," I said, and then handed my Diet Coke back to her. "Can you bring me another one with less ice? And a lemon. Or actually, can we get a little cup of lemons or something?"

"You want another Diet Coke, but with less ice, and a plate of lemons. Is that all?"

"And the muffins."

When she left, Ross announced, "I'm not waiting for Ethan. When she comes back, I am ordering steak and eggs."

I told him, "It's rude to order before everyone gets here."

"It's also rude to be late everywhere."

I picked up his phone from the table and handed it to him. "Here. You text him to move him along. He's ignoring me."

He didn't. The room began to fill with the after-church crowd. Couples, families, and children all dressed in nice dresses and nice jeans congregated around the hostess stand. Complimentary coffee carafes were set up by the door. The restaurant was a blend of sounds: tables being pushed together, crying babies, booming choir baritones greeting people with a "Hey! How y'all this morning?" and the local country music station playing some Carrie Underwood song.

I spotted Ethan worming his way through the crowd. "There he is. You can order now."

When I stood up and waved him in, my shawl slipped onto the floor and when I bent down to pick it up, I found a boot print where I had accidentally stepped back on it. I brushed off the dirt and stood to see a blonde woman standing at our table next to Ethan.

My first thought was: *That girl is naked.*

She wasn't actually; she was fully clothed. She had on yoga pants and a zip-up jacket. I knew I was being silly, but that's what I saw when I looked at her: a naked woman. She was short, so she held her back straight and her head high. Her stacked sneakers added another two inches to her. But when she stood still, she pushed her hips back so her butt and boobs stuck out.

Hoochie. That's the word I couldn't think of that day. She was hoochie.

Ross leaned over to me and whispered, "Be nice."

I whispered back, "I'm always nice."

People were always telling me to "be nice." I don't recall ever once being mean. I know when to smile even when I don't mean it. I know how to not raise my voice and still get what I need. I don't know how to be any nicer when I am looking at something that's not right and needs to be fixed immediately. And if that means I don't get invitations to sororities, bachelorette parties, and girlfriend getaways ... so be it. They're always in my office or pulling me aside when they want to dish about their mothers-in-law, their co-workers, or any of the *Real Housewives.*

I removed my tote bag from the extra chair to make room for Ethan's little friend. "Good morning! I'm Jenna."

Ethan tossed his sunglasses on the table. He then pulled out the chair for his companion. She said, "Hey! I'm Gabbi!"

Of course you are.

I was staring at her. I was not trying to. She and Ethan glowed together. They were there in front of us, but really miles away together somewhere else. It was weird. I hope me and Ross aren't like that in public: two dopey teens who can't stop mooning over each other. Ross reached over and shook her hand.

Meeting the girlfriends is the worst. None of them stick around long, so it's not something I have to deal with often, but every once in a while he gets serious about someone and he brings them to me and Ross. Usually Ethan gives me a little warning. I show up prepared with interesting questions based on what he's told me about her: her family, her hobbies, her church, her favorite TV show, where they met. But today, I had nothing. I was so mad that Ethan just sprung her on me like that.

I was wracking my brain for conversation points while Ross was telling them about pre-ordering drinks.

"Yes," I agreed only to interject. "We should order before Ross wastes away to nothing." I dug around in my tote and removed a purse hook from the side pocket. In a swift maneuver, I stuck the hook to the side of the table and hung my bag from it.

I realized Gabbi was watching me. I said, "I'm sorry. I don't have an extra if you need it. But I guess you didn't bring a purse in?"

"No. I've just never seen anyone use those before. I've only seen the ads on TV." She seemed to be studying the bag hanging from the hook. I was getting annoyed at her judgy eyes. Not even fake bags need to sit on the floor in the dirt. She giggled, which I learned was how she responded to every-thing. "I guess I just left everything at Ethan's." A swatch of pink appeared across the bridge of her nose. Ethan reached over and placed his hand on Gabbi's thigh.

They made googly eyes at each other.

I hate it when couples do that: act like other people aren't in the room. If you're not able to be around normal people, then don't come out at all.

"How long have you two known each other?"

"A while. Gabbi lives in Tillman."

"I've heard so much about both of you." Gabbi sounded fake, like she was unaware that Ethan had any friends at all.

The waitress appeared with my Diet Coke. This one had zero ice in it, which I think she did just out of spite. I squeezed lemons into it while she took everyone's orders. I swear to God, all Gabbi ordered was a cup of hot water with a lemon, a fruit cup and one—count it, one—scrambled egg white. I mean, who eats like that? I ordered Banana's Foster French Toast just out of spite. Both the boys got steak and eggs.

When noon rolled around, the waitress appeared with the Bloody Marys we ordered. I stuck with my Diet Coke. Gabbi had been telling me about her job, some kind of online fitness coaching or something. She was also telling me about her apartment being sold and how she was looking for a new place to live. When she started talking about how she pulled a tarot card out of her deck that meant "good fortune," I just checked out a little. It was hard following her anyway. From what I could tell, she didn't watch TV, shop for anything other than fitness clothes, and didn't eat real food. What on Earth did we have to talk about over brunch?

The boys were discussing something that was getting heated. I heard Ethan tell Ross that he was going to need to "man up," so when the waitress appeared passing out drinks, Ethan looked relieved.

Ross was complaining about his neck, and the next thing I

know, Gabbi made everyone switch seats so she could do some kind of spine adjustment on him. And I'll tell you what, Ethan did not appreciate it when she placed her hands on Ross's back and then plopped down beside him to show off pictures from her website where she's doing all these human pretzel poses. I tried to distract Ethan from what was going on but it was not working.

I turned to Gabbi and said, "Are you not getting a drink? It's okay. I always drive everywhere. We can drop y'all off." I wanted her to not have to worry about driving home. That was me being nice.

"No. I'm good."

"Oh," I whispered, for her privacy. "Are you like, in recovery? Are you an alcoholic or something?"

"That's rude, Jenna," Ethan warned.

And there it was—again. But I was just being considerate of her needs. "It's just a question."

Gabbi giggled, because apparently she giggles when anyone asks her anything. "No. I'm not an alcoholic. It's just that alcohol doesn't really support my journey right now."

"What's that? What's your journey?"

"It's like my glow up. I'm only engaging with activities that lead me closer to my goals. Besides, my polarity is backwards anyway. When I drink, I get amped. The opposite of chilled and relaxed …"

Good Lord, she sounded like my aunt who wears only copper jewelry and sells herbal supplements on Facebook.

And she was still talking.

"… you know, alcohol is mostly sugar, and all those empty calories just add unnecessary pounds."

Ethan cleared his throat. "Hey, don't judge. I'm still carrying my winter weight."

Gabbi pushed against his shoulder. "Stop it." He took her

hand and kissed it. And they did it again, they went someplace else together in their gross little couple bubble. How is that not rude? At least Gabbi realized it and said, "Besides, many successful women choose not to drink. J.Lo. And she looks amazing. Also, Kim Kardashian."

Kim Kardashian. I mean, is this woman serious? I shrugged. "I guess you gotta stay fit for when your sex tape leaks."

She turned to Ethan. "Did you leak our sex tape from this morning?"

Ethan blushed. "Okay, okay. Here." He swapped his Bloody Mary with my Diet Coke. "We are going to get Jenna a drink because this Diet Coke has her too keyed up."

"Stop it." I waved him away and took back my Diet Coke. "I'm not keyed up. I don't need your drink. I'm just getting to know your friend. Besides, Gabbi knows I'm joking. See? We're good."

"We're fine." Gabbi smiled at me, and I knew that smile. I'd seen girls flash me that smile a million times before. It's always some power play, but guess what, girl? I always win.

I just could not get over her and Ethan. It was the only thing I could talk about on the drive home. Ross was a little tipsy, and he was still irritated with Ethan because of whatever they were hunkered down discussing.

"Man up. I am a man. I'm all man." He was pressing the buttons on the radio, trying to escape commercials for car dealers, plumbers, and a jingle for some sausage company out of Louisville.

"Of course you're a man. But where on Earth did she come from?"

"He said she was from Tillman."

"No. She lives in Tillman. She's probably from Kanton or

somewhere out in the country or … ugh … do you think she's from St. Louis?"

"You were not nice. We said to be nice."

"I was nice. They were the ones being weird. They got up and, like, disappeared for, like, ever. Where did they even go?"

"They were having sex in the bathroom, Jenna."

"Oh." It took me a minute to compute what he said. "Ew, gross…and then they just came back like nothing happened? There were kids all over that place."

Ross kicked his foot up on the dash and scrolled on his phone. "I swear to God, Ross. If you scuff my leather dash, I am going to be so mad at you."

He removed his foot and slumped in the seat. "Your dash is fine."

I was so … I don't even know how people have sex in public. Is it that they want to get caught? Or that they just can't wait? Can't control themselves until they get home? Ethan always said I was a prude about stuff like that. I am not a prude. I have awesome sex. But why do I need to swing from the rafters and bone somebody at a well-populated brunch spot to keep from being a prude?

And Gabbi can't even blame it on being drunk and horny, because she sat there and sipped warm water with freaking lemon, like some weirdo. Does water with lemon make you horny? Or is she, like, horny all the time? Isn't that what makes somebody a sex addict?

And then I looked over at Ross and I'm like, *We've never done that. We've never even made out in a restaurant or bar.* "You don't want that, do you?"

"Want what?" he scrolled through his apps.

"Sex. At O'Charley's."

"No." He dropped his phone in the cupholder. "It wouldn't be fun."

"Why?"

"Because you wouldn't be comfortable and I wouldn't be comfortable. We're fine. It's not for me."

"If our sex life is boring, you'll let me know, yes?"

"Of course. But it's not boring." He looked out the window. "When we get home, we will have sex."

"Who says?"

"I do. Because I am a man, who has plans for his woman. I'm going to play the big room!"

And we did. He was on one. We spent the rest of the day in bed.

THE OFFICIAL STATEMENT ON GABBI'S WEBSITE AND SOCIAL MEDIA ACCOUNTS

Hello Friends,

First, I want to be clear about this … I didn't kill Ethan.

It's not my way, it's not in my nature to kill anything. I'm the kind of person who scoops up spiders and releases them out into the wild. I never went hunting as a kid. I have never eaten deer meat. I don't condone fur. So how anyone could think that I would do anything as insane as kill my boyfriend is beyond me.

I'm the kind of person who believes that everything is part of a bigger plan, and I don't always get to control what happens, but my job is to make sure that I keep a high vibe frequency that will attract what I need to be in service of others.

And to be honest, that's been a real struggle right now.

I loved Ethan. We were together off and on for a long time. We had a very passionate connection. He would walk into a room and all my hairs would stand on end; we had this electricity between us, and when we touched, sometimes I thought I would burst into flames.

Y'all … It was hot.

And now he's gone, and I don't know how to process that. We had plans. We encouraged each other. When things were good, we boosted each other.

Ethan was one of those guys who really cared what other people thought about him. He needed to be taken care of, and if certain people didn't approve of me, well, he would start pulling away.

I don't know what their problem was. I know that some people are jealous of me. I'm aware of how I look. I work hard at it. I love going to the gym. If you love something, and it helps you look fit, then it's the process more than the reward that is beneficial. And anyone else can do it. I'm not special. So I don't understand why anyone would be jealous of that. It's not a scam. I make the time to go to the gym three hours a day. And I love it.

But let's be real, y'all. You can't be an attractive woman anymore without someone saying something about it. And it's mostly women. You'd be amazed at the things that people think they can say to me—*you must be lucky, you must have a high metabolism, you must be blessed, you have too much time on your hands* ... or what's worse, *you must be on drugs, you must have an eating disorder, you must have had plastic surgery. Have a chip and live!* Like to my face and on my social profiles. It's ridiculous.

And when they tell me these things, I just smile, because I know they're struggling.

But none of that makes me a murderer. I loved Ethan.

As a result of the toxic messages I have been receiving online, I'm taking a step back. Under the advice of my attorney, this will be the last I have to say about the subject. My fitness coaching website, GabbiFixMe.com, will not be updated, but you can still peruse the archives for meal planning, grocery store checklists, fitness videos, gym strategies, and fitness calendars—all downloadable PDFs.

I have no reason to be defensive or scared about the outcome of this trial. As Celeste Sullivan says, "Outcomes are irrelevant." I know the Universe is looking out for me, and the outcome will be what it is intended to be.

I am not scared because I have told the truth. There's nothing else to talk about.

GABBI

Here's what you need to know about Kentucky girls—they're all princesses.

I'm not talking about being rich, because Lord knows, they're not. These princesses will spend money they do not have to buy new boots, they will expect their parents to take out a loan so they can drive a new Lexus, and they will expect all men to fall head over heels in love with them. Every woman I have met who has been raised in Kentucky has two things in common: they believe deep down in their heart of hearts that they will get whatever it is they want, and they believe they know everything.

This is not a judgment. When we pass judgment, we separate ourselves from love. And I did love those girls. I grew up with those girls. But I also recognize who they are. Princesses.

My first encounter with a Kentucky princess was in college. My roommate was from a tiny town in Northern Kentucky outside Cincinnati. She was city, as my mama would say. She grew up in the suburbs, thought all the tobacco barns on the drive down were "quaint", and owned every fragrance that

Bath and Body Works produced that season. Our room smelled like "Sweater Weather" all the time.

She didn't work, she didn't go to class, and she cried every time a boy said he was going to call and didn't.

She was a princess.

And I realized that I was surrounded by them. The girls across the hallway who came to college together and scheduled all their classes around *Days of Our Lives*. The girl in our suite whose boyfriend's parents paid for her cell phone. The girl in my class who "borrowed" her grandfather's handicapped parking permit so she would always get a space close to the building. Princesses held positions of power in their sorority, ran for student council, and were named editors of the newspaper. And not because they had to fight tooth and nail for it, but because they knew it would be theirs. Their daddy or mama said they could have it, and they believed they could.

If ever in any situation they did not get the thing they desired, they would pivot and proclaim, "I never really wanted that anyway."

I didn't understand how they got there. What kind of parents did they have to create the level of self-esteem these girls possessed to assume that the world revolved around them?

But the most princess of all the princesses was Briana. Briana wasn't much to look at. She had delicate features on a squat body. Her skin was so fair that she was practically see-through. While the rest of us were all getting fake baked, she shone as white as the moon. Briana carried herself in a way that announced that she was not to be trifled with. She deployed all the tools in the princess handbook to ensure she got her way: flattery, cajoling, cooing, smiling, and eventually the cold shoulder. And sometimes, flat-out denial.

One time, I mentioned that she had once dated someone I knew, and how he was heartbroken over the situation. She looked through me and said, "We never dated." I was so confused. Not only had he told me that she was his girlfriend, but he once asked me to drop him at her dorm to meet her one night. She even flew with a group of us on a school trip— piggybacking on our group rate—and they had sat cozily together on the plane. But face to face with me, she declared, "We were only ever friends. We never dated. Like, nothing ever happened between us."

It took me a while to realize that all those gestures he made indicating how much he liked her—the texting, the drop-ins, the introducing her to his parents—in her princess mind, that's how all people should treat her. With reverence. Everyone wanted to spend time with her. It didn't mean she owed them anything.

And that's how it went. I never once saw her without a boyfriend. She never once questioned how she would pay her rent. She never once uttered the phrase, "I want this, but I don't know if I can afford it." She would wrap a leash around her cat's neck and walk it around her neighborhood like it was a dog, because why not. On the rare instances that she was feeling a little low, she would test drive new cars because she wanted to spend the day with salesmen flattering her.

What was intriguing was how she never demanded anything. She would decide that she wanted something and then patiently wait for someone to make sure it happened for her. She wanted a boyfriend, she got a fiancé. She wanted a house after they married—because no crummy apartment life for her—so, they immediately bought a house. She wanted a job, she got three offers. Briana returned to the community that raised her and purchased a nice house near her parents where she started to have babies.

Because the problem with being a princess is you are still beholden to the kingdom. Princesses are taken care of. Their parents were paying their bills, so they had to follow their rules. And despite the fact that many of them left home for college—like many princesses before them—eventually, they had to return home. They set up their own castles to rule their own tiny little kingdoms on the ends of culs-de-sac and farm roads to care for the retiring kings and queens, or to raise other little princes and princesses and repeat the pattern all over again.

Eventually, I realized that I didn't want to be a princess. I wanted to be a queen.

And that's when the real work began.

I was dating Roger at the time. He was a periodontist that I'd met at the gym, because he would run on the treadmill next to mine. For a guy in his forties, he was keeping it tight. But he was balding a little and overcompensated by talking about his Mazzeratti.

I knew he was married. He didn't hide it. I spotted his wedding band right away, but I was dating a lot of married guys back then.

I liked sneaking around. There was something really sexy about the fact that these guys would leave their perfectly organized homes decorated top to bottom in Hobby Lobby bric-a-brak to nail me in their truck behind a Captain D's.

Roger asked me to go with him to a conference in Cincinnati, and I had nothing better to do, so I joined him. He paid for my ticket, but we traveled separately. He left my name at the desk, and I met him in his room. During the day, he would go to his breakout sessions, and at night we would go to dinner, share the in-room jacuzzi, and have lots of sex. He couldn't take Viagra because of an underlying heart murmur, but he did his best.

Cincinnati is boring, but the hotel had a pool. I was going to spend the whole day poolside drinking margaritas and charging all my drinks to Roger's room. But the pool was harder to find than I thought.

I walked downstairs in this cute neon pink string bikini—I had a super tan then and that pink looked real good against it—and a sheer lace kimono over it. When I walked past people, I imagined that they could see me moving in slow motion—my platform sandals hitting the marble and my kimono billowing behind me. I even threw in a gentle toss of my long blonde hair over my shoulder.

I was trying to avoid the convention crowd, but somehow ended up down a hall next to Conference Room K. A group of people were sitting behind a table stacked with books all from the same author, Celeste Sullivan. A promotional banner with a woman's face and the words *You Can Have It! Permission to Receive What You Desire* hung behind them. From inside the conference room, I could hear a woman speaking into a microphone.

She was standing on a platform in a tidy suit; she looked chic—practically French—with a high-necked collar full of ruffles. She was tall in her nude pumps. She wasn't young, but mature. Her blonde hair had shimmers of silver in her dark roots. It framed her face with bangs and a natural wave. I have never been a fan of that injection-face look of all the reality show personalities. This woman looked like someone who had good genes and the confidence of wisdom.

I was drawn into the room. Something about her voice. She wasn't southern. It was missing the lyrical rhythm or twang of a southern accent. Maybe midwestern or up-state New York. I don't have a good ear for accents. I could only tell that she didn't carry herself with the preacher tone of other speakers. Her voice was strong, but also soft. She didn't need to shout.

She was saying, "It was that moment that I realized all the ways I was sabotaging my life … the jobs I took were not my passion … I filled my body with sugar and caffeine … and then sleep aides at night—those Ambien stories are no joke. I shut out those who loved me because I always felt like that love came with conditions, and then my romantic life … well … they were unworthy. I chose these things under the illusion, or delusion, that this was all I deserved. That was the lie I was telling myself …

"We don't like to admit all the lies we tell ourselves—take this job because it's all you're qualified for. Take this relationship because it's the one in front of you…you deserve better. You deserve more. If you want it, you can have it."

I felt a hand on my arm and jerked back in surprise. I turned to see it was a young woman that had startled me. She whispered, "You should go in and sit down."

"I'm sorry. I didn't sign up or pay …"

"Don't worry. Celeste never turns anyone away. You can sit there in the back."

So I did. They had rows of chairs set up with cushions, probably from the hotel's wedding collection. I looked around the room and I saw mostly women, a few men, nearly all middle-aged. They had these looks on their faces—abject admiration.

Celeste paced around the platform as she spoke. "First, you must rid yourself of these delusions—the ones that tell you to compromise. Shed yourself of all that does not spark passion. Align your thinking so when an opportunity knocks, you won't mistake that it has come for someone else. It is there for you. And you must shed yourself of the obligation to go along with the world. Don't drag yourself down with other people's expectations. They don't make the rules or set your pace. You do. And finally, resist that impulse to be on call for others—" In the corner of the room, a member of the crowd made a noise and people giggled. "Oh, I heard an amen! You understand what I mean then."

She asked everyone to close their eyes for a guided meditation. At first I wouldn't close my eyes, but, reluctantly, I gave in. It felt like the room emptied. She was instructing us to look inside, deep down at that place where the center of our being resided. I searched and it was like at that moment Celeste Sullivan was speaking directly to me. I could imagine that she reached into my chest and pulled out my heart, but instead of my heart, it was a tiny bluebird. "Are you willing to let your heart fly?" I imagined she set the bird in my hands. But I couldn't let it go. I clutched it to me, scared that if I let it go, I would never see it again. And then I realized I was crying.

All of a sudden, the crowd was applauding and the lecture was over. I looked down at my empty hands and wiped my face with my kimono. I am rarely self-conscious, but I became very aware that I was practically naked. It was also like something inside of me had shifted. What am I doing? Like, what am I doing with my life? Celeste had left the stage and people started to gather their things.

A woman wearing a T-shirt paired with a flowy shirt and lanyard took the stage. She tried to capture the attention of the departing crowd. "Quickly, before you leave, I want to remind you that Celeste will be signing books in about 10 minutes. Let's give a round of applause to our sponsor, Xena Books!" A smattering of applause joined the murmur of voices. "Also, I want to remind you all that Celeste is hosting a weekend-long seminar in St. Louis in September. Registration tables are set up in the back along with our merchandise tables."

I waited for people to leave before I stood. I was still so

dazed from the experience. When the crowd had mostly relocated or were distracted with their own group conversations, I tried to slip away. However, the young woman from earlier stepped into my path.

"Hi!" She held out her hand. "I'm Amber!" She was one of those girls that you knew sent text messages loaded with exclamation points and heart emojis. She looked sharp. Dark, lob haircut. A-line skirt. Navy chemise blouse with a pattern loaded with tiny white horses.

"Hey." I shook her hand and introduced myself. "This is so weird. I'm not even supposed to be here. I got lost looking for the pool."

"Kismet. Celeste says getting lost is merely the Universe rerouting you to where you need to be instead of where you think you need to be."

"It was … uh … what is this, exactly?"

"This is one of many stops of her speaking tour. Have you never heard of Celeste Sullivan?"

I shook my head.

"Definitely kismet. What did you think?"

"It was … " I wasn't sure what I thought about it. I was embarrassed and confused about crying in a room full of strangers like it was some Southern Baptist revival. I had never thought about kismet outside of Hallmark movies and good parking spaces. "I'm intrigued, I guess."

"You came at the right time. We're offering a reduced rate to anyone who attends this conference for our fall weekend intensive retreat in St. Louis in October. It's only $2,000, and that includes a private room and food."

Just then Celeste emerged from the crowd and stood next to Amber. She had a gentle smile and smelled like jasmine. "Amber, darling, would you please fetch me some water?"

There she was. Standing so close to this woman after her

speech made me feel even more naked. Now that I was closer to her, I could see the fine material of her clothing. It must have been purchased at one of those high-class stores like Bergdorf Goodman. And here I was in a Target bikini like I was on Spring Break. A bikini I thought was pretty bougie because it didn't come from Walmart this time.

"Of course. Celeste," Amber said, "this is Gabbi. She dropped in for the talk and I was just about to tell her about the weekend intensive."

"Wonderful." Celeste took my hands into both of hers, with their perfectly manicured nails: short, nude, and sensible length. They felt so warm. "The weekend intensives are a fantastic way to meet other women who are on their journey to claim their power."

I blurted a nervous laugh. "I'm not sure I'm on a journey."

"Of course you are, darling." She winked at me. "Or else you would have made it to the pool … Now, I must sign these books and say hello to these lovely people."

She let go of my hand and accepted from Amber a bottle of what looked like a German mineral water. "Thank you. So good to meet you, Gabbi."

I watched her glide away. Her body was lithe and confident as it wove through the crowd. She must do pilates. Celeste took her seat at the table and waved the first person in line closer to her.

Amber said, "Dazzling is the word you're looking for."

"She's gotta be a total bitch, right?"

"We don't use that word. That word is the opposite of claiming your power. It's diminishing someone else only to make yourself feel better." Amber tucked her blouse tighter into her skirt. "I've been on her team for the past six months and since then I've been knocking out goals left and right."

"Boyfriend?"

"Yep."

"Cash?"

"Uh-huh." Amber grabbed a plastic bottle of Nestlé water and took a sip. "She pays well and supports my Etsy store. I make wall art of inspirational quotes. I also just started selling stickers." Amber handed me a hot pink business card. Her Etsy store was called *Say it with Style*.

But the weekend was going to cost $2,000. And it was in two months. I didn't have that kind of money to spend on anything, much less a weekend retreat with a bunch of strange women. And I didn't have enough time to save for it.

"If you don't want to attend an intensive, I totally get it." Amber handed me a copy from the top of the nearest stack. "At least read her book and join her Facebook group. I'm in it and it's full of fun, motivated women."

Again, I laughed nervously. "That's the problem. Women don't like me."

"That's clearly not true, because I like you."

I knew I was getting played, but it was nice. Kind of like when the guys who work the kiosks at the mall tell you how beautiful your hair is so you'll stop and let them try their curling irons on you or rub you down with lotion. It felt nice to be around a woman who didn't comment on my body. I was standing there in a bikini and no one made a joke or a weird judgy face. Like, Celeste had mentioned it, but in such a fun way. It was nice to be invited somewhere with a group of women and not out of some obligation—because I'm dating someone's brother or cousin.

The cover of the book was white and bright pink. A much younger Celeste in a glamour photo was printed with the words, *You Deserve What You Get*. I tucked Amber's card into the book and found a place in line.

The book grew heavy in my arms. I placed it back on the

table and looked back toward the exit. *I mean what was I even doing anyway?* But I lifted the copy back off the table and moved along in the line like the others. Along the way, I noticed that the table was loaded with other things, not only the book I was holding but other books, too: *The Only Way Out is Through: A Twelve-Step Process to Obtain the Life You Want; It's Not Them, It's You (And a Little Them);* and the latest, *You Can Have It! Permission to Receive What You Desire.* They were also selling these boxes of something called affirmation cards that were the same size as my tarot deck. Celeste had written books about money, sex, romance, and bravery. I paid the cashier who directed me to the line for Celeste to sign my book.

When I finally reached Celeste, the bottle of the German sparkling water was mostly empty. Celeste tapped her fingers against the tabletop, like a pianist longing to play.

"Gabbi! So good to see you're still here."

How on earth did she remember my name? She'd signed twenty books at this point. I told her, "I was interested in what you said about being stuck in a self-sabotaging pattern. It's like I only go after things I know are going to end in disaster."

Celeste's face was gentle and calm when she listened. She swept her pen along the first page of the book, fast and large. "When you are caught in a self-sabotaging pattern, it's usually fueled by a sense of feeling unworthy of all the Universe provides. When you identify you are stuck, you can start to make small changes in your choices to get you unstuck."

She relocated Amber's card to a specific section of the book. "Start reading here. This will benefit you the most." She slapped the book closed and slid it back to me. "I'm so glad you got lost. Now you can find yourself. Enjoy your journey."

"Wait." And then I told her about my guided meditation. I don't know why I told her, but I described the little bird. "Is that good? Was this right? Did I do it right?"

"Did it feel right?"

"Yes."

"Then it was right. You're on a journey now. Don't forget to enjoy the view. Thank you for coming."

I accepted the book and stepped away, stunned. I turned to the section Celeste had marked. It was titled "Break Out of the Pattern." I started to read as I walked down the hall to the elevator.

Recognize when you're bored, when you're lonely, when you're restless, hungry, horny—you possess a body that has all of these endless needs. Most of the time our frustrations are a result of our responses to those needs. You are more than mere bodily functions.

I found the pool. I grabbed a towel and located the first shady chair I could find. When the waiter came to see if I wanted to order food, I asked if the hotel carried any of that German mineral water, but they said they'd never heard of it. I ordered a club soda with lime instead. I didn't want to drink margaritas and float in the pool anymore. I read for the rest of the day. The chapters flew by. I grabbed one of the free hotel pens and underlined passages I wanted to remember.

Stop giving purpose to your pain.

Change one small thing. Small changes make a big difference.

How do you want to feel when you wake in the morning?

I was so immersed in the book that I didn't notice when a man sat down beside me. He cleared his throat to get my attention. I ignored him. He was overly tan and shirtless. He was in his 40s, but I knew he was about to tell me he was in his 30s. I kept trying to read. When his Michelob Ultra was delivered, he made this big show of thanking and tipping the waiter.

Finally, he said, "Must be a good book."

I was annoyed, but I slapped the book closed anyway. "It is." And I asked myself: *Why don't I tell this guy to go away?* I never do that. I'm always afraid they'll think I'm being rude. And then he smiled at me, and I felt this familiar flutter I get whenever a guy smiles at me. *Why do I like this? He's clearly gross and I'm here with someone else.* I was trapped. He asked me my name, and I automatically told him.

"Gabbi with an 'i'? I like that. Girls with 'i' names are fun."

I'd heard that one before.

He said, "You have very long legs."

"Do I?" I said like this observation was some kind of compliment. I was short but I was all leg.

He said, "I'm a chiropractor. I notice these things. You're very symmetrical. Do you have a regular chiropractor that you see?"

"I've seen a few chiropractors in my time." I swear to God, a giggle popped out of my mouth, like an involuntary stress response. I know it encourages them. And normally, I do encourage them. But today I didn't want to. It's like I couldn't stop myself. It was some weird reflex or something.

I didn't realize it in the moment, but I now understand that the reason I was incapable of telling a man no, *this* man no, was because I was terrified he would go away. I was like all the other Kentucky princesses: I was looking for a man—a daddy, a boyfriend, a husband, whatever—to take care of me. If I rejected them, they might not protect me. They might not want to rescue me: from a boring evening, from a job, from having to change my own tires or having to do my own taxes. I was relying on men to do the work for me, because I didn't believe I was capable of standing on my own.

But, back then, I didn't really want to stand on my own. I didn't want to change my own tires or do my own taxes. I bet Celeste Sullivan has never once changed a tire, but she doesn't need to please someone to make that happen. She was a queen. She ruled.

I didn't want to be a princess anymore; I wanted to be a Queen. I would reign.

I could instantly see where this conversation with this guy was leading: he was going to keep talking and move closer to me. When he moved closer to me, he would become more comfortable touching me. He would buy me drinks and then suggest we go to his room. And before, I would have allowed all of those things to happen. I would have been charmed and wooed by his presence and allowed him to have sex with me. If he took my number, we might text sexy things for a while and then he would disappear from my life. I could already see it ending in disaster. And I heard Celeste's voice, *One small change.*

I reached like I was going to touch his arm, and spilled his beer on the table. The foamy beer splattered my bathing suit and kimono, and a bit on his trunks. He laughed and called out "Party Foul!" I leapt up and grabbed my things and exclaimed "Oh no! Now I'm going to smell like a brewery!" and fled the pool.

Back in my room, I took a shower and changed. Before I could settle back with my book, Roger texted me, telling me he was skipping his afternoon session, along with a series of eggplant and squirting emojis.

I didn't tell him about Celeste Sullivan until we were at dinner. He was drinking scotch on the rocks. At first it seemed like he was listening, stroking my arm from across the table.

He said, "I'm glad you found a way to entertain yourself," in that way that indicated he wanted to change the subject, but I didn't want to change the subject. I was already thinking about what I wanted to do with my life, what I would be good at. I mentioned the trip to St. Louis in October. "I'm not sure how I'm going to come up with $2,000."

"Whoa. Hold on. What exactly are you getting for $2,000?"

"From what I understand, it's a whole weekend including food and hotel room—"

"You can't do that."

"Why not?"

"Because you're a fool to hand $2,000 to a charlatan who you just met in the conference room of a Ramada."

"We're at a Hyatt," I corrected him.

"Whatever … To do what? To help you sort out your feelings?" he chuckled. "I mean get a therapist. See a professional. Not some … *internet guru*," and he laughed at his own joke. The whole thing seemed to be incredibly funny to him. "This is how people end up in cults. I'm just trying to protect you." He placed his hand on mine.

I told him that he was probably right and that I was being silly.

When the waiter came around, I ordered the most expensive steak on the menu.

"I thought you just wanted a salad."

"I just suddenly realized how hungry I was." I ordered him another scotch and the $115 bottle of burgundy. "You know red wine makes me feel sexy."

I got him laughing and kept asking the waiter to refill his drink. I pretended to sip the wine and when he wasn't looking, chugged water. He drank the scotch and whole bottle of red. I filled out the credit card receipt for him, asking him to sign his name. He was seeing double by the time we left.

He was sloshy and staggering back to the room, feeling me up in the elevator. He couldn't even get his keycard from his wallet. I had to open the door. In the room, I told him to wait for me to change into something sexy.

And then I just waited him out.

I knew as soon as he sat down on the bed, he would be out like a light. Once I could hear him snoring, I pushed all of my things into my suitcase and wheeled my ass out of there. I found a credit card that wasn't maxed out and got my own room for the night. On the plane back to Nashville, I pulled out a notepad and started working on a plan to come up with $2,000.

Roger texted me all night and the next day. At first they were concerned texts and then they became aggressive. He accused me of scamming him with the expensive dinner. I guess he considered it payment for sex he never received. I was used to men making me feel like I owed them. I swore it would be the last time.

I was not a whore.

I was a queen.

CHAPTER 3

THE AFTERNOON AFTER THE MURDER

Lindy grabbed her phone and listened to her voicemail messages. She had one from Rouse. Their police station was small; he could have wandered over if he had a question. Rouse handled a little bit of everything, but he was dogged about white collar crimes and fraud. A month ago he'd been heavily investigating a tech company that conspired with an area school representative to offer exclusive contracts in exchange for "gifts" like speedboats, jewelry, and cars. Right before Rouse broke it open, the FBI swooped in and hijacked his bust. Rouse was consistently bitter. Lindy dialed his number but it went straight to voicemail. She made a note to get back with him. "Is Rouse related to our vic?"

"Could be," Boggs sat across from her.

"Did he call you?"

"I haven't gone through my messages." He picked up the receiver and entered his code.

"He could just be a nosy bitch," Lindy suggested. "Are we going to call the ex?"

"You mean, *am I* going to call the ex?"

"Yes. Are you going to call the ex?" Lindy clicked on the form to contact AT&T for access to the phone records. The victim's phone was found in the bedroom plugged into the charger. It was currently in an evidence bag. Jenna had handed over every passcode she had, which was several. But they still had to complete the paperwork for any additional cloud accounts she might not have had access to.

Boggs whistled. "Check her out."

He turned his monitor so Lindy could see it. On the screen, a large image of a blonde woman using a fly machine in a gym. It was a black and white image. Her back was muscular but not ripped like a bodybuilder. The website was called GabbiFixMe.com. She had links to multiple social media accounts, a contact page, blog posts, and lots of photos of the same attractive young woman.

"No wonder he was hooked." Boggs snatched the receiver and dialed.

"Oh, now you want to interview the ex." Lindy clicked on the feed from the Instagram account. Photos of Gabbi drinking green tea from a glass mug. Photos of Gabbi at the gym doing reps with a set of free weights. She was strong. Photos of Gabbi on a yoga mat standing on one leg and holding the other curled high behind her, her torso pressed out into a bow. "Wait. We should take the call in the interview room. Put her on speaker."

He shrugged. "Hello, this is Detective Ian Boggs from the Pleasant Springs Police Department ... " He left a benign message with a phone number and asked her to call him back.

Lindy clicked on the link to the Instagram account. Gabbi's highlights had labels like "Inspiration," "Food is Fuel," and "Strong is Sexy." Lindy scrolled down the page, spotting self-ies, food photos, fitness clothing hauls, green drinks, sneaker shots, and workout notes.

Gabbi took a photo of everything. Lindy took hardly any photos. She had some saved on her phone of Ella, but most of the photos on her phone were of stupid things like where she parked her car at the mall.

From Lindy's desk she could see the other officers had framed photos of their families, friends, and a few hunting trophy shots on their desks, where her own desk remained mostly empty of personal effects. She didn't even have a photo from her wedding.

Boggs asked, "When was the last time she posted anything about Ethan?"

Lindy scrolled until she found his face—actually, it was the two of their faces squished together. The lighting made it seem like a night spot—date night or possibly a wedding reception. She was glowing. He looked glassy-eyed. "Here we go." She clicked on the photo and saw the posting date. "September." Three months ago. Lindy scrolled up and saw a gap in the time between postings. She clicked on her Twitter and Facebook pages—same story. In September, this woman was posting happy couple photos and then a total media blackout for two weeks. The posts became far less personal. Generic quotes and food images. Fewer selfies until earlier this month.

"Anything?"

"It looks like they broke up and she was getting over it."

"What about his accounts?" Boggs walked around the desk and pulled up a chair next to Lindy. His accounts weren't personal at all. No snarky comments or silly memes. All of his posts were about his business: images from member events, promotional information, images from around Pleasant Springs proclaiming what a fantastic town it was to launch a small business.

"He's keeping it really clean online."

"Yep."

"You know what that means."

"Yep." I pushed him away and pressed the submit button to send the form to AT&T. "I can't wait to see what's in the DMs."

GABBI

How'd I meet Ethan?

Oh my gosh, it was one of those moments that you know it was meant to be.

First, when I woke up that morning, I did a card pull from my tarot deck. So there I am in my breakfast nook drinking green tea, and I pull … the six of cups.

I know, right? Cups are good. Cups mean prosperity, romance, love. Even reversed it means independence and moving forward. It was an excellent sign.

And I needed an excellent sign because everything seemed to be going wrong. My apartment was being sold out from under me. I lived in an old house that had been split into apartments that was now being renovated into one large home. The neighborhood where I was living was on the come up, so the owners wanted to restore it back to a single-family home and sell it for a million. And it sucked because I couldn't afford a house of my own. I needed to find a new apartment, but I was also ready to make a move, to buy a condo. What I wouldn't give to live in one of the cool renovated condos downtown above the little shops and the bakery, but the only people who can afford them are ... well, let's just say ... they real rich. And I had literally nothing in my savings account.

My wellness coaching business hadn't quite taken off. After I attended the Celeste Sullivan intensive last October, I'd spent the last five months devoting all of my energy into making myself a health and fitness coach and doing my best to pay off the credit card that I opened so I could pay for the retreat. And then, I found a guy who set up my website for me, but I was never pleased with how it looked. And then after the first installment I read all this stuff online about how I could have done it all myself. It was so frustrating, but I had made the leap.

Facing a loss after a risk is not punishment, it's just the consequence of taking a risk. You have to learn from it. That's from Celeste Sullivan.

When I woke up, I had gotten a message in the night from the moderator on my Celeste Sullivan Mastermind Group. One of the things we learned at the retreat was to post about our journey, because it made us accountable to the goals we set. But we had this monstrous woman who nailed me for every tiny infraction. Her name is Ashley and she's based out of ... I don't know ... I think Pennsylvania or something—someplace that's cold. Like, what is it now, Ashley?

Everyone always asks me why I don't get along with women. And the fact is that women do not like me. I have dealt with it my whole life. Women are instantly looking to tear me down. Except Reneé, who I've known since we were girls.

The email from Ashley said:

You have been warned twice about posting material that is inappropriate and unacceptable to the values of the Celeste Sullivan Facebook group. Please review the group guidelines, section 3A, if you have questions about why you are receiving this notice. (IE: Your nipples are visible through your shirt)

Failure to adhere to the guidelines will result in a suspension of your access to the group.

I am sending this because no one wants the group to be flagged and land all of us in "Facebook Jail." This group is too important for that.

Group Guidelines section 3A states: All photos posted by group members must adhere to the guidelines of FB, but also the values of upholding women in the best light while they claim their power on their journey. Please avoid nudity, drunkenness, slovenliness, or the glorification of substances that are, for the most part, still illegal in 26 states.

I had posted a photo of myself in my nightshirt. I was telling everyone about a serum that I really liked, and posted about how an inner glow is better than any foundation you could buy at the store. I thought I looked amazing in the mirror selfie. I didn't even notice my nipples. Then she posted a catty comment about how, "It must be nice to have time to give myself a nightly facial."

This is what I'm saying about women. All the other comments on the photo were positive. I got many fire emojis, questions about where I purchased the serum, and not one person mentioned my body. Ashley's tacky comment got 39 likes and a thumbs up. When Ashley's in charge, I'm offensive.

My other social media stats had stagnated as well. I looked through my analytics for my website, and I had gotten three views the day before, and one of those had clicked on my homepage and then immediately left. Like they opened the closet door when they needed the bathroom. I can only assume they were robots. My Facebook and Instagram posts were likes from former classmates or former coworkers. Reneé always liked and commented, "Get it, Girl!" which made me happy. But I needed more followers and bigger numbers if I was ever going to take off.

I was in that place where I felt like I couldn't do anything right. Something needed to happen, and fast. I reminded myself, *When you think you've released all outcomes, think again.*

I was incredibly happy to see the six of cups come out of my deck.

I just needed to trust and let the Universe do its work.

At the time, I was working for Berry Hill Chiropractic. I'd been a receptionist there for a few years. It offered some benefits and all the alignment work I wanted. They also gave me a little bonus for managing their Facebook page. But it wasn't enough. I still hadn't gotten my first wellness coaching client. That's where the money was. If I could just get one bite, I would be golden. Clients are on contract. I could charge a monthly rate, and then I'd have a steady income. Right now I was only getting a few bucks at a time when people down-loaded either my workout or meal plans.

But I knew something big was heading my way. I was about to get more people to coach or I was going to win the lottery. I was open to both possibilities.

I'm a positive person. Which is why I know I was not moping at work. But I did ask for a massage between clients.

Jack, one of my bosses, was always offering. He was what I would call dashing. He had this fantastic salt and pepper hair and a round, inviting face. He had great teeth that he keep incredibly white by going to the dentist regularly. He had welcoming energy, with a little bit of sliminess. He made you feel pretty and sexy, but also made you know he was a little nasty. He was the best salesperson for the clinic because he put people at ease just enough to get them in the door. However, no one really wanted him touching them. His brother Chad was actually the better chiropractor. Chad was incredibly closed off and private. Jack bragged about his college days, his guys' weekends in Vegas, and how he used to sing karaoke at some bar downtown, and everyone said he sounded just like Blake Shelton. And he loved to talk to me.

Sometimes it was a distraction. He'd hang around the reception desk and ask me a million questions about who I was dating, and whether I was on Tinder, and which of our clients were hot. When I walked in the clinic that morning and saw Jack at my desk drinking coffee and checking the appointment log, I took him up on that massage.

"What's happening, girl? Why are you so stressed?"

I was sitting in the massage chair, with my face pressed against the pillow ring. I directed all my answers to my feet. I told him my frustrations about not finding clients and wondering if I needed to relocate to a larger city. He rubbed his thumbs into the muscles next to my shoulder blades and I felt a release.

He said, "I'm shocked that people are not banging down your door for wellness coaching. I mean, look at you."

"Thank you!" I told him about Ashley and her warning. "Whenever I do get people looking at me, I'm flagged for it."

"Don't let that bitch yellow card you. You're putting yourself out there, and that's very brave."

"Well, anyway. The more pressing issue is I've got ninety days to vacate my place. Which means I have ninety days to find a new apartment. I don't even know where to start."

He rubbed down to my lower back, close to my hips. "You know, we have a condo downtown that we only use every once in a while. Maybe we could work out something where you could live there."

I did know about Jack's condo. They bought it and renovated it with the idea of it being an AirB&B and even listed it a few times, but his wife, Allison, was disgusted by the idea of strangers being naked anywhere near the furnishings she picked out. I think she wanted it to be like some dollhouse or something. She never went there. I was interested but didn't want to come across as desperate. "Oh, yeah? Like, what would you think about charging for rent?"

"Why don't you and I meet up tonight for dinner and we can work something out."

Oh.

I'd been here before. I knew exactly how this was going to go. We were going to go to dinner and he was going to tell me that he can't stand to see me struggle, and how he cares about me, and then he would take me downtown to show me the condo, and then he'd say, "This can be our place." And *boom*, I'm kept.

And honestly, I considered it. When I split with Roger, I was like, "Okay. No more married men!" But this wasn't just a married man—this was banging a married man specifically to get a free condo. Yes, the sneaking around is always fun, but this wasn't sneaking around for fun. It was sneaking around for a place to live. Sneaking around for survival. Would I ever feel comfortable worrying that his wife could show up at any moment where I lived? That she could put me out? But I was the one who asked the Universe for a solution and this is what I got.

He wanted to meet out of town. He suggested heading up to The Boat, which is what everyone called the casino across the state line in Illinois. It used to be a riverboat that actually went out on the water, which is why—at the time—gambling was allowed. Now the rules have changed and they don't have to go along with the pretense. Also, we get it. These are river cities. There are boats and barges and the Queen Anne tour docks twice a year, bringing in tourists to the downtown shops. Now, The Boat is a huge Harrah's casino with a mile-long buffet and a hotel. Neither Jack's wife nor any of her friends would be caught dead there.

I agreed to meet him in the bar. I arrived early, which was a mistake because you can't sit at the bar and enjoy a drink without being forced to stare at a video poker game. The place was already crowded. When I asked the bartender for a club soda with lime, she informed me, "If you're going to sit here, you have to play the game."

"Can I stand near the bar if I don't want to play the game?" She shrugged. I removed myself from the chair and fixed myself between two spaces so I wasn't directly in front of a game.

This place was not good for my vibe. I'd recently self-diagnosed myself as an HSP. A Highly Sensitive Person. I am especially sensitive to things like lights, crowds, sounds, and people's energy. Just standing in this blinking room was sucking all the life from me. But again, I still hadn't figured out how to tell a man no, so there I was.

In an attempt to avoid all the blinking lights, I pulled out my phone and checked my website analytics again. I had a tendency to fixate on my numbers. Why did my food posts get more likes than my gym photos? Why did my mirror selfies only get horn dogs? Why were my coaching promo posts always ignored?

Over my shoulder I heard this alarm and shouts, and it was this cluster of women about my age, all decked out in their nicest clothes. They were laughing and squealing, and I was like, *How does that even work? You get all dressed up just to be with a bunch of women?* And I had to be honest, I was a little jealous. I've never been part of a girl squad. I honestly think Reneé keeps me away from her other female friends.

I turned to smile at the bartender, who left my club soda and lime on the bar for me. She didn't acknowledge me. However, I realized an incredibly handsome man had sat next to me. He was also nose deep in his phone, but no one was hassling him to play video poker or find a new seat.

Anyone who has eyes knows that Ethan was a handsome man. He had thick, dark hair and these icy blue eyes. Like Prince Eric from *The Little Mermaid*. I think I honed in on his shoulders. He had nice, strong, broad shoulders, not the beefy ones I see at the gym all the time. He was lean strong. I wanted to be in those arms, to at least know what it was like to be in those arms … or to have my legs wrapped around them.

And that's when he caught me staring at him. I was so embarrassed, because I'm pretty sure I was leering at him. I might have been acting a little gross. I hadn't dated anyone since I started my glow up. He smiled and said, "Hey."

"Did you know you're not allowed to sit here unless you're going to play the game?"

"I did. But they know me here and know I'm just taking a little break."

"So if I'm sitting with you, they won't hassle me either?"

"Let's try it." He pulled out the chair, inviting me to sit next to him.

I thanked him and explained that I was checking my analytics while I waited for someone. He asked to see them. He told me he was a marketing and promotions manager or something like that. We talked about strategies, and he told me something I will never forget. He said, "Promoting yourself and your services is not selling. Selling is inauthentic. To share yourself, to share what you are doing, what your goals are, what your passions are … that's what attracts people."

I mean, he was so on my level. "Do you believe that you attract the energy you send out?"

"Absolutely."

"Don't you think it's scary, though? Letting people see you, like the real you?"

"Yes. It's terrifying. But it works."

So I put it out there for him and I asked for his advice. "I have this business that I want to launch. But I also have this job. It's a good job. It's a steady check. But I also want to make a real go at this business. You know what I mean?"

"It sounds like you don't trust that you can make it happen." He took the last sip of his drink. It smelled like bourbon and I was dying to taste it. "Remember what they say. Leap and the net will appear. You want big things, you gotta make big moves."

And then he reached over and took my phone. While he was typing, a balding man in a sports jacket approached him and clasped him on the shoulder. "Ethan, I can't stay for all the festivities, so can you send my host gift to the right table?" And he started shoving cash into Ethan's hands. Like, a wad of cash. Ethan gestured for the bartender to hand him something to put the cash in. She dug up an old-school plastic cup they used to use to collect coins from the slot machines and passed it to him. The guy was staggering drunk and looked a little green. Ethan assured him, "Yeah, I got ya. I got ya," as he worked all the bills into the cup.

"People just hand you cash. Are you a stripper?"

He laughed, "Would you come to my show?"

"Do you have props? Like a cowboy hat or matador costume?"

"I would probably go deep Kentucky country boy—some

breakaway Real Tree camo or something." He handed my phone back to me and showed me where he had entered his number into my phone. "What's your name?"

"Gabbi."

"I have to get back into my event. Why don't you text me later? You know, when you're done here."

"How do you know I'm not on a date? What makes you think I'm even available later?"

"I don't. I'm taking a risk." He touched my hand and said, "I'll see you later."

And he left. Just disappeared into the crowd. I was sizzling. I downed my club soda because I was warm all over. And it wasn't just him. I mean … it was, I'm not going to lie. But also, what he said. I was like, *Why don't I trust myself enough to go for it? Why don't I believe in myself?*

Jack arrived soon after. I could tell he showered, shaved, and put on what I guess he thought was a cool shirt. It had silver stitching on it. We walked together to the restaurant.

I was so distracted. I just kept thinking, *Okay, if I trust myself to make my business a go, what do I need?*

When Jack mentioned the condo, I told him that I didn't think I would need it. I couldn't imagine having sex with Jack to get a condo when I knew that I had so much of my own untapped potential that I hadn't tried. It would be cheapening myself and all the work I'd been doing. I was not a whore.

So, I lied and said that a friend had called me earlier asking me to move into a house with them and help with the mortgage. "Besides, you know, you might need that condo. Even if it's just a place where you and Allison can go and be together without the kids. I mean honestly, I feel kind of bad. I haven't called her since she had that last baby to see how they're doing. I should call her."

"No," he said quickly. He didn't want me calling her. But I couldn't resist tormenting him a little.

"No? I just feel so guilty. Y'all have been so sweet to me and I never talk to her anymore."

"Well, the kids keep her real busy."

"Exactly. And here I am monopolizing her husband. Taking him away from her and, what is it now, three kids? It just doesn't seem fair."

That squashed all talk about the condo, and he was ready to go then. He didn't even suggest dessert.

I ducked into the ladies' room, giving Jack enough time to leave the casino. On my phone, I saw Ethan had sent me a text:

U done w/that guy yet?

Yep. Where can I find you?

CHAPTER 4

THE DAY AFTER THE MURDER

Lindy and Boggs drove to Ethan's family's house out in the country near Eddyville. Boggs drove through the sleety rain across the Land Between the Lakes Bridge. The windy road took them past bare trees, choppy water, barges in the distance, and gray skies. At one point, a deer sprinted across the road, making Boggs pump the brakes.

Kentucky has more counties than any other state, which means it has the most jurisdictions and pockets of power. It creates areas with different hierarchies, values, and structure. And while the state registrants are blue, in Presidential elections, they mostly vote red, creating a contradictory area-wide classification of Conservative Democrats.

And all these kids from these different areas mix and mingle when they go to college. They compare similarities and differences while also assuming that their proclamation of "I grew up in (insert hometown name here)," is enough to explain away their entire personality.

When Ethan told his new friends, "I'm from Lake City," many of them might have assumed: well-off, country, conservative Baptist. On the other hand, when his ex-girlfriend told people she was from Maynard County, many might assume low-income, redneck, and a mixed bag of pro-cannabis Protestantism.

Not to mention, mostly white.

In Pleasant Springs, the population of persons of color is close to 13% and that includes the university population.

Transportation between all these counties requires long drives in the country on windy roads, over bridges, and past soy, corn, and cotton fields.

Out in this part of the country, holiday decorations were sparse. It was difficult to determine during the daylight hours whether homes were decorated for the holiday at all. Only a few homes had half-deflated Snoopys or Santas drooped on the lawn. One house had a pressboard train painted black, and after dark probably had a ring of running lights on the wheels.

The sky was white like it could snow at any time but none of it was on the forecast. It was just cold with the potential for ice.

Again, Lindy reached into the pockets of her coat for her gloves, and came up short. She ticked the heat up one notch.

The Moll family was a multigenerational clan. Tobacco farmers transitioned into small business owners, who invested in oil. The family provided gasoline to three franchise gas station chains.

They were rich. But it was country rich.

Ethan's parents lived on a renovated farm estate that was inherited from the generation before it. It was set way back off the road, a dark wooden horse fence lining the property, although no horses were anywhere in sight. The Molls were presenting themselves as old money but missing the legacy of the antiques. Everything on the property was new but looked old. A tire swing hung from a bare tree in the side yard. Currently it was acting as the de facto gathering spot for all the aunts, uncles, cousins, neighbors and church friends. They'd come to drop off casseroles, cry, and sit a spell, like an ongoing sprawl of a funeral before the actual funeral.

The fields near the home had been turned into a parking lot —diesel trucks, SUVs, and Lexuses were being managed by a band of North Face-wearing teens who waved people into available spots. Boggs pulled behind a Chevy SuperCab. When they approached the house, a passel of men stood on the porch in Carhartt coats and toboggan hats. Boggs blended with the men on the porch, paying condolences and shaking hands. Lindy meandered inside.

All the rooms buzzed with the sounds of women. As Boggs would explain to Lindy on the drive back, "Baptists love to keep themselves busy. It must keep them from drinking and dancing." In the kitchen, a group was uncovering sandwich trays from Walmart. Some washed dishes. Another group gathered in the dining room where they organized flower arrangements, fruit baskets, and plants along the walls. A woman sat at the dining room table among rotisserie chickens, veggie trays, and a vat of barbeque. She was taking inventory of the gifts in a schoolhouse notebook for thank you cards to be written at a later date. Upstairs, someone was vacuuming. Lindy could hear the *whoosh* of the washing machine in the distance. Other women mingled around the house holding red Solo cups and tiny paper plates. Women held each other up, handed each other tissues, and fetched sweet tea for others.

The house had been decorated for the holidays. The bannister and mantle were draped with greenery, cream candles, and red velvet bows. In the corner was a large Christmas tree outfitted with coordinating cream and red ornaments.

On the couch, in the center of this hive, Ethan's mother sat on the sable-colored couch and stared at a spot on the floor in front of her. She was small, newly gray, and wore a sweater that had been embroidered with a poinsettia design.

"Mrs. Moll." Lindy crouched down and held the woman's hand with both of hers. "I am so sorry for your loss. I'm Detective D'Arnaud. I am investigating your son's case. Can I speak to you for a moment?"

The woman placed her limp hand in Lindy's and turned to the young woman sitting next to her. "Brittany, can you please get the detective a glass of tea?" The young woman sitting next to Mrs. Moll made herself scarce and Lindy took her place.

"These are all my daughters and granddaughters." She gestured around the room, then, as if realizing for the first time how full her home was, amended it to, "... and friends, I guess."

"How many daughters?"

"Six. And then Ethan," she choked. "Ethan was the last."

Lindy nodded.

"Ethan lived in Pleasant Springs, but the family lives here. That's a little drive."

"He loved living near that school. He said there was always something going on. Something about that town, though."

Which was exactly how Lindy ended up there. Her wife grew up in Pleasant Springs. She rushed home as much as she could—it had some kind of pull on her.

Despite how many times Lindy insisted that they were better served living in an urban community—a place that had a larger LGBTQ+ community, and all their friends—the second that April started talking babies, she insisted on going back home. Lindy loved her too much to say no.

Mrs. Moll weakly clasped Lindy's hand. "Officer. Who could have done this to my boy?"

"That's what we're trying to find out. Did you know of any trouble that Ethan might have been in? Anyone who had hard feelings?"

"No. Everyone loved Ethan."

"Did he have a girlfriend? Anyone he was seeing?"

She shook her head. "No one special."

"What about his work? Do you know anything about his clients?"

Mrs. Moll wiped her face with a Kleenex. "He was a booster. He motivated people."

"What exactly did he motivate them to do?"

"He could never explain it to me in a way that I could understand it," she said. "These kids don't have jobs like we did. They seem to have all these made up names. Jenna could probably explain it better."

Lindy followed Mrs. Moll's eye-line into the kitchen, where Jenna was staring Lindy down and chatting with a dark-haired woman. Jenna had a downturned mouth, a permanent natural frown. When she realized they were talking about her, she nodded and walked toward them.

"Detective," Jenna crouched down to Mrs. Moll's level.

"Jenna—hon, can you explain to the detective what it was that Ethan did for a living?"

"He was the head networking associate for Local Business Integrations. Remember? He was in charge of the networking events."

Mrs. Moll nodded like she was remembering it all. "He liked it when people had a good time." Mrs. Moll said to Lindy, "At Christmas, he was the one who always came up with all the games or got everybody laughing over something silly."

She began crying again, looking around helpless, like she needed one of them to stop it all from happening.

Jenna reached out for her hand, "Miss Anna, would you like me to fetch you another sweet tea?"

"No, thank you. I'm about to float away on it." She excused herself and disappeared into a different room. When she moved from the couch, Jenna stood at her full height, which as Lindy was just reminded, was taller than she allowed people to see her. She crossed her arms over her chest and scanned the crowd.

Lindy stood to meet her level, but was at least two inches short. "I didn't realize you would be here."

"Ethan and I grew up together. We went to the same church. You want me to fix you a plate or something?" She said it like she was expected to be courteous like that but didn't really want to.

"No thanks. So you and Ethan were childhood friends?"

"We ran in different circles. We didn't become close until college." Jenna turned and walked toward the dining room. The woman who had been sitting next to Lindy placed her hand on her arm. "Aren't you the cop who ma– who's with the Robertson girl. The one with the baby?"

People around here struggle with the word "married" when it comes to two women. Some of them are straight-up homophobes. Some of them just don't know the terminology. "I am." Lindy sat back down. "Would you like to see a picture?"

These women could all be prejudiced as hell, but none of them are going to pass up looking at baby pictures. As people like to say around here, *It would just be tacky.*

The women at the Moll homestead all had stories about Ethan and many of them were of him convincing them to either do something, give him something, or buy him something. He raised the most funds for every school fundraiser. Many of the women laughed at how their freezers were still full of cookie dough that he'd convinced them that they'd be sorry if they didn't buy. He started his own lawn-mowing service. He lifeguarded at the YMCA. He worked toward Eagle Scout but didn't quite make it. Everyone was pleased to tell stories about him. No one could think of anyone who would want to do anything like this to him. Boggs was still walking the perimeter with the men.

While waiting in line for the bathroom, a woman with bloodshot eyes pulled her to the side. "Hey," she hissed, getting Lindy's attention. She had the whiff of marijuana on her. "Has everyone around here painted him as the perfect angel?"

"Not quite perfect." Lindy studied the woman's face. "Are you one of the sisters?"

"I'm Aimee." She nodded. "I guess you've figured it all out, right?"

"Figured out what?"

"Ethan was the only boy of six sisters." She held out her hands as if that was the answer. "Now what does that tell you?"

Lindy knew better to answer rhetorical questions posed by people who were clearly high.

"That they kept trying until they had a boy." Aimee developed the wide-eyed knowledgeable look of someone who doesn't get high often, but when they do, they think they're a genius. "We all knew it. They needed that heir. It's so backward. And then by the time Ethan arrived there were so many complications. He was under-developed and everyone was worried he wouldn't make it. So Daddy's little helper turned into the family doll."

A baby boy passed from mother to oldest sister, to younger

sister, to younger sister, and on down the line to a toddler-sized Aimee. Lindy was struggling enough with one baby, let alone a brood. April would be thrilled to have a brood.

"You two were close then?"

"I guess. He was trying to get me to rent out his spare room."

"Was he short on cash?"

"He would never admit it, but I think so. He started hounding me about it a month or so ago. 'Move in with me! It'll be fun! I never see you!' Like, he didn't say rent out his room, but I figured that's what he wanted."

"Were you thinking about it?"

"Like I wanted to live in Pleasant Springs? Partying with rowdy-ass, drunk college kids is not my scene. Besides, I don't get along with his girlfriend." She nodded her head toward the door that led to the kitchen. Jenna was leaning against the counter showing someone a photo on her phone.

"Jenna said that she and Ethan are just friends."

"I don't mean like girlfriend, girlfriend, but come on."

"You think something more is going on?"

"She's not my brother's type," Aimee sighed and stared off into the distance as if lost in her own thoughts. "I feel sorry for her, really. Ethan was used to having women do everything for him, but he also resented it when a woman tried to tell him anything. That's what he was always accusing me of doing. He said my negativity was toxic. I'm not negative," she took a step closer to Lindy, and Lindy tried to step back but her back was at the wall. She rattled a few photo frames. "I'm a realist. I warned him."

"Warned him of what?"

"I told him he was taking too much on. The house was too much. The SUV payments. The boat he bought."

"He owned a boat?"

"And two SeaDoos. But he sold those to Clark. That's Chrissy's husband "

Lindy hadn't seen his financials yet. "So you think he was broke?"

"He must have been. He was doing what he could to sell off his stuff."

"Where did his money go? Do you think he was doing drugs? Gambling?"

"No. Nothing like that. I mean he's done drugs," she dropped her voice, "I mean, who hasn't, right? But he wasn't a druggie. He spent time on the Boat, but that was for work stuff."

"Do you know if he was seeing anyone?"

She smiled. "I know he was seeing this girl in Tillman, and they were like … intense."

"Intense how?"

"They would be super hot and heavy, and then nothing. And then he'd be burning up the road to see her again."

"Did you ever meet her?"

"No. But I found her on Instagram. She was hot. That's probably why Jenna kept doing stuff to run her off. The last I heard, Jenna was working really hard to get him hooked up with Hillary."

"Who's that?"

"She's a local girl. Sweet. Part of their whole contemporary Christian crew."

Lindy looked puzzled.

"You know, church every Sunday and Wednesday. All their Instagram posts are Bible verses or raising money for mission work. Jenna's boyfriend's brother—what's his name—is in a Christian rock band. They like everyone to think that they're straight edge, but they do the same shit as everyone else. They just keep it tasteful or hidden. You know. They're the wine after Sunday School crowd."

"I guess that's not you."

"I'm real." She was holding her phone and fidgeting with the case, popping the corner of the phone out and then popping it back in. "But the whole Jenna and Ethan thing was a little twisted. It's just classic codependent behavior. Jenna was used to taking care of people—adults—and Ethan needed to be taken care of. Codependents need narcissists."

"You think your brother was a narcissist?"

"Well, not a malignant one!" she said. "He was…Ethan. He was addicted to attention. He didn't want to just make a bunch of money—I mean, we grew up with money. He wanted to be iconic. The kind of guy everyone told stories about. He was really charming and he always got what he wanted, and sometimes, to do that, he would cut corners or cut you down. Everyone always said I was jealous of him because he was the baby, but I was the only one who would call him out on his shit."

Lindy took her hand. She knew anger, even anger at the dead for having the audacity to be dead. Aimee was always in her brother's shadow and would be forever more because he didn't just die, but was murdered. Aimee leaned on Lindy, placed her head on her shoulder and softly wept.

Then she slid her hand around Lindy's waist. "So … you want to go see my room?" She lifted her head and smiled, then tried to intertwine her fingers with Lindy's.

Lindy pushed her back gently. "I'm married."

"Oh," she said. "But it's like, an open marriage, right?"

"No. And we just had a baby. Would you like to see pictures of her?" Pictures of Ella were like a social multi-tool kit.

"Yes!" She pushed against Lindy's shoulder in a *Get out*

gesture. "And I have a million questions. But first, I need to get some chicken and chips. I'm starving."

Finally, Lindy could go to the bathroom.

In the car on the drive back, Lindy wrote notes and debriefed Boggs on what she learned. "One of the sisters tried to make out with me."

"Which one?" he asked.

"Aimee."

"Me, too!"

"That's fun. Apparently her type is 'cops,'" Lindy said. "Anyway, when she wasn't coming on to me, she dished about Ethan's financial situation. She thinks he was flat broke. It seems like he had a spending problem."

"It did look like he had a lot of toys around the house."

"According to her, he had a boat."

"And two SeaDoos. Clark was telling me he just bought them from him. When he asked him why he was selling them, he said, 'for an engagement ring.'"

"Aimee knew about Gabbi and described it as 'intense.' She also said Jenna kept running her off. Oh, and I got another name of a completely different girlfriend—Hillary. So who was the engagement ring for and who was it definitely not for?"

"Clark thought he was just messing with him. Everyone I talked to made it seem like he had no plans on settling down."

"Did you talk about his job with anyone?"

"They were under the impression that he was going to join the family business at the end of the year."

"Aimee didn't mention that part."

"They spoke like Ethan was coming back home."

Lindy tapped her pen against the dash. "If his job was

going so great, why would he come home to work for Daddy?"

"At this point," Boggs said, "what we know is he may have been broke, which means he could have owed someone money. He may have had multiple girlfriends, which means someone could have been jealous." Boggs's phone lit up with a notification. He reached into the console and picked it up. "And it seems we have the murder weapon."

They drove back to the station, dropped the keys off, and headed to their desks. Boggs listened to a message from forensics and then called Hanson at home. Lindy waited at her desk, listening to one side of the conversation.

When he hung up, he said, "They found the knife. It was wiped down and stored back in the weapons locker. They found two different blood types on it. They've processed it, and now we wait on the DNA."

"That'll take forever," she said. "So you're thinking what I'm thinking, right?"

"Yep, slippage."

Blood is messy and slippery. That hand slips off the handle and will slice up the assailant's hand.

"Have you seen any cuts on anyone we've spoken to?"

"No."

"It could be old blood. He was a hunter. He could have been using it to clean a wild turkey and cut up his own hand. But Hanson said all the other weapons were clean."

"Would they be able to tell if it was animal blood already?"

"Not yet." He grabbed a rubber band ball he kept on his desk and tossed it in the air. "Okay, so we knew he was stabbed before. Now we think he was stabbed with his own knife and whoever did it probably cut themselves when they did it. And, they were familiar enough with him and his house that they were able to put it back with his things."

Lindy stood from her desk and snatched the ball from the air. "We need to talk to the girlfriend."

"Yeah. But which one?"

Lindy tossed the ball back to him and announced that she was going home.

When they moved to Pleasant Springs, April had wanted a place close to her parents, but they weren't ready to purchase land out in the country to build a new house on. They took a reduced-priced home in one of the undeveloped subdivisions. Each house looked the same: red brick, garage in the front, tiny front porch with just enough room for one rocking chair. Inside, everything was builder basic: pine cabinets, linoleum floors, carpet. April's mom picked out all the furniture, from the fake leather sectional to the *Live, Laugh, Love* wall art. Lindy and April treated it like it was a college rental. They didn't make improvements. They didn't worry about stains. Sometimes they sliced veggies directly on the counter without a cutting board. They told each other that they'd get it ready for resale once Ella was no longer throwing food everywhere. It was another thing in Lindy's life that felt temporary.

Ella was working her way around the coffee table when Lindy walked in the door. April called, "Hey, babe!" from the kitchen. Lindy unstrapped, locked up her gun, and washed her hands before scooping Ella into a squealing hug.

April had saved her a plate. Babies eat early like old people, and April had developed that habit as well. She had also developed a desire to learn how to make traditional Southern dishes and called her mom all the time for recipes. This desire was in direct conflict with her continued efforts to take off lingering baby weight, so she was constantly making modifications to account for calories and carbs.

"What are we having?"

"I made chicken and dumplings, but no dumplings."

"So you made chicken soup?"

"Basically," she said. "However, you can have six Triscuits to go with it."

"Six whole Triscuits! What a treat!"

April cleaned while Lindy ate. Ella stayed in the living room with her scattered blocks, activity pad, pink Duplos, and assorted stuffed animals. But the little girl was clearly on a mission to lap the coffee table a number of times unknown to her caregivers. Lindy always sat at the seat at the dining table where she could view each room.

"How was the family?"

"Like you would expect. Grieving. Confused. Angry."

"Did you see Cara?"

"I met them all. Cara was one of the twins?"

"Yes. She was at UK when we were there."

Lindy shrugged. It seemed like most of those who went to college around here either went to the University of Kentucky or Southwest Kentucky University. Lots of other schools, but it's like none of the kids here had ever heard of them.

"She was in my Economics class with me. That was the one where we got a new professor mid-semester because the first professor was fired for trading grades for sex. You don't remember that?"

"At this moment, no. But am I surprised that yet another scandal in the great Commonwealth of Kentucky was revealed because somebody had their dick out? No."

"Don't talk like that in front of Ella."

"She's in the other room. She doesn't even know what these words mean."

April walked over to where Lindy sat at the table. She slid her hands down Lindy's hair and placed her hands on her shoulders and began rubbing her neck. "I don't like it when kids cuss. It's tacky. And she picks up on everything we say."

"Really?" She softly moaned then asked, "So you've stopped calling bad drivers moronic twats?"

April told her to shut up and tried to stomp off, but Lindy pulled her back to her and pulled her into her lap.

April pulled away and sat down in the chair next to Lindy. "I just feel so bad for that family. I mean, what if it was some crazy person who's just looking for open doors? His house was right next to the fraternity house. They could have blended in with the crowd, and no one would have noticed."

Lindy took both of April's hands. "Babe. You don't have to worry. All the evidence so far indicates that it was someone who knew him."

April's face turned paler. She let go of Lindy's hands and turned away. "That's even scarier."

Lindy volunteered to put Ella to bed. She changed her, put her in pajamas, dimmed the lights, and held her close. At night she would hold Ella's little body against hers and sway, comforted in the knowledge that if anyone dared hurt her, that Lindy would not hesitate to put a bullet between their eyes. Possibly the same desire lingered at the Moll household, hoping to take down whoever took their son out of the world. Ella patted her tiny hand against Lindy's chest near her heart. Eventually, Ella let Lindy lay her down, giving her a bitch- I'm-not-even-tired look before slumping onto the mattress and rolling onto her side. Lindy reached into the crib holding a binky and Ella snatched it out of her hand like a crocodile.

Lindy sat in the rocker and waited for Ella's chest to rise

and fall with the breaths of a deep sleep. On April's nights, she'd read one of her books about academics and leadership. On Lindy's nights, she put together puzzles in her brain.

April was right. The assailant could have blended in with the party crowd. And if they did, they would be reasonably young.

She pulled out her phone and texted Boggs:

> We need to review the home surveillance footage again.

He didn't respond. She didn't even see three dots. He was clocked out.

Ella was finally snoozing. The nightlight shined stars on the ceiling. Lindy's phone's light was illuminating her face. She placed it in her pocket and went to her bedroom.

April was in bed. She'd swept her hair in a messy bun and slipped into one of the rayon nightgowns she bought from Kohl's when she was pregnant. Her face was shiny from her cleansers and moisturizers. She was reading her phone. Lately she'd joined multiple online groups about planning Disney World vacations. She was excited to take Ella to meet Mickey Mouse, regardless of how many times Lindy has explained that Ella would be terrified of a giant mouse with dead eyes.

Lindy climbed in the bed and pulled the phone from her hand.

"What are you doing?"

"I am about to take a shower and I want you to join me."

"Okay. But I don't want to get my hair wet."

●   ●   ●

For a long time, Lindy tried to hide her heart from April. Her friends had warned her. They worried that April was a tourist, that she was experimenting, that she wasn't really one of *them* because she was bi. Even now, Lindy's friends would ask her if she was really happy in this same-sex, heteronormative fantasy after 15 years.

It was rude. But nothing anyone said ever mattered to Lindy.

She was wrecked for April.

She wanted to hold her and protect her until she died.

April was drying her hair. She was pretending to be annoyed about the fact that she had to break out the hairdryer, but her smile told me that she wasn't so annoyed that we couldn't go at it again. Then she went and ruined the mood.

"Remember that Jeff's coming to town this weekend. I gotta make sure the house is presentable."

"Right," Lindy stepped from the shower and wrapped herself in a towel. She placed her hand on April's waist and kissed her on the neck.

"He's going to talk to his daddy about joining the family firm."

Lindy stood back and looked at April in the mirror. "So he's moving here."

She wasn't focused on Lindy, only her hair. "If they can come to an agreement. He also said something about wanting to take Ella to meet his parents."

The heat kicked on, making the lights flick and the shower fan lag for half a second. One of those things about her home that always unsettled her that April was oblivious to.

"Wait," Lindy said, having processed what April just told her. "Are you saying that he wants to co-parent with us now?"

"He didn't say anything like that." April slipped her night-gown over her head. The dampness from her skin made the rayon fabric translucent.

"Because you didn't ask him," Lindy sharpened her tone. "We have a contract that says we're the primary parents."

Lindy followed April out of the bathroom into the bedroom and dropped her towel. "I have adopted Ella. He's the one who drew up the paperwork."

"Which is why I didn't ask. I know all about the contract. I signed it, too." April climbed into the bed. "Honestly, I don't see the harm in having another set of hands around here."

"Are we not fine? Your mom and dad are, like, constantly available. We have daycare and soon preschool ..." Lindy threw on a sleep T-shirt and a pair of shorts.

"But imagine if our daughter had an even larger network of people who love her."

"Extended family is overrated." Lindy hadn't spoken to her biological family since she sent out the invitations to their wedding and received them right back stamped undeliverable. "Besides, Ella is never going to lack for love. She has us." Lindy climbed in the bed and adjusted her pillows. She was the one who picked out every sheet, blanket and pillow in their home. Her bed was her sanctuary and the conversation was killing her sleepy-time vibe. "I can't believe how comfortable you are with this."

"I don't see what the big deal is."

"Of course not, April. Because you are Ella's biological mother and Jeff is—"

"Just the sperm donor."

"Then why is he taking Ella to meet his parents?"

April looked straight ahead and fussed with the blanket.

"If he decides to void the contract, takes it to a judge, then where am I? Where are my parental rights? If, God forbid, something happens to you, then Jeff could fight for custody as the biological parent."

"Which is why we have the contract."

"This is Kentucky, April. When have the rules ever stopped anyone from doing anything around here?"

When gay marriage was legalized, it was an eastern Kentucky county clerk who refused to award marriage licenses, citing it was against her religion.

"You're overreacting, okay? Jeff has no interest in parenting Ella. But he and I have been friends for … ever. His parents know my parents. I'm shocked they haven't already asked me to come over with the baby."

Lindy wasn't. Jeff's family were the Tankersleys. They were the law firm that represented the hospital, the city and county school boards, and the University. Lindy suspected that insemination was not their idea of a grandchild.

But April couldn't fathom anyone not accepting her daughter. Lindy heard all the micro-aggressive comments about their "test tube baby," questions about their "ceremony" instead of wedding, and stumbling over whether they use the word "partner" or "wife." Lindy got fired up over it one day, shouting, "Our marriage is legally and spiritually valid. I am your wife, and you are my wife. I am not your partner. We didn't open a goddamned cupcake shop together."

April would always say when someone was clearly being snide, "People just don't know."

Whenever these moments happened, Lindy was reminded that if April chose to slip back into a heteronormie life, it would be like Lindy never existed. It would just confirm to everyone that April had just been going through a phase.

"Ella is your baby. We have a legal document confirming that. Jeff does not want to be a parent. But …"

"What?"

"While he's here, maybe we can talk about ..."

"No."

"We always said we wanted Ella to have a sibling."

"Not when he might be changing the contract. Not this weekend. Not right now." Lindy jumped from the bed and headed to the door.

"Where are you going?"

"To get six more goddamned Triscuits!"

After that first night, me and Ethan were *together*. We texted back and forth all week, and then on Friday night he was knocking on my door. It was so exciting getting my place ready for him: my best sheets, my best perfume, my best lingerie. It was way more fun than sneaking around. It was like homecoming every week.

In the meantime, I was hustling. I was looking at apartment listings. I was hanging up flyers and business cards at every gym, church bulletin board, and community center all over town. I was talking up my coaching services to anyone who walked in the clinic. Jack was no longer lingering around my desk, which was fine by me.

I also posted double-time on all my socials. I thought about what Ethan had said about "sharing" instead of "selling," and showing vulnerability. I posted a video of me falling out of a headstand. Like I had gone up, but I couldn't get settled, and boom, I was on my back. I had just rolled in a ball and laughed my ass off. I got, like, 100 likes immediately. I would have never allowed myself to post that before.

And Ethan had this great idea that I should get to know the concierges at all the big hotels because Tillman gets tourists. And he said I should see about setting up at the annual Bridal Expo and get these folks who are #sweatingforthewedding.

But he was so distracting. I would start working on a list of hotels to visit, and then I'd end up setting up a bunch of sexy selfies for him.

He told me my place was cute one morning while he was standing in my kitchen wearing only his boxers. He was keeping me entertained while I made him a smoothie.

"Don't get too comfortable with the place," I poured coconut water into my blender. "I have to move out soon."

"Have you found any place you like yet?"

"Not really. I'm looking at apartments, but all the ones in my price range are not … I don't know. I just don't like them."

"Why don't you buy?" He was nosing around my pantry. "Then at least you'd be building up some equity."

"You're funny." If he was paying attention to this place at all, he'd realize I was living paycheck to paycheck.

"How much do you have saved?"

"Nothing."

"What about your parents? Can they front the down payment?"

I actually laughed out loud. I hadn't asked my mama for a dime since I turned eighteen years old. Hell, one time I sent *her* $500 because she got behind on some credit cards. I dumped a bag of frozen bananas and berries into the blender. "No. My parents aren't like yours."

"What's that?"

I could only sigh. If I said rich, he'd think I paid attention to stuff like that. Like I'm shallow or a gold-digger. Instead I said, "Supportive. Now, hand me the spinach."

He passed me the plastic bag from my fridge and

muttered something about how his parents only seemed supportive because they were worried what others would think if they didn't support him. Then he asked me how much I could borrow and started talking about first time home buyer incentives, percentages, HOAs, and other acronyms that I'd never heard of before. He even suggested I buy a foreclosure and live in it while I fix it up and flip it. He was so smart and full of ideas. Just a million ideas all the time.

"C'mon," he slapped his hands together. "Get dressed!"

I ignored him and poured smoothies into cups.

"Seriously, go get dressed!" He removed the blender carafe from my hand and dropped it in the sink. "Go put on something nice. Not yoga pants."

"You love my yoga pants."

"I love your ass in yoga pants."

"You love my ass in everything."

"You're still not getting dressed." He clapped his hands together and pushed me out of the room. "Let's go."

"Your smoothie!"

He kissed me on the head and said, "Oh baby, you really are crazy if you ever thought I was going to drink that."

He was like that, too. Placating, but only up to a point. Bossy but nice about it.

I had this great boho caftan: pink and paisley. I put on some strappy sandals. He wore a nice button-up and khakis.

Ethan grabbed some old bronze-tinted aviators from my dresser and placed them on my face before we walked out the door. I asked him, "Are you auditioning to be my stylist?"

"You just need the right look for where we're going."

"And where is that?"

"It's a surprise." He loved surprising people. But really, I think that he loved knowing more than other people.

In his SUV, he keyed into the navigational system. He entered an address that I didn't recognize.

"I do live here. I can drive."

"No, no. I have to drive. Besides, it'll ruin the surprise."

The automated voice instructed him to turn left, turn right, hop on the interstate … We were practically out in the country near where my mama lived. Next thing I know, we were in a new condo development by the Harley Davidson Superstore. A sign on the condo building said, *Live, Shop, Work.* He pulled behind a Prius just like mine. A red sign next to a cluster of balloons announced "Open House."

"Ethan. Seriously. I can't go in there. I don't have any savings. There is no way I can afford something like this."

"Not with that attitude. Besides, no one here is forcing you to buy. You won't know what to ask for if you don't know what's out there." He kissed me on the nose. "Trust me. This will be fun."

He was right. It was fun.

We hit five different open houses that day. We gushed over hardwood floors and laughed at gaudy paint colors. And my wishlist started to come together. But by the time we finished, it had grown from reasonable to ridiculous: steam showers, vaulted ceilings, wine fridge … I don't even drink wine.

Ethan talked me up to every realtor like I was some sort of celebrity. Everything was "she needs" or "she requires." And all in connection to my work. He wasn't pretending to be my spouse or sugar daddy. It was more like he was my agent or manager.

I overheard him tell one of the realtors, "She's going to need a dedicated space for gym equipment, but also a space for filming her yoga videos. She'll also be holding virtual classes, so what's the WiFi situation in this building?" And I was like, *What a smart idea.* If I had my Yoga Teacher Training certificate, I could teach classes without needing to be part of a studio.

He told them I needed a clean-lined kitchen for meal prep videos and lots of storage. "You wouldn't believe the amount of flaxseed she goes through."

It's like he remembered every little nugget of information I had ever told him about who I wanted to be and used it to convince these people that I was already a success.

When we drove back to my place, I told him, "That was crazy. I have never felt so … You're a very good salesman to convince them that any of that was real."

"It's real. But you have to believe it." He reached over and took my hand. "First, you believe that it's possible. Then you make it happen."

We were happy.

I thought we were happy.

I was happy.

But I pushed it. I realized he was always coming to me. He'd come in on Friday nights and we'd hang out at my place. Sometimes we'd go downtown and walk around. He'd get a few drinks in him and make friends with everyone in the bar.

It was fun, but I started to feel like he was being a tourist in my life instead of a boyfriend. He hadn't changed his relationship status on his socials. He never posted anything about me. I never met his friends. I sure as hell hadn't met Jenna. I now realize that he was probably terrified of that.

I was tired and starting to get annoyed. He wasn't letting me into his life.

I hadn't said anything, yet.

He'd come in one weekend and picked up some bourbon on the way. I didn't even bother with my nice sheets and lingerie anymore. I wore an old T-shirt and some sweatpants that I had cut off into shorts. We were going to bed, and I roll over and see him on his phone, smiling. I looked over his shoulder to see what made him smile and I realized that he was on Tinder!

"What the fu—?" I pushed him until he bounced right out of the bed and onto the floor.

I can't even recall all the words I used, I was just so enraged. Eventually, I told him to pack up his shit and get out. But he was clinging to the side of the bed and kind of laughing. He was like, "Babe. Babe. Babe … this isn't for me. It's for us. Look!"

I was too pissed off to even listen. I started scrambling for what I recognized was his in my room: his overnight bag in the corner, his pants on the floor, the nice button-up shirt hanging outside my closet. I started snatching the clothes and crammed them into the bag, which I realized was heavy for something that looked so light. But he took it from me and thrust his phone into my face. I saw that it was a Tinder account set up in *my* name and with *my* photo. Under preferences, it said *Women Seeking Women*.

"I'm not a woman seeking a woman."

"I know," he placed the bag back on the floor, never breaking eye contact with me. "We are a couple seeking a woman."

I was swiping through the photos he had posted. All the selfies that I had sent him. They were for him and he was using them like bait.

"I thought it would be fun. Do you even realize how sexy you would be with your hands on another woman?"

"Yeah. Actually I know exactly how much you'd like to see that."

"I thought you'd be excited. You've had a threesome before."

"I mean, yeah, but that was like forever ago." It was way before my empowerment journey. And what I learned from the experience was that it wasn't for me. It was fine. I pretended to be turned on by this woman because it was my boyfriend's birthday. I faked the whole thing. And when he wouldn't stop talking about it and how we should do it again, I broke up with him. But I wasn't going to tell Ethan that. I learned a long time ago to lie to guys about things they want me to like, and that included threesomes, blow jobs, and sex in the shower right before I leave for work.

I was standing there in my pajamas, holding his phone and trying to figure out how to explain to him why this bugged me without breaking down this image he'd built around me.

I handed him his phone back and told him, "I know you love surprises, but this is one of those surprises I don't like. You set all this up without me. You were getting it all in place so I couldn't say no." He moved to the side of the bed closer to where I was standing. "We've never talked about having a threesome, or foursome, or whatever. And if we did, why do you assume that I wouldn't want another guy in here?"

"Oh no, honey. This is a one penis party."

"And right now, it's a one vagina party."

"Okay. Honest, Gabbi...I swear to God...I really thought you would be into this."

In my head I thought, *No. You thought you'd be into it.* I went on to explain, "And this is my town. It would be different if we were trying to do this in Vegas or something."

He reached out and took my hands. "Do you want to go to Vegas? Because I can set that up."

I had a flash in my brain and wanted to ask, *Is that a propos-*

al?, but I didn't because I knew it wasn't. "That's not the point. I live in a small city and you have me matching with lesbians in my area! I have flyers up all over town with my face on them. People are weird about that stuff here." I don't know why I had to explain it to him. He grew up here. He knew. You have the church folks preaching their anti-gay nonsense, posting on Facebook about gay marriage being wrong, but at the same time it's okay if two hot women get their freak on as long as another man is there and no one else knows about it. Someone sees my face on Tinder associated with this unicorn hunt, and then those anti-gay, church-going women will refuse to work with me.

He grabbed the phone from the bed. "Fine. I get it. I overstepped. Look, I'm deleting it. It's going. Look! It's gone." He stood and tried to pull me close to him, kissed my hands and tried to bring me in for a hug. I wouldn't accept it. "I promise, I didn't mean to make you angry. I'm sorry." He kissed me on the back of the neck.

But it was just one of so many things. Despite the fact that he had repurposed my photos and tried to manipulate me into a group sex party, he also was not letting me into his life.

I pulled away. "Why are you always coming here?"

"Because you live here."

"That's a cute answer, but seriously, you're always coming here. And when you come here, you stop by my work and chat up my coworkers. You've met Reneé. You've gone to my gym. The barista at the coffeeshop down the street knows your name and your order on sight. You know all about me but not once have you suggested that I come see you. See your house. Meet your friends."

"My house? My town? … " I heard a grumble of *Oh my God* as if explaining this to me was exhausting. "It's boring. It's just some stupid college town with fraternity parties and not much else."

"So is that why you're here? You're bored?"

"Well, yeah." He sat back down on the bed. "I'm excited to come here and hang out with you. We always have fun."

"I know. I don't see why we can't have fun at your house."

"We don't even have a Starbucks. You get that right? No Planet Fitness. I have to purchase an overpriced membership at the University to use the free weights. Until a year ago, it was a dry county. Our O'Charley's is brand new. The bars, the music, the people, it's all here."

"Then why do you live there if it's so boring, and so lame, and so not fun?"

"Because it's home. I'm, like, working on something big there. I understand the place." He reached out for my hand again. "You know what? It's fine. I've changed my mind. You've convinced me. Come stay with me next weekend."

"Really?"

"Yes. But the second you get bored, we are getting right in the car and coming back here."

But I wasn't over it yet. I was still annoyed that he was trolling for someone else when he was getting it whenever he wanted it. I was *not* a lousy lay. The fact that he was looking to bring someone new into our bedroom this early in the relation-ship was a little insulting. Like we were bored with each other already? He made me feel like I had something to prove. I had to pull out what me and Reneé call Magic Pussy ... sorry. That's probably inappropriate. It just means I needed to show him how lucky he had it – that the kegels were working, that my tits were still fly, and that I was an excellent lay. I was not some sex doll who is just going to lay there and take it.

That Friday, I made the drive. It was barely 45 minutes on the highway. And it was right past where I grew up in Kanton. I knew about his town. Half of my high school class went to college in Pleasant Springs. It's a small town. Big deal. I kind of get why he would think I would be bored, but I was no stranger to small town and country living. This place had a Kohl's, a Kroger, and a Walmart. It's nice. But that's typical of Ethan. Nothing was ever just nice. He was always craving the exciting thing that was happening somewhere else. He was spoiled that way.

He literally swept me off my feet when he met me at my car. Picked me up and carried me across the threshold. Then I had to send him back for my bags.

All of our house hunting had educated me on how to spot a home's footprint. His home was a master on main, detached two-story, with four bedrooms and a basement. Each room was decorated in Kentucky chic. Black and white artwork of horses. Silver replicas of Derby cups. Wooden photos in frames of Ethan and his family. Tapestry throw blankets tossed over the one thing that looked like Ethan had picked it out himself, the bro-y brown leather sectional couch that looked like a bed.

He showed me around and brought me a glass of water. His kitchen had little else in it except coffee. On the back porch, he showed me where he wanted to put in a hot tub.

"I was thinking about a pool when I moved in, but I just don't think I have the space to put in the one I want."

I was fixated on the view. All the houses' backyards were visible: no fences separated anyone. Everyone could see in everyone else's backyards. Directly across his backyard, a short distance through some sparse trees, I could see cars. "Is that the Walmart parking lot?"

"Yeah," he sighed. "They need to plant some more trees. Maybe they'll do that when they move out the fraternity at the end of the street." He pulled me close to him and hugged me from behind. I could see it—this place as our first place. I could practice yoga on this porch. We could convert the basement into a gym. He needed fresh food in his fridge, and a furry throw for that leather couch. He needed soft things. Supple things. Natural things.

I started laying hints. "This is such a big house. What are you doing with the other bedrooms?"

"One of the rooms is an office, but I'd much rather use my laptop on the couch or go to work." He pulled me in for a kiss but I pulled back.

"So why did you buy such a big house?"

He shook his head and pulled me inside. "Because I wanted it. Now, are you going to kiss me or not?"

We spent the rest of the evening cuddled on that couch. I felt so at home. It was like I had lived there the whole time.

I was comfortable at his place, but I still needed to be me. I'm an active person and not used to laying around in bed all day. If we were back at my place, we would run down to my gym, or run errands together, or do something. It was raining when we woke, which crushed my outdoor yoga plans. I ran through my morning sequence in his living room instead.

Eventually, I told him that I was feeling restless, which he assumed was a request for sex. Afterwards, I suggested that we go to his gym. He stalled. First, he said, "Sure," but then when I asked when, he put me off.

He said, "I'm not sure how my visitor's pass works."

"Okay, well I need some cardio." It wasn't raining anymore.

"Do you want to go down to the basement and do some burpees or something?"

I was already pulling my shoes from my overnight bag. "I'd rather go for a run. I'll just do a few laps around your neighborhood."

He stood up and took a step closer to me. He was wearing

a pair of cozy lounge pants and a soft blue T-shirt. I could smell the crisp scent of his shower gel when he pulled me close to him. He said, "My neighbors might not feel comfortable seeing a stranger running around their neighborhood."

I've always run around wherever I wanted, so I didn't know what his neighbors' problem was. "Okay. Go with me. If they see me with you, it won't be weird."

He whined about not wanting to leave the house at all that day. We'd worked out together before; I didn't understand what he was being such a baby about. I was strapping my cell phone to my arm and he wasn't even dressed. "If you don't want to go, I'll go on my own. I grew up in the country. I'm not a stranger to creative fitness plans … ooh, creative fitness plans … I should do a country fitness sequence for my website. Like a no-equipment, gravel road, outpacing the tractor thing. Yeah?"

"Sounds great, babe." He shoved his hands in his pants pockets.

"I'll be back in an hour."

"No," he said and walked down the hall. "Let me put on some shorts."

I went out on the front lawn and stretched my ankles while I waited. A woman next door was outside fussing with the ferns on her front porch. She spotted us and waved.

We walked a little and then jogged down to the end of his street, past the fraternity house that looked empty. He explained how all the kids around here head home on the weekends, so all the parties were on Thursday nights before everyone left town. He said the neighbors complained about the kids parking on their street and walking to the Nu house, so the cops started ticketing. The students started parking at Walmart, skipped over the ditch, and walked to the parties from a clearing at the end of the cul-de-sac. Once the Nu house was finally relocated closer to campus, they hoped the drama would stop.

Ethan waved at every car that passed. I couldn't tell if he was being courteous or if he knew all of them. Outside of his subdivision, we were able to cross the highway leading south out of town to the sidewalks that surrounded the University. I could see the recreation center and the window of his gym. I pointed that out to him and said, "We could go in and ask about the visitor's passes. See if they'll let us in."

"I don't have my card or anything."

Small towns. Or maybe it was boys. I rarely walked out of my apartment without my cell phone, my ID, and my debit card. I knew many women who wouldn't head out without pepper spray in their hidden pocket. Hell, not too long ago, I had been sent an ad for a pair of running shorts with a built in gun holster. But no, boys can go run and do whatever and not worry about making it home. Everything always works out for them.

We passed the stadium and a Hardee's. I could see the student residences, also quiet on a Saturday morning. It was a pretty town. There were chichi boutiques and big old Ford F-350s sucking down gas at Speedway. It was like a fantasy place, a little too good to be true.

I always thought Pleasant Springs people were stuck up. Even as kids, they were loud-mouthed know-it-alls who bragged about everything nice they had: their schools, their big houses, even their fancy-pants vacations. Even though Ethan grew up wealthy in the country, here he was, trying to impress the great people of Pleasant Springs.

When we got back to his street, Ethan got this idea that we should race. I don't know why. He was already struggling to keep up with my pace. I had slowed myself as much as I could and not be walking. He was fit, but he didn't do cardio. He would warm up for five minutes on the treadmill and then hit the weights. I'm not crazy fast, but I've at least run a 5K before. He wasn't going to beat me.

"Okay. From where to where?"

"From here to the house."

He counted us off and then he took off. He started off too fast. As soon as the adrenaline burned off, he slowed down and I smoked him. I slapped his mailbox when I reached it and spun around to see him walking and holding his side.

"I'm fast like a bunny!" I called to him. "Hop, hop, hop!" I shook my tail at him.

He was pissy. I thought it was funny. "What's my prize?" I danced around him. "What's my prize for winning?"

He wouldn't answer me. And I realized he was really mad about it. I was nervous. I'd pushed it. I was always pushing him and now he was mad.

I reached out for him and said, "Oh, baby."

"Is this how you coach people?" He dodged me. "By rubbing it in their face when they can't keep up with you? That's mean, Gabbi. That's really mean."

"I'm sorry." Before he could get away from me again, I wrapped my arms around his sweaty torso. We were funky, but I loved that earthy, gamey smell. I nuzzled him until he kissed me. He finally smiled and said, "You know, my mama told me to stay away from fast girls."

"I bet she did." I trotted ahead of him a little and wagged my tail at him. "C'mon. Catch the bunny! C'mon." I let him rush me and scoop me up into his arms and into the house.

I'd forgotten the first rule: Never best a man, even if you were the best.

The next morning, he woke me up and said, "Let's go to brunch!"

He never told me we were meeting his friends. I even had a cute outfit picked out in case we did go out or meet up with people. But he said brunch, and I figured it would be the two of us someplace secluded. I hopped in the shower and threw on some yoga pants and a hoodie.

When we arrived at the hostess stand at O'Charley's, he didn't even stop. He just pulled me behind him. The next thing I knew, I was standing next to a table with these two people I'd never met before.

Jenna didn't look like what I had imagined. She had been described as this strong, powerful force to be reckoned with, but she looked … off. She was doughy and abrasive. But I get why he wasn't into her. She was like a forty-year-old school teacher in a twenty-year-old's body. She had this mom energy, like she was going to pull juice boxes from her big tote purse. She was covered in all these layers and accessories: a cardigan with the handkerchief hem, a tunic, leggings, a drapy scarf. It was a shame, because she was tall and could have a power-house of a body. And her colors were all wrong, too. She was wearing these peaches and pastels that made her look even paler than she already was. And don't even get me started on the hair. Too damn long. She needed something short and sharp. I almost went to beauty school. I have an eye for these things.

She moved her tote to allow me a place to sit. "You didn't bring a purse in?"

I felt like she was examining me. "Oh. No. I guess I left everything at Ethan's." I really had. No phone. No ID. No cash. He rushed me out so quickly. He reached over and placed his hand on my leg. I covered it with my own. He was good about reminding me that we were in something together.

The waitress appeared and took their orders. There wasn't much on the menu that I could eat. Jenna ordered Banana's

Foster French Toast, which explained why she was a fan of all the layers. When I ordered warm water with a lemon wedge, I felt her look.

The boys huddled up in that way that boys do. I heard the words "business" and "risk." Jenna had a lot of questions about my job, which always makes me feel awkward. All Ethan's friends were career-minded. They graduated college and had goals. I didn't want to tell them that I was a receptionist at a chiropractor, so I focused on the fitness coach business. I mentioned the chiropractor like an afterthought, like I was just putting in a few hours for a friend who had a growing business.

She wasn't listening anyway. It was one of those moments where someone was looking me right in the eye, but they were really listening to the conversation in the background. I kept talking. "And I'm looking for a new apartment. Where I'm at now is being sold, so Ethan's been taking me around to open houses and things ... and you know, I'm working hard to get clients and just putting good energy out in the Universe. I pulled a Ten of Cups from my deck the other day, and that means wealth and prosperity, so I know that I just need to be patient. I'm just working on my journey."

Jenna snapped to attention now. "What's that? What's your journey?"

"It's like my glow up. I'm only engaging with activities that lead me closer to my goals. Repeating affirmations, filling my body with good fuel, a lot of yoga. When I pulled my card yesterday, I got The Lovers, which is very fortuitous."

"Card?" Jenna repeated everything back to me like I was speaking a different language or she was hard of hearing. Like she knew the words I was using but not in this context.

I humored her. "Yeah. I pull a tarot card from my deck in

the mornings. It's a morning routine thing. What do you do in the mornings to prepare for your day?"

Jenna scrunched up her nose. "Coffee … immediately. And I guess I used to read a verse from the Bible or a devotional book."

"Right. It's the same thing."

"It's not the same thing."

"It grounds you. It helps you prepare for the day. Usually affirms that you're on the right path, right?

Jenna said, "Right." She looked me over. It was a look I was familiar with. She was trying to determine whether I was dumb or crazy.

The waitress appeared with the cocktail hour drinks. Ethan looked pleased, but Ross still looked uncomfortable. I was nervous, so I rubbed my hand against Ethan's thigh.

Jenna leaned over and whispered to Ross, and he replied, "Yeah, my neck's just bothering me again."

Finally, a way I could contribute. "Do you carry a lot of tension there?"

He sipped from his drink. "It's from sitting behind a monitor all day."

"We see a lot of people in our office with the desk hump. Do you mind if I show you something?" I nudged for Ethan to move. "Switch spots with me."

Ethan laughed and conceded. I could see Jenna's eyes on me when I reached out to Ross's back.

"So here, this vertebrae is bending forward because these muscles," I placed my other hand on his stomach, "are not helping hold you up. If these were stronger, you would naturally sit up straighter at your desk." I placed my hand on the back of his neck. "And here, your neck is extended from screen use. You're on your phone a lot, right?"

He nodded.

"I don't know if you go to the gym or what your routine is, but you would benefit from the ab extender and the fly. If you don't like the gym, I'd recommend more lunges or mountain climbers."

Ross smiled. He had a nice smile. His hair was a little over-styled, with his whole modern nerd vibe going on. He had striking blue eyes. He said, "I don't disagree with you. I'm just not a fitness person."

I giggled. It's a default mechanism when men disagree with me. I can't very well tell him, *Don't be an idiot.* "Then you'd probably like a good yoga sequence. I could assemble a few for you." I grabbed my phone and pulled up my website.

"I didn't think guys did yoga. I thought it was just for … you know … people who look like you."

My stupid website was too hard to navigate on mobile. I knew that's why I wasn't getting any clients. "Here. Here's my website. And you can see some of my sequences …" I tapped on the screen "Here. Something like this."

I held out the screen so we could look at it together. I pointed out some of the moves on the page. "See, this is plank. In this pose, you tighten your core. That's the area you want to work on. See how I'm now on my side, that's side plank. It'll take practice, but I can show you modifications."

"Whoa! How'd you do that?"

"I don't know. What did I do?" I didn't even notice what he was talking about. I think I was in flying pigeon post, where I'm inverted and balancing one leg on my forearm while the other is extended straight into the air. It's the impressive poses that get the most likes, but it's not like an everyday pose. I'll admit, my legs looked long and my glutes firm. My arms are strong enough to hold me in this pose. Why more people didn't want to learn from me with a body like that astounds me. So frustrating.

"That's impressive."

"Thank you."

"Do you post these every day?"

"Some. I'm starting to post them more. Trying to be less stylized and more authentic, which is great because I was burning through so much time editing everything to be perfect.

"Who built your site?"

"This jerk who overcharged me. I wish it was more sleek and minimalistic. And I wish I could update it myself."

"You know, I can show you a few things."

I grabbed his arm without thinking about it. "Really? That would be amazing! We could even work out a trade? I can coach you and you can help me build my website."

He shrugged, "I would be open to that. And then you can pass my info along to any of your friends?"

"Totally. Why don't you come home with us and we can swap some ideas?"

Jenna's voice broke through. "You mean Ethan's house?

"Yeah. Ethan's house."

Jenna tossed her head back. "Because you said home. You said 'Come home with us'. Have you moved in?"

My other defense mechanism kicked in—the receptionist one—smiling when someone was being needlessly rude. "No. But I'm that person who says home when they mean hotel. It's just a thing I do. It usually means where I'm sleeping that night."

"Do you sleep in a lot of strange beds?"

Ross barked at her, "That's rude, Jenna."

But Ethan laughed, like he was amused by all this posturing. He swapped his Bloody Mary with Jenna's Diet Coke. "Obviously you need this more than I do. You're a little uptight today."

"No." She swapped the drinks back. "No. No. I don't need it. Besides, I'm driving today. Here, give it to Gabbi. I'm sorry. You drink this and I can drive you guys home. It wouldn't be the first time I hauled their drunk asses home after brunch."

"No," I waved my hand to decline. "No thank you. I don't drink."

"Oh. Are you an alcoholic?"

Both Ethan and Ross jumped her this time. "Jenna!"

"No. Not an alcoholic. I just always feel bloated and sleepy when I drink. It doesn't do anything for me. Besides, many successful women don't drink alcohol. J.Lo ... Kim Kardashian—"

"I guess you gotta stay fit for when that sex tape leaks."

I turned to Ethan, "Did you leak our sex tape this morning?"

He blushed, and laughed again to himself. "I am ... I ... I wonder where our food is."

And then the waitress appeared, as if he'd summoned it. In the hullabaloo, I slipped away to the restroom. I was livid. What a cheap blow! One of the most famous, most beautiful women in the world. Took a scandal and became a household name...and supported her whole family. It's all the same garbage that I was getting from that bitch on Facebook. Or when Jack's wife would come into the office and tell me, "I feel bad just looking at you," while she shoves complimentary M&M's in her mouth. The teacher who told me that she was sure "all the boys appreciated" the skirt I wore to class, which was a perfectly reasonable finger-tip length, and the last clean item in my closet.

This is why I say women don't like me. And today, I don't like women right back. More women have sent me weeping into a ladies' room than any dumb man.

When I came out of the stall, Ethan was leaning against the

sinks waiting on me. I washed my hands and told him he wasn't supposed to be there.

"I locked the door. No one's coming in."

I blotted my eyes and cheeks with one of the hand towels. My face was blotchy. "You need to talk to your girl."

"I told her she was being rude," he said. "She doesn't know how to act. I don't bring women back to my town. When I'm here, I have to be … a certain way … people expect … anyway, they aren't used to seeing me with someone."

I considered what he said. I guess he didn't tell them I was coming. They'd probably never even heard my name before.

He said, "Besides, it's not like it helped that you were pawing at her boyfriend."

I recognized that tone. He had a lot of nerve coming in here being mad at me.

He said, "You did have your hands all over Ross. You were rubbing on him—"

"Okay," I held up my hand and heard the country in me about to come out. "I was showing him where his spine was out of alignment. That's the same thing I do at work."

"You're a receptionist. You don't lay hands on clients."

"I can't even with you right now. Your girl has been nothing but rude to me all morning." I was amping up into a real cussing and I couldn't stop myself, and I was trying to hold the flow of it back. "And he offered to help me upgrade my website. I was going to trade coaching services. I'm doing my job. This jealousy bullshit—" And it was like alarm bells going off in my brain, *Leave him … no, kiss him … no, leave him. No one talks to you this way!*

I tried to move past him, but he placed his hand against the wall, boxing me in. I was pinned by the hand dryer.

He said, "You don't get it. I mean, don't you know what you do to me … what having you here is doing to me…what you do to people? There isn't a man, and probably half the women, who wouldn't want to trade places with me right now. To be able to stand this close to you. To know what you taste like."

"That doesn't mean they get to," I said.

I didn't ask for this attention, despite what people think. Earlier, I would have thought maybe he understood—that it was a pain in the ass most of the time. But now, hearing him say my presence made him lose that cool facade he has in front of other people. Maybe I do know the real him. If the Ethan I knew was different from the one his friends knew … well, I kind of loved that.

He was so close, leaning in that way like he was going to kiss me any second, the sweet anticipation of what was about to go down.

"I don't like you touching other men."

"I don't like touching other men."

"You're mine."

"And you're mine." I placed my hand over his heart. "This piece that you don't show anyone else, that's mine."

He hoisted me into the air and pressed me against the wall. I wrapped my legs around him. We were ripping away our clothes. He lowered me and bent me over the sink. My hands slipped on the soapy counter. I could see him smiling at himself in the mirror as he took me from behind. I tried not to moan, not to draw any more attention to us. But I came … hard.

When we were finished, we put our clothes back in their proper places. He was flushed and I smoothed down my hair. Before he unlocked the door and slipped out ahead of me, he said, "I can't wait to get you home."

Jenna and Ross barely noticed. We ate quickly and paid the check, rushing back to Ethan's house.

That next week, I texted him and he wouldn't reply. Or the few times he did, his responses were robotic. On Thursday I asked flat out if he was coming to my place that weekend or if I should plan to come to his house.

He texted, "I don't know. I'll call you."

The blow off. I couldn't believe it. His social media status still proudly proclaimed, *Single*.

CHAPTER 5

FOUR DAYS AFTER THE MURDER

Lindy drove Boggs to Integrated Business Solutions, LLC. It was located on a gravel lot strip mall off the highway, nestled between an abandoned Curves for Women and a State Farm Agent—both empty now. The ghosts of commerce. Inside the old Curves, a banner drooped so low it almost touched the floor.

They were starting with the vic's place of work. All effort to track down the girlfriend led them nowhere. They'd left messages, but her last Instagram post geotagged her at a yoga retreat in Puerto Via, Mexico. Luckily for them, she posted that morning that she was on her way back. Until they could speak with her, they were running the vic's financial statements and waiting for the cell phone records. Until those documents became available, they were going to chat with the vic's former boss.

The space inside Integrated Business Solutions was massive—a large bullpen area that was occupied by a large, plastic, round buffet table with folding chairs around it. Along the teal green walls, open cardboard boxes spilled their contents: T-shirts, lanyards, stress balls, and plastic cups.

In the right corner of the building, two offices had been erected with picture windows to allow anyone outside the room to see what the person inside was doing—no real privacy. A man emerged from one holding a breakfast sandwich wrapped in wax paper. "Can I help you?"

"Is this your company?"

"It is," he popped the last bite into his mouth and brushed his hands on his polo shirt. "I'm Ned Rockford. How you doing?" He was slick, like a car salesman. The man was carrot orange with white rims around his eyes. They introduced themselves. After he shook their hands, Lindy looked to her palms for evidence of self-tanning lotion. Perhaps he had a tanning bed in his house, a leftover from the late eighties.

"Oh no. Is this about Ethan? Please, please come in." He waved them to the round tables and indicated for them to please sit down. His voice shook when he spoke. "I already miss him so much. I'm not ever going to be able to replace him."

He offered them a coffee from the Keurig machine or a bottle of water; they both declined. He grabbed a nearby fast food cup that condensated with beads of sweat. The ice rattled inside as he slurped from the straw.

Boggs started. "What exactly is this business?"

"We help small businesses and entrepreneurs connect with more established businesses for networking opportunities, as well as helping them optimize their digital marketing."

Lindy asked, "Isn't that what the Chamber of Commerce does?"

"Ideally. No, our Chamber is far too concerned with big fish. When the Tappen factory left, they put all their efforts into bringing Pella Windows. They want another Pella. As a result, small businesses don't get the attention they need. Passing the alcohol ordinance was a big push, but it's all chains:

O'Charley's, Kohl's, Culver's. What about our local go-getters?"

He kept pitching. "Chains come into a town and close up at the first sign of trouble. Years ago, Tillman lost their World Market because gas prices rose too high, and they realized it wasn't worth the cost to send trucks that way. They come in, build a brand new building, and then abandon it. What are we supposed to do with a chain building designed to look like a hacienda? Local business owners go to church here, send their kids to our schools, pay taxes here: they are invested in the community. And we are invested in helping them."

Lindy, again, ready to argue, "And you think digital marketing is the answer?"

"Folks around here don't know the first thing about SEO. But Ethan did. It's all about getting eyes on your business in the most convenient way possible. People have smartphones, they go to your website, they go to your business. But his mission was connecting solopreneurs with corporations. Say you just graduated from our illustrious architecture program at SWKU. These kids don't want to slave at a firm for years. They want to hit it now. Ethan helps them design their webpage, gets their online presence built, and then connects them with industries like the hospital, the schools, the university. When they put in their bids, they won't be dismissed. Their company name is already making the rounds. We get them looking sleek and established, and then we get them in a room with CEOs, executives—and then they see who asks them to dance."

The folly of youth and those who exploit it. A 22-year-old architect who's never built anything outside his garage is going to be in charge of the new hospital wing? It was an interesting sell.

"So, where is this room? How do you get them together?"

"We host monthly networking events at Harrah's in Metropolis. It gets the small business owners together with our larger business sponsors. It's good for everyone. And we always have a big time."

"And you always do this on the Boat? Why not here, closer to the businesses you are promoting?"

"That was Ethan's idea. It's an all-in-one. Good music, good food, and if some want to gamble a little, who's to stop them? They're all adults having a good time. Some even bring their spouses."

"Sounds expensive."

"We get a package—the room, buffet tickets, and slot credits."

"What did Ethan do?"

"That kid was a recruitment star. He had the gift of gab. If I could have bottled it, I would have. I'd be a millionaire twice over."

Similar to what the family had told them. The kid had a gift and everyone loved him for it.

"Do you think he was struggling over anything? Was anyone who came in here angry with him?"

"No. I'm telling you, this kid could talk the panties off a nun. No one left mad."

"Do you think he was spending a lot of money? Like maybe he was gambling, or got in with the wrong people?"

"I never saw him gambling. He would spend the whole night talking to people. One night he talked himself plumb hoarse."

"You don't think he was in any financial trouble?"

"Well ..."

Lindy was becoming familiar with this pause, the vocal transition from just the facts to gossip. It was the first thing she learned—everyone here gossiped. It was as good as cash in this town. If you had the dirt on someone, it basically paid for your lunches moving forward. The most commonly uttered phrase in this town was, "You didn't hear it from me."

But he did hesitate, like maybe he was betraying some kind of trust. "He liked his toys. I told him to slow down, but you can't tell these kids anything." He ruffled his hair. "I was worried about him. We were in the middle of a little dip in revenue. It's not uncommon. We're not the hot new thing anymore, so we had to hustle a little to expand our reach. We were talking about setting up extension offices in Tillman so we could have better access to both southern Illinois and east Missouri. All of west Kentucky could have been our oyster. It has so much potential, but we're just two guys here. We aren't in a position to bring on another associate. We don't even have a receptionist. He was complaining that his bank account took a dip. He was not happy about it at all."

"Do you think he would do something … reckless?"

"I don't think so. He was pretty level-headed for someone so young."

"Do you mind if we look around his office?"

"Normally, I would say yes. But we keep files on our members and some of that information is confidential."

"We can go get a warrant."

"You're going to need to." He said it coolly. No tone. No bite.

Boggs stood and sighed. "Okay. We'll do that. I'm just surprised that you would make us go through all those steps considering how close you were. For all you know, one of your sponsors is involved."

"Or not. I already heard it was the girlfriend, but y'all can't find her cause she's in Mexico."

"That what you heard?" Boggs chuckled.

"Yes, sir." Teeth-baring smile. Too cool for both of them.

"You ever met her?"

"Yeah. A few times. She'd stop by here when she would come to town. She was a lot like him. She just chatted along like a little songbird. Together they could have … well, you never really know people, do you?"

"Who told you it was the girlfriend?"

"Who didn't?" He flipped his phone over on the table, effectively silencing the notifications that were making it light up periodically. "I've had several calls and messages from people who heard that hot young thing he was dating had done it. I don't believe half of it. I also heard she was a little snow bunny and some big dudes were looking for some cash she owed them."

Pretty girls and cocaine. That sounded a little too cliché. But clichés exist for a reason. Lindy asked, "Why would they come after Ethan if she owed them money?"

"Because Ethan kept cash all over that house. He didn't believe in credit cards."

He probably also didn't like claiming things on his taxes.

Boggs asked. "You know that for a fact?"

"He stopped using cards years ago. Said it was a Dave Ramsey thing. A bunch of folks have been doing that for a while now. You see the women at Kroger with their envelope system in their purse. He had a debit card, but all I ever saw was a wallet full of cash. One day he was out and he said he had to 'run to the ATM,' which was a safe in his house."

"Did everybody know this?"

"Everybody who knew him," he shrugged. "Be mighty tempting."

Lindy and Boggs had found no evidence of a robbery. Wallet, TV, laptop, guns—the safe was unmarred and empty, but it also wasn't cracked open. If anyone wanted to rob him, they'd have taken everything, not just what was in the safe.

Boggs said, "We heard he didn't have a dime to his name anymore. He was selling his jet skis and things."

"Nah. He might have been tightening up, but he wasn't broke."

"It would be really helpful if you would let us go through his office. He might have left a card or a number in there that might help us."

"Well, ain't y'all got his phone?" The longer they talked the more folksy he was becoming. "He kept everything in that phone. I can barely figure mine out."

"These tech companies are worse than criminals for getting information." Boggs was still working to get into that office. "We need someone who has the password."

"Can't Jenna help you with that?"

"You know Jenna?" Lindy asked.

"She's everywhere Ethan goes. I've never seen a woman take care of a man who wasn't trying to get a ring out of it. They met for lunch several times a week. Sometimes she would even drive him to work."

"Do you think Jenna's the jealous type?"

"Never met a woman who wasn't."

Lindy growled under her breath to Boggs. *"Get me the fuck out of here."* She covered it best she could with a cough.

"But I heard the girlfriend was jealous. That he called it quits and Gabbi wouldn't let go." He tapped against his phone back and said, "I'm not going to talk ugly about nobody ..." the folksiness was about as sticky as syrup. "But I heard them girls almost came to blows in the middle of Kohl's. Jenna told her to stay the hell away from Ethan. I mean, if that had happened late one night at the bar, nobody would have said a word. But it was the middle of the day and everything. And that's just tacky."

Boggs asked, "Did they actually tussle, like roll around on

the floor and pull hair?" Lindy had watched Boggs do this before, lean into the underlying sexism and fetishism.

"Nah, but I would have liked to have seen it. I'm gonna tell ya, though, Ethan was real put out over it. I told him, 'Look man, you wanna have a wife and a girlfriend, you gotta make sure they're both on board. Otherwise you gotta let one go.'"

"You sound like you speak from experience."

"Y'all ain't gonna entrap me. Both the current and former Mrs. Rockford will attest that I do not have time for girlfriends, boyfriends, or any other friends."

Later in the car, Boggs told Lindy that the transition between the former Mrs. Rockford and the current one was when the former hired the current to be a full time housekeeper. Lindy would bet good money that the current Mrs. Rockford would rather die than allow another woman to clean her house. Apparently, the Rockford children did not make the transition nearly as well. Supposedly, Ned only sees his kids on the holidays.

"Maybe Ethan was a surrogate son for him."

"Possibly. It seemed like he was quick to throw the girlfriend under the bus."

"Yeah, but that just makes me more suspicious. He seems like the guy who likes to talk his way out of his problems."

"I'd feel better about him if he let us search the office."

Lindy said, "But he is shady, right?"

"Oh yeah," Boggs said. "Rockford used to be the president of the Chamber of Commerce around here, but suddenly resigned to 'spend more time with his family.'"

"And then he started this business."

"Yep. No one can touch him."

"Is he being protected?"

"I think there's probably a reason why he's never been busted." Boggs said. "Good to know what the town is saying."

"Town or him?"

"I got this while we were talking to him," Boggs swiped open his phone and showed Lindy a screenshot message that his wife, Jackie, had texted to him. It had been posted by Jenna. It said, "When are the cops going to get off their butts and arrest the Crazy Ex-Girlfriend!!" Underneath the post were hundreds of comments. The first one said, *They know that bitches be crazy!*

She was calling them out. They would be in for it when they got back to the house.

At the station, Lindy checked her messages. She had another message from Rouse. But before she could make a note to herself, the lieutenant called them into his office.

Lieutenant Delphrain collected University of Tennessee sports memorabilia. His family lived right over the line in Paris, Tennessee, and much like other young people they crossed it to go to school at Southwest Kentucky State—then on to the police academy, and then back home. Pleasant Springs might have an allure, it drew people back to it. But sports allegiances were cemented at birth—his blood was as orange as anyone who attended UT. As was his office. The walls decked out in banners, ties, hat racks, framed renderings of Peyton Manning, footballs in acrylic boxes. Nearly all were gifts from his mother.

Lindy slumped in a nearby chair. She always positioned herself this way when she was called to the principal's office—which was all this was. Boggs, pad and notes ready, sat up like the apple-polisher he was.

He closed the door behind them and gestured for them to

sit down. Behind his desk, he poured two gel capsules from a bottle of Naproxen on his desk and popped them in his mouth. Through his teeth he said, "The chief wants to know where you are in the case."

"We're pretty sure we got the murder weapon. It's a 12" serrated hunting knife that we found when they inventoried the vic's hunting gear. Whoever it was knew where he kept his knives. They tried to clean it, but it lit up like a Christmas tree. We also found blood on the handle."

"Could be animal blood."

"That's why we're running prints and DNA on it now. You know that's going to take a while. We've talked to friends and family—"

"Were you at Integrated Business Solutions?"

"Yeah," she said. "It's the vic's workplace."

Boggs asked, "Did Rockford call and tattle on us?"

"Before you even made it to the car."

Boggs cursed under his breath.

Lindy sat at the edge of the chair. "So this guy's protected."

They ignored her question. Boggs told the lieutenant, "He pushed for the warrant."

"You won't get it."

"We have to at least go through the motions."

Lindy pushed, "Seriously? Is Rockford cousins with the mayor or something?"

The lieutenant said, "Fill out the form. See if you can find a judge, but step lightly."

"Judge Harris might sign it," Boggs offered.

The lieutenant stood and walked around the desk to lead them out. "Judge Harris is up for reelection just like the rest. Work around it."

Lindy stood up. "If we wait, he could be in there destroying evidence."

The lieutenant shook his head and opened the door. "Then find a quicker workaround. Besides, he asked about the girl-friend. What do you know about her?"

Boggs swiped on his phone. "According to her Instagram, she has been geotagged in Puerto Via."

"Sweet baby Jesus, are you telling me that you two sat on your hands long enough for her to flee the country?"

"We don't know that. She's at a yoga retreat."

"Oh yeah? When did she leave?"

Lindy and Boggs looked elsewhere. "The day after the murder."

The lieutenant flung the door closed and marched back behind his desk, perfectly positioned for the cussing he'd been holding back for days. Lindy and Boggs just stood there and absorbed each curse word, insult, derogatory remark, and general roaring. He was at least clever. Boggs was a douche canoe while Lindy was an apathetic fuckwad. When he'd exhausted himself, Boggs said, "She's on a plane back. She posted a few hours ago from her layover at the Atlanta airport. She used the hashtag 'homeward bound.'" He flipped his phone around to show the lieutenant.

He reached his hand toward the phone. "Let me see that."

The lieutenant swiped the screen of the phone. He said, "Good God, that's gorgeous!"

Lindy looked at Boggs, who reached for his phone back.

"Look at that view." He handed the phone back to Boggs. Lindy leaned over to spy the photo. It was of a young blonde woman on the beach, her arms raised to the sky, her chest flexed out, one leg tucked beneath her and the other extended behind her. She wore an emerald green bikini with a gold chain around her waist. Her hair was swept up into a pineapple messy bun. The perspiration on her breastbone, the pose emphasizing her round glutes. In the background, a glorious view of the Gulf of Mexico.

Everyone in that room would happily drink this woman's bathwater, set up camp in her laundry hamper, and be her yoga mat. None of them were admiring the palm trees in the distance.

"Go round her up! Before she takes off somewhere else." The lieutenant said.

Lindy paused. "Hold on. Can we at least discuss Integrated Business Solutions?"

"What about it?"

"There's something bugging me about the vic's job. Like, I don't get what it is. It sounds like he's still his fraternity's social chair."

"You talk to Rouse?"

"He left me a message."

"He's been looking for a reason to nail Rockford for years, but he can't really prove anything. Doesn't matter. Go talk to the girlfriend."

CHAPTER 6
EIGHT DAYS AFTER THE MURDER

After a quick stop at the gas station at the edge of the city limits, Lindy and Boggs drove north of town. They sipped from their big sodas and ate salty peanuts from a plastic package that Boggs poured down his neck while he drove.

Pleasant Springs is smack dab in the middle of nowhere. In order to get even a glimpse of "big city" life, its people must drive 45 minutes north to Tillman where there are bars, fancy restaurants, and an emerging art scene.

In between, it's nothing but empty fields, small farms, commercial farms, unincorporated communities, and access to a few other small towns. Getting stranded on the side of the road would leave someone waiting for a long time. Cell service is spotty and gas stations are sparse.

In the spring, the hills are covered with vibrant green Kentucky bluegrass.

On this day, the drive was desolate and gray.

Lindy felt the vibration of her phone. A text appeared across her screen that read:

Jeff wants to come over for dinner tonight.

Lindy typed onto her screen:

I don't know how long this will take.

After she hit send, she texted:

Don't wait on me. Tell Jeff I said hey.

Boggs asked, "The house?"

"No. April. Jeff's in town. He's coming over for dinner."

"That sounds *fun*."

"It ain't great."

"Why didn't y'all just go with an anonymous donor?"

"You'd have to go to a clinic in Nashville or Lexington. The whole process is expensive."

Tillman offered options but it didn't offer everything. They had IVF clinics, but they catered to hetero couples with fertility issues. It didn't matter. April didn't want to go the anonymous route anyway, worried they'd get the sperm of some weirdo looking for cash. "The description might say LSU grad, but it won't say schizophrenia."

Lindy tried to explain that a good clinic would provide family history profiles, but April would never consider it.

When April started making arrangements to use Jeff's sperm, sitting at the table with her calendar and ovulation charts, she was wondering aloud whether she was going to book a room or travel to Lexington where he was living then. "If you travel, I would need to take leave to go with you."

"You're not going with me," her words matter of fact, as if Lindy was being ridiculous.

"Why wouldn't I be there?"

Lindy watched her sitting before the papers, highlighters, and an ovulation kit box. She never looked up, but reached out, placing her hands over the pile, as if somewhere on one of those pieces of paper was the right answer to this question.

"Why don't you want me there?"

"Because it's not … because I … I wouldn't be comfortable. If we went to a clinic, it's not like you'd be in there with me."

"Of course I would. I'd be allowed to go in and hold your hand."

"But I … it's not a clinic and I wouldn't be comfortable. It would be uncomfortable … for me … you being there. It would be like having you there while I get a pap smear."

"You'll be doing this in a suite at the Hyatt. Hardly the pap smear environment. Besides, you're the one who's always telling me how magical and beautiful this experience will be."

"I can't have you in the room when I am injecting my vagina with semen. I can't. I can't have you watching that!"

Lindy had never been suspicious of April and Jeff until that moment. And here it was, the road diverging. Would she let it go or ask the question that was lingering over them, *Are you planning to fuck Jeff to make this baby?*

Lindy was trained—no, it was her nature before her training even began—to run toward gunfire. Asking flat out would be running right into the shootout, gun out, looking for a target. Her gut said April was up to something, but she didn't know how far to push it.

Lindy was disconnected from anyone who could offer any answers. She no longer spoke to her biological family, and all her friends—her community—lived far and wide in different places. She had created a family with April, but at the cost of community.

What little representation that existed in their college town was predominantly male, which meant the focus was on predominantly gay male issues. Lindy couldn't wander into her friendly neighborhood lesbian bar because there were none. Not even a secret one that she knew of. The few queer women she had encountered only stayed for a short time or sequestered themselves far out in the country.

She missed community, Pride events, and conversations with queer women in person, rather than on Reddit.

Lindy insisted on being present. She told April that she didn't have to be in the room, but she at least wanted to be in the house. Jeff would stay with them, they'd do their thing, and freeze what they could in case it didn't take the first time.

"Not take?" April asked. "Why wouldn't it take?"

"Because sometimes it doesn't." Lindy wondered if April had read anything at all about the process.

"I don't want to store that in my freezer," April said. "And it will take because I don't want to do this again."

And then April changed the plan.

Lindy was called out on a case—a meth head was roaming the county with a shotgun after shooting his girlfriend, who he'd accused of stealing his stash. It was all hands on deck, and Lindy didn't know when she would be back. April had peed on her ovulation stick and called in her stud without Lindy.

When Lindy finally came home, April told her it was done.

Lindy was livid. In a fit of rage, she stripped every bed in the house and wiped every surface with Clorox wipes. There was no talking. That night, Lindy slept on the couch.

She almost walked out. But where would she go? Get a hotel room? So everyone in town would talk? No. She had to just deal. She volunteered for extra shifts, slept at the station, and showered at the gym.

Lindy learned the fertilization took via text message. April sent a photo of the pregnancy test with double lines and the words:

COME HOME, PLEASE.

April was waiting for her in the living room, fondling the test. "I know you think I fucked him."

"Well, did you?"

"No." She threw the test on the coffee table. "I know you don't believe me."

"I don't. You've been acting shady as hell. Are we not in this together? Are we not a team here?"

"Yes. But you weren't listening to me. I said I wouldn't be comfortable with you there and I meant that, but you kept pushing. I didn't fuck him but I took advantage of an opportunity. That's it."

"You cut me out. Straight couples have conception stories. Gay couples who have babies have conception stories. They might be different, but they have them."

"What story?" April rolled her eyes. "It was cold and embarrassing. Like using tampons for the first time."

April continued, "I couldn't get past it. I had a baby story in my head. I never knew if I wanted to get married, but I knew someday I wanted a baby. And I wasn't going to be able to ever say, 'We're not trying but we're not *not* trying,' or ever have that … realization of feeling not great and then *surprise*. If it couldn't be natural, then it needed to be as clinical as possible."

It made no sense to Lindy. It could have been clinical. They could have saved their money and gone with an anonymous donor. It was April who fought so hard for Jeff. Lindy said, "But it could have been our own. We could have made it our own story."

"Aren't you so goddamn exhausted having to blaze a new trail to get anywhere. We have to invent everything? Everything has to be on our terms. Do you see how that makes everything harder?"

"Yes. Blazing new trails is hard, except it's not blazing a new trail. Other queer women have done this. You didn't even seek out anyone in our community. I mean …" Lindy stopped herself from lecturing her for not knowing her queer history, for not seeking a queer community, on all the things that had irritated her for years. It was pointless to go through it all now. "Fuck it. Whatever. It's done. You didn't want to share this experience with me. So what now? Is this your baby or ours?"

"Ours! Our baby. You're going to be here every day. Isn't that more important?"

Lindy ran her hand through her hair and stood. She stepped away to walk into the kitchen for some water, and April grabbed her hand, perhaps reading it as a step to walk away forever. "You have to forgive me. You have to. We have to get through this, because I'm going to have this baby, and I am freaking out right now."

Lindy sat back down next to her and pulled her into a hug. She cradled her head and let April cry on her shirt. Lindy waited until the tears slowed then asked, "What did Jeff say when you texted him?"

"I didn't. You're the only one I've told."

So Lindy let it go. She decided to let the past be in the past. Except the past was not in the past; it was going to be in her living room tonight holding Ella.

Boggs flipped through the songs, and Lindy barked, "No country."

"Aw, come on." He landed on an old George Strait song and nudged her, "Come on. Sing it with me!"

The Tillman PD allowed them to use one of their interrogation rooms, but not before asking a million questions and making them fill out fifteen different forms. The station was nice: sleek, updated, with tiny cameras in the rooms instead of a clunky digital relic mounted on a conspicuous tripod. Lindy and Boggs eyeballed all of it. The Tillman Chief of Police greeted them, and also laughed his ass off when he heard they'd let their primary suspect fly off to Mexico.

"She came back!" Lindy said while Boggs filled out the final paperwork. She sounded like an angsty teen. Right now she was an angsty teen. Her best girl had a boyfriend, just like back when she was sneaking around with Jennifer Reynolds in high school, and ended up leaping from her bedroom window and running through the woods to get away from Jennifer's power forward boyfriend and the rest of the starting lineup.

Gabbi answered the summons in a timely fashion. She entered the station right on time, on a cloud of delicate body spray. When she spoke to the desk sergeant, she leaned onto her forearms pushing her breasts together. All her clothing looked like it'd been rolled onto her body with a paint brush; her stretchy yoga pants and three-quarter zip were a bright lilac. Her sneakers matched, with a slight touch of neon green. She possessed effortless sportiness as she walked through the bullpen, was escorted to the cold room, and shown to the chair across from the camera.

Lindy sat down across from her. Boggs sat at the corner of the table. Gabbi smiled and didn't say hello. She was tan from her trip, except for her hands, which were splotched purple from cold.

"Miss Edwards," Lindy began. "Thank you for coming in today."

"It's fine." She placed her head into her hand and leaned toward Boggs, smiling. "But would it be possible for someone to bring me some warm water? It's so frigid in this room."

Gabbi kept her gaze on Boggs, like he was a plate of whatever type of food she no longer allowed herself to eat.

Lindy had seen this before. All the time, actually. Women who thought they could bat their eyelashes to get out of tickets, possession charges, solicitation. And then they would turn snide as soon as Lindy would start with the questions.

When one's only tool is a vagina, every problem looks like a penis.

They just assumed that Lindy was a sexless shrew sent to ruin the party. Lindy leaned into the role: the schoolmarm, the killjoy, the bitch. As did Boggs.

He clasped his hand over Gabbi's, "You're cold."

"See. You know," she looked up at him through her lashes, "humans release a chemical when they touch. So the instant even hands touch, those two become bonded."

"We're bonded now?" he asked. His Kentucky accent became more melodic.

"Yes. When you think of me, you'll remember holding my hand, and you'll release that love chemical."

Lindy interrupted their bond. "Miss Edwards." Gabbi was still giggling, like someone called out in class. Lindy sharpened her tone. When Boggs released Gabbi's hand, he turned it over so Lindy could get a glimpse of it. On the palm of Gabbi's hand was a cut in the middle of healing, pink and white. She'd likely have that scar for a lifetime.

Boggs asked, "Hey, what happened here? That looks like it was bad."

She smiled, "Oh, that happened when I was in Mexico.

There was a broken tile in the pool where I stayed, and I sliced my hand on it. You wouldn't believe the forms you have to sign when you get hurt at a fancy hotel."

It didn't look like a shallow cut. It looked deep and possibly made with a serrated blade. But Lindy was not an expert on cuts.

"We're going to need to take a photo of that, Miss Edwards," Lindy said.

She shrugged, "Fine." She pulled her hands into her lap in a slow, deliberate motion, like she was in a bad play and had just finished miming pouring tea into cups for her guests. It was delicate, but forced.

Lindy went back to her script. "We wanted to ask you about your relationship with Ethan Moll."

"We dated. I thought we were serious. But it didn't work out."

"When was that?"

"A few months ago."

"And did you two see each other after the official break up?"

"No."

"What about calls or texts?" Boggs asked.

"Probably," Gabbi said. "I was trying to get a hold of him before I left on my retreat, but he wasn't responding."

"Why?" Lindy asked.

"I don't know. I was getting on the plane the next day, I was going for a reset, and I was going to be doing a digital detox, so I wanted to make sure we were officially done."

Boggs said, "You could have just texted him that."

"I mean, yeah, but I didn't want it to be like that."

"But you never heard from him?" Lindy asked.

"No."

"What was your plan, to just ghost him when you got back?"

Gabbi said, "Why not? Essentially, he was ghosting me."

Boggs asked, "Did anyone tell you he died before we called?"

"No, but my friend Joey … our friend Joey … he called me after y'all did."

Lindy asked, "You were both friends with Joey?"

"Yeah. It's all just so …" she squinted and fanned her eyes. She whisked her hands across her dry cheeks and cleared her throat. "I mean, who would want to kill him?"

Boggs answered, "That's what we're trying to find out. Was he in trouble? Did he gamble or owe anyone money?"

Gabbi shook her head. "I don't think so. Sometimes we talked about going away. He had a boat. But it was at the lake. He had this fantasy that we would sneak off and live on a boat somewhere."

"Why?" Lindy asked. "He had family, friends … why would he run away?"

"No one told Ethan that he should build a life that he doesn't need to escape from."

Boggs looked down at his notes. Lindy searched Gabbi's face. Everything about this person seemed so inauthentic. Lindy asked, "Is that a Pinterest quote?"

Gabbi shrugged. "Ethan told me once that he always had to be two people—who he was where he lived and then who he was everywhere else."

"Everywhere else with you." Lindy was the one becoming snide. Something about Gabbi was needling her, the deliberate hand motions, the quotes instead of communicating. She was a phony.

"Me, Joey, his team of bros. Ask Joey about it. He's got stories from long before I came on the scene."

Boggs asked, "What kind of stories?"

"Drinking. Coke. Strip clubs … but that wasn't with me. He only drank around me. I don't drink anymore, and he knew that." It sounded like a brag. "When we met, I was in the middle of my glow up and trying to get my coaching business off the ground, so no alcohol, no sugar, no gluten … I never saw him get too crazy."

Lindy asked, "Where were you the night that Ethan died?"

"At home. Packing. Then I drove to the airport."

"Can anyone vouch for that?" Boggs asked. "Did you have a friend helping you, or maybe your new boyfriend?"

She shook her head and slid her hands under her thighs.

"We've been told that you didn't take the break up very well. That you were spending time in Pleasant Springs even after the breakup."

"You've been talking to Jenna."

Boggs said, "She's not your biggest fan."

"That girl has issues." A glimmer of the human underneath the facade peeked out. Gabbi crossed her arms over her chest but then dropped them. She shook her head and rolled her shoulders, then smiled. "But I still recognize the light in her."

"Were you looking for a job in Pleasant Springs? Were you planning on moving there even after the breakup?"

"I'm a lifestyle coach and fitness coach, and I saw some opportunities in Pleasant Springs, but ultimately I decided to stay here in Tillman."

Boggs tried to lead her, "It would make sense if you were hung up on a guy and wanted to be close to him—everybody's done a psycho drive-by every once in a while."

"I did not do a psycho drive-by. We broke up, and I started working on improving my life. I was not hung up."

"You're not leaving the country again any time soon, are you?"

"I can't. I have a yoga studio to open."

They reminded her about the photo they needed to take of her palm, and she laid her hand on the table.

"Actually, we need to get a series of photos. Detective Boggs is going to leave and another female officer will come in. You'll undress and we'll get a series of photos."

"Oh. No. I'm not comfortable with that. I'm not someone who just takes off their clothes unless it's for my gynie appointment."

Boggs said, "It would be helpful so we can eliminate you—"

"You can take a photo of my hand, but unless you arrest me, or have some paperwork like a—what do they call it?—a warrant? I won't take off my clothes."

Lindy left and got the camera. On the other side of the door she could hear Gabbi's giggles, goaded by Boggs. They didn't want to push too hard or else she would lawyer up. Leaving her with Boggs would allow him to smooth over any awkwardness and keep her on his call list.

Lindy was annoyed when they finally left. She drove them directly to the closest drive-up coffee shop and marched inside. She ordered two drinks and eyed the brownies in the display case.

In the car, Boggs flipped through his notes. Lindy jammed the keys in the ignition and drove them out of town.

"She's full of shit, right?"

"She's not genuine," Boggs said. He looked at his notes. "She grew up in Oak's Bluff, which is like a nothing spot outside of Kanton. That's all Maynard County rednecks."

"It's like she's hiding all that redneck nature under all her new-age, guru nonsense."

Boggs said, "We don't have anything that puts her in Pleasant Springs yet."

"I know."

"But nothing that puts her in Tillman either."

"So what now? Go talk to Joey?"

"If she went to Pleasant Springs, she would have to put gas in her car. We should check the cameras at the gas stations."

"What's she drive?

"A Prius."

"Figures." Lindy sipped from her drink. "Okay, so we'll check the ones by her house, and the ones off the exits."

Boggs asked, "Do you think she's good for it?"

"I think she's full of shit and has a big cut on her hand," she said. "We'll have Hansen look over the photos to see what he thinks, if he doesn't bitch too much over the quality of our photography skills."

"It looked like a jagged cut."

"We can contact the place where she stayed. If she had to sign a bunch of insurance forms, they'd be able to tell us."

"Let's go see this Joey guy while we're in town. Maybe he can tell us more about Ethan's party time."

They waited for Joey in a glass-covered conference room in a building downtown. It was a retrofitted building paid for with state-supplemented initiatives to bring more business into the downtown area. A young assistant type, possibly wearing the first tie he'd ever purchased on his own, offered them a choice of still or sparkling water, Nespresso, or Red Bull, and then left them alone. While they waited, Lindy stood at the windows overlooking the downtown. From their vantage point, they could see people milling around on the sidewalks and drivers struggling to parallel park. She watched a car turn onto the cobblestone one-way street, then slam on the brakes, and throw it in reverse.

"Idiots," Lindy muttered.

When Joey eventually entered the room, he looked haggard. His suit was wrinkled, his eyes had double-bags, and were bloodshot. A stain on his left sleeve is either ketchup or cherry syrup. Too bright red to be dried blood.

Joey sat at the head of the table. Lindy and Boggs sat across from each other on either side of him. His voice was shaky as he spoke. "This has just been so fucked up. I'm sorry. That's rude. I apologize." He directed the apology to Lindy with a nod. Poor Joey.

"We need to know more about Ethan so we can determine who did this. When was the last time you two talked?"

"It was mostly texts. Like we texted almost every day," Joey removed his phone from his pocket and unlocked it. "I was texting him … oh, God. I was texting him after he died. Asking him where he was. That's so … We were talking about hanging out soon, but he said he had to go to this wedding first. He was running some game on this hometown girl."

Boggs asked, "Do you know her name?"

Joey shook his head. "Girls don't get names unless he's serious about them. But I think he was trying to impress her by taking her to this wedding."

Lindy asked how long they had known each other, and they were regaled with a tearful tale of two pledges bonding over their shared time going through the unsanctioned hazing week.

"You went to school with the whole crew: Jenna, Ross—"

"Yeah, but I didn't really know them. Ethan was really good at keeping his life compartmentalized."

Lindy asked, "How's that?"

"Ethan just didn't like to mix his different worlds. So like, back in the day, if we wanted to do something, we would meet at the house or out somewhere. We never hung out at that house he shared with Jenna and Ross."

Boggs nodded as if he got it, but Lindy pushed. "So who was he hiding? You from Jenna or Jenna from you?"

"I don't think he was hiding as much as he just didn't feel comfortable because he didn't know *how* to be. It's like placing a chameleon on a plaid shirt."

Lindy asked, "So what was he like when he was with you?"

Joey smiled, but a pained smile. "I mean we'd get around," he cleared his throat. "But back in Pleasant Springs, all that stuff is don't ask, don't tell. So, like, this one time, we take off for Nashville, and we're at this place downtown straight up doing shots. It might have been bottle service or something. I don't remember. We're covered in girls. Just having fun, right? And all of a sudden, I look up to see Jenna walking through the place. Except I didn't recognize her at first. Jenna's kind of buttoned up. You've seen her. She looks like a student ambassador or one of those mean high school teachers, right?"

Lindy said, "I can see that," and Boggs nodded.

"Right, so she's wearing this sexy top and some tight-ass jeans, and these boots with super tall heels on them. She's got her hair down in these bouncy curls. I thought maybe her and Ross broke up or something because she looked like she was on the prowl. And I might have even taken a run at her, but before I could even say, 'Damn, Jenna,' Ethan's sending her to the bar to get a drink. Then he tells me to round up the girls and head to the bar down the street. Now, I don't like to change locations because it's too easy to lose people on the walk. But he was pushing, 'I gotta get rid of Jenna.' So, here I am, rounding up girls like some cattleman. We hit up the next place. Pretty quick after that, he found us and acted like it never happened. I asked about Jenna and all he said was, 'She went home.' And that was it."

Boggs asked, "So what happened there? Did he run her off?"

"I don't know. Probably. There's knowing, and then there's knowing. And I think he didn't want her to see what we were getting into. My question is: where was Ross? If they're all hunky-dory, then why was she walking into the place like she was DTF?" He held his hands up like he had presented some insight for the police to ponder.

Boggs asked, "What do you think was happening there?"

"I think she was taking her shot."

Lindy asked, "So you also think Jenna wanted to be with Ethan?"

"I think she might have wanted to get the full package, but even if he was interested in her that way, she wouldn't have been happy with it."

"Do you think she was jealous?"

"I don't know. I don't really know her."

Boggs asked, "What about Ethan and all this partying? Was he doing drugs? Coke? Oxy? Xanax?"

Joey shook his head. "I'm going to have to plead the fifth on that one. Ethan wasn't into drugs as much as he was into taking whatever was around. Nothing for home use."

Boggs asked, "What about gambling? Hoops? Horses?"

"Nah."

Lindy asked, "So what was his vice?"

"Girls." Joey stretched his arms over his head. "Let's just say we've hung out over 100 times and he's never once crashed at my place. We've been out together here, in Nash-ville, on the Boat, and at the end of the night, he's going home with some girl … I know this is a bad question, but did they say whether he was eat up with venereal diseases?"

Neither Lindy nor Boggs said anything; mostly they stared at Joey, unsure how to respond.

"You're right. That's tacky. I don't know why I asked that. I don't actually need to know that."

Boggs said, "I mean, if there were so many girls, then he must have gotten some jealous boyfriends riled up, right?"

"I mean maybe a while back, but he and Gabbi have been hot and heavy."

"You know Gabbi?" Lindy asked.

"Yeah. I mean she was the only girl he ever dated that he let me be around. Like, girlfriend, girlfriend anyway."

"But they split."

"Yeah. But they always found their way back to each other. They had one of those doomed romance things going on. They would get close, but then he'd back off for a while, and then he'd split again. I told him it wasn't fair to keep jerking her around like that."

"So they were still kind of together."

"If you asked either one of them, they would say no. But not in a way where you ever believed them. I was surprised when he started spending time with that hometown girl."

"Did Gabbi know about this new girl?"

He shrugged. "I don't think so. But maybe."

"Don't you think that would make her mad? She's got this guy whose family comes from money—he's like Prince Charming—and he's going to drop her for some schoolteacher?"

"I guess, maybe. But if she was just looking for a guy with money, I mean look no further." He smiled, all teeth. "I make more money than Ethan ever did."

"I thought he was doing well with his company ... he owns his home, has a boat—"

"That was all show. He had no insurance. He had no

savings. I have a 401K and stock options. Ethan was living on charm and favors. If Gabbi's a gold digger, she's a really bad one."

Lindy asked, "Did you peg her for the jealous type?"

Joey expelled air from his lips like a trumpet buzzing. "Yeah, but I mean, snatch-a-weave jealous. Not crazy-ex-girl-friend jealous."

Boggs leaned back in his chair, "That's funny because so far, you're the only one who has said that."

"None of those people in Pleasant Springs know her. She's actually really sweet. We work out together sometimes."

Boggs said, "I bet she makes the gym real fun."

"Yeah! You've seen her. And man, I tried to get in when her and Ethan split, but she wasn't having it. I was BAM," he crossed his arms in front of his face, "locked in the friendzone. She said she needed to get serious about her coaching or whatever."

Lindy asked, "Did she call you when they broke up?"

"Nah. I just saw where her Insta got real introspective, like a bunch of those inspirational quotes. And then Ethan said he was taking another girl to that wedding. I figured that was it."

Lindy asked, "Have you seen Gabbi around much?"

"Only online. I think she just got back from a yoga retreat … I mean … y'all can't seriously be thinking Gabbi had anything to do with this?"

"A lot of people around town are saying she was stalking him. Creeping around town."

"I don't know about that … But I wouldn't be surprised if he told people they had split when they were still together."

Boggs asked, "Do you think he was embarrassed of her?"

"Gabbi's hot. But with her crystals and her vibes and sh … I mean … does she look like a Sunday school teacher? A former beauty queen? Do you think she's ready for the whole-some Christmas photo shoots?"

Boggs said, "Nooo."

"Thank you. You get it."

Lindy said, "I'm sorry, but I don't. Are you saying Ethan didn't want to bring Gabbi home to Mama?"

"Pretty much. Gabbi's fun. Ethan leaves that little Pleasant Springs bubble to have fun. Mixing those worlds, bringing her home to his parents and their First Baptist crew, his sisters, Jenna? Nope. He wanted to keep Gabbi in a pretty little box on the shelf."

Lindy took a few notes. All of the archaic reasoning sounded so Kentucky. It's all about the surface. Lindy was also once the girl people didn't want to bring home to Mama, or even meet in daylight, or in public. Logically, Gabbi could get tired of that pretty little box and lash out.

"Hey, Joey. You said Ethan didn't have any money," Lindy dug in. "Do you have any idea what it was Ethan did for a living?"

"He sold marketing consultations. I think it was like that business fraternity … what do they call it? … BNI? Like some membership-based networking group. But he always said the real moneymaker was the members' parties on the Boat."

Boggs leaned in, "But be real. Do you think he was getting girls and drugs for these members?"

"Maybe. But if he was, he wouldn't be bragging to me about it. Pleasant Springs has a bigger cone of silence than Vegas."

When they left, Joey stood and leaned in, as if he was expecting a hug. That boy needed to call some friends or get a therapist.

On their way out of town, they stopped at a few gas stations, the more likely ones Gabbi would have passed on the way to Ethan's house. They looked at their surveillance cameras and had the files emailed back to the station.

They rode in silence for a while. It had started to rain on their drive back, a smattering of drizzly mist that wasn't even enough to keep the wipers at a low speed. Lindy manually hit the wipers on and off as she needed them. The sound of the damp drag of rubber against glass mirrored their mood.

Boggs asked, "What are you thinking?"

"I think … that Joey might be the only person we've talked to who's telling the truth."

"That kid was messed up." Boggs tapped the passenger side door with his key fob. "He kept texting the vic after his death. He clearly didn't know. But Gabbi stopped texting him on her trip, which could mean she knew he wouldn't respond. She mentioned a digital detox, but Joey said she was posting to Instagram."

"And she has the cut."

"That she said happened in Mexico."

"Okay, so she was already out of the country. If she was guilty, why wouldn't she just stay in Mexico?"

"Good question. I mean as many people are pointing at Jenna as they are Gabbi."

"Why does it have to be a woman at all? I have a bad feeling about this job of his. It sounds—"

"Sketchy as hell. I agree," he said. "Okay, what if she comes to town before her trip. One last hurrah. They knock one out, he's in the shower, she sees the messages from the other girl, she snaps, grabs his knife. She would know where it is if they dated as seriously as she said. She confronts him in the shower and stab, stab, stab."

"There are too many iffy things. She would have to go into

his closet, push aside all the clothes, unlock the weapons safe—"

"Are we sure he kept his hunting knife in a weapons safe? It could easily have been with his hunting gear in the garage."

"What if he'd left it lying around?"

"In the bedroom? Maybe. Makes more sense for it to be in the kitchen or living room. Like he was sharpening it."

"He seems like the kind of guy who leaves stuff around."

"But we found it in the gun safe."

"And everything else was in the garage."

"Why open a safe and grab a knife when you could grab a gun?"

"The knife had to already be in the bedroom for it to work. Stab, stab, stab, wipe the blade—"

"Cutting themselves on removal and then returning it to the weapons safe like nothing ever happened."

"Okay. But why? Something other than the crazy ex-girlfriend theory." Lindy posed. "No gambling, no drugs ... so debt? Joey said girls were his weakness."

"But he also said Gabbi cured him of that."

"Well, then she must have sugar cooch," Lindy said. "Because there is no cure for someone whose addiction is pretty girls. Gabbi said he was looking to escape. Do you buy that? Escape from what?"

"One of his sisters said he tried to sell his boat. Said it was for a ring. Maybe that was a lie. Maybe he was running away."

"Right. But away from what?" Lindy went back to the wipers. They mutually pondered in silence. She asked Boggs, "You grew up here. Does any of that compartmentalizing make any sense?"

"Sure. But that's not just here, that's everywhere." He flipped through his portfolio at his notes. "Didn't you ever date anyone who you didn't want your mom to meet?"

"I was an openly gay teen in eastern Kentucky. I was everyone else's secret."

"Right," he said. "Well maybe I should teach you about the straight world."

"Oh please, do, because your customs are so difficult for me to understand. I heard you actually try to put your penis inside of vaginas? I mean that's just crazy!"

"You started this conversation, thank you very much."

"Well, you don't have to be so fucking smug about it."

"What I am trying to tell you is sometimes a guy might want to be with a girl because of what she can do for him instead of building a life together."

"I'm not confused about the idea that a girl is a freak and you don't want to be in a relationship with them. But he was in a relationship with her. Why would he be embarrassed by her? Because, what? His family would disapprove? That sounds dumb. Why would he be in the closet?"

"The family seems to be well off, outstanding in the community. Possibly his parents have put pressure on him to find a 'nice girl.'"

"Nice girl. Do you know how many nice girls turn out to be total nightmares?"

"Everything Joey said made sense to me. Some guys like to keep girls around because they have fun with them, and then they have other girls they want to settle down with. He didn't want to settle down with the girl he was having fun with."

"And people want to say my love-match is invalid?"

He shrugged. "You asked."

"But would that make her snap?"

"People have snapped for much less."

"Right now, we got nothing. We need to go through the surveillance tapes from the gas stations, and see what Hansen says about that cut."

JENNA

That whole thing about all girls in Kentucky being princesses is total bullshit. No one takes care of me. I'm a grown-ass woman. I pay my own bills. I work hard to do so.

Maybe that's true for those girls who grew up in the bigger cities like Louisville or Lexington. Girls who *ooh* and *ahhh* over Derby hats and wake up at the crack of dawn to watch a royal wedding. Maybe in the suburbs. But I grew up in the country. I wore jeans and T-shirts to school. The only hats I wear are baseball hats when I get on a boat or if I'm helping my mama in the garden.

I mean, I've seen those girls; I've known those girls who expect the world to take care of them. I worked with this one girl who was the most guileless person I have ever met. She was honest and truly believed that humans were good. She never suspected any one of ever lying to her. We were an interesting contrast in the office. I mean, we were in sales, for crying out loud. But that's what worked for her. Everyone believed her, so they trusted she would never intentionally screw them over. That girl never once missed a sales quota.

But she also had a complete disregard for both her space

and common spaces. Her office was a mess. She left dirty dishes in the sink in the break room. She would leave half-drunk Starbucks cups in other people's offices if she stopped by to chat. Her vehicle was in complete chaos. And it never bothered her, because at some point someone would come up behind her and toss out her trash. I asked her once, "Girl, you left an oatmeal bowl in the sink. Are you not going to wash that?"

"Why? Don't we have someone who does that for us?"

"No. The cleaning staff only takes out the garbage and vacuums the floor."

"Well, it's always cleaned when I come in the next morning, so they must do that too."

"No. I do. I am the one cleaning your bowl."

She didn't apologize. She simply said she didn't know. But for the next few weeks, she'd walk past my office and announce that she had washed the bowl that morning. She was so proud of herself, as if I should put a sticker on her shirt.

So yes, I am aware that some girls who live in Kentucky think the world exists to clean up after them.

But that's not me.

GABBI

Eventually, Ethan texted me after that disastrous weekend with his friends.

> Hey beautiful.

He was sweet, sexy, and we fell right back into our old habits.

I suggested that I come back to visit him at his place. Like a do-over, right? And again, he was like, "No. It'll be more fun at your place."

But I wanted that chance to do it over again. I wanted to be in his space. I wanted to be curled up in a blanket with him on that awful leather couch. I wanted him to want me there. I explained that I wasn't working Friday. I could come in on Thursday afternoon after my shift ended and we'd have a whole extra day together. Finally, he agreed. "Fine. You can come to my boring-ass town again."

"It'll be fun," I insisted. "Don't worry."

He wasn't worried. I know that now.

So I headed to his house on Thursday afternoon. I woke up

the next morning and he was already gone to work and there's nothing in his house. I had asked him to pick me up a box of green tea and some fresh bananas before I arrived, which he "forgot." Typical. I was pissed because I had brought him a bottle of bourbon. And that cost way more than a silly box of tea. I went to Kroger. I picked up some stuff for dinner. He had this huge gas grill on his porch that he had never used. I also got his favorite granola bars.

But he was all weird about it. When he got home and saw the granola bars, he started packing up all his stuff.

I told him, "I just got here last night, why would we go all the way back?"

"Because it's just so much more fun at your place."

It was easier not to argue with him when he got like that. I packed up all my stuff and all the groceries I bought, except for the granola bars. He grabbed one before we headed out.

"You're welcome," I said, loudly, because he had yet to show any gratitude. But that was Ethan, right? Everything was his. Everyone doted on him. Everyone wanted to take care of him. If I didn't love him, it would have been sickening.

He pulled me in close in his kitchen and pulled the granola bar from his mouth. "Thank you, baby." And he kissed me on the head, munching on the bar.

"Gross. Do not even tell me that you got granola in my hair!"

"You're good," he smoothed his hand down my hair. I couldn't *not* go wherever he wanted to go. I would have followed him anywhere. I was that nuts over him. He pushed me toward the door and slapped me on the ass. "Let's go!"

He was 100% more relaxed when we were out of town. He was energized and handsy. When he placed the bottle of bourbon on the counter in my kitchen, it looked like a good amount of it was gone. But did he drink it the night before or in the car on the drive?

I asked, "Did you spill this?" I guess I was a little more annoyed about the money.

He didn't taste like bourbon. We didn't even go out on the town. When we were at his place, I had planned to grill some eggplant and broccoli rabe on his grill. Instead, I roasted it in my oven. After we ate, we cuddled on my saggy, second-hand sofa that I covered with an old bedspread. It wasn't until then that I saw him pour a little bourbon in an old jelly jar that I used to sip on green juice. He never seemed drunk.

The next morning we went to the gym together. I'd sit on the leg press and he'd film me showing proper technique. I was so excited to post it all on my socials later. Then we met Joey for a late lunch.

I don't care what anyone else says, I was not pressuring Ethan to let me move in with him. It was Joey who brought up my apartment situation.

He said, "What's happening with your apartment? That whole neighborhood is on the come up."

"I have to find a new place," I shrugged. I mean, there was nothing else I could do. There was always Jack, but I didn't think he'd let me now that Ethan was in the picture. "I just don't really like anything in my budget." Fine. It was a little lie. I had stopped looking. Not because I was trying to "trap" Ethan, but because I was distracted. I hadn't really looked.

"Come live with me!" Joey loved to brag about his huge house on the south end of Tillman. He said he had a room with its own exit and I could throw in some rent until I found a place of my own. Joey was like that. He was a the-more-the-merrier kind of guy. But Ethan had this weird freak out over it.

"You're not moving in with him."

"What's wrong with me?"

"Gabbi should be … well, she should stay the hell away from you."

"That's rude."

I jumped in because it was starting to get personal. "You know guys, I think I'll keep looking. Because I'm sure something is out there. Thank you, Joey. That's very kind."

But Joey wouldn't drop it. He looked right at Ethan and said, "It's not like you're offering her a place to stay."

And then Ethan got all defensive, "I don't live here—"

"Exactly."

"I might not even stay here," I waved my hands frantically to get them to focus on me for a second. "I am not locked in to Tillman. I could run my coaching services pretty much anywhere. I could do it all remotely. That's the point of online coaching. It's very mobile."

"Besides," Joey suggested, "You might be better off in a city. Some place like Nashville. No, Nashville's no longer the spot. It's too crowded. Have you looked into Austin?"

Ethan was in a mood all day after that. We went back to my place and he just laid down in front of the TV watching some show about car racing. Eventually, I went to bed without him. I could feel all this gray, staticky energy radiating from him. Like he was a spinning wheel of indecision on the screen.

The next morning, I woke up to the sound of him packing up. He made some flimsy excuse and took off. I tried to get him to talk to me, to talk about what was bothering me, but no…he just bolted.

He didn't even send me a courtesy text to tell me he made it home okay. I had to text him. And he just stopped responding. I sent him a message asking if we were doing anything that weekend. But I already knew, I was being ghosted.

It was so cowardly. If you place your penis inside of someone, they deserve a goodbye. That's just the kind thing to do.

I spent next the weekend alone and miserable.

And then Reneé was getting married. So that didn't help.

I love Reneé and I love her fiancé Robert as much as I can love anyone who is marrying Reneé—no man will ever be good enough for her. And she's so goofy in love with him. But I was not in the mood to celebrate anyone's love.

Reneé wanted to have a blowout bachelorette party. Or at least her sister Katie did. I would have been fine if we'd piled down in a cabin by the lake, but everybody else on the group chat kept posting:

> New Orleans!

> YASSS! New Orleans 🐊 🎷 🥖

> OMG, YES!

Reneé's friend Margaret was all of a sudden posting prices and flights. She'd already found a hotel. She was sending maps that showed the short walking distance to Bourbon Street. I mean, there was nothing else I could do except say yes.

We met at the airport and flew out together—just a crew of rowdy girls. And I was still dragging my heart behind me because of the Ethan brush off. I didn't texted him. He wasn't talking to me, so I wasn't talking to him right back. Jerk. But it was driving me crazy. I kept checking my phone in case he texted me, liked a photo, or posted something.

I didn't know all the girls on the trip that well. I knew Katie. When we were kids, Katie was the cool, older sister who would drive us around and teach us how to not get caught. Katie always had a boyfriend, always had a car, always had money because she always had a job, and always kept a tiny cooler of wine coolers in the back of her car.

Where Katie was curvy—all country-girl ass—Reneé was scrawny, walking around on nothing but bones. Katie was loud; Reneé was quiet. Katie wanted to be the boss; Reneé went with the flow. But they loved each other in that way that it would have never occurred to them not to. I never had a sister, so I had no concept of how it worked.

Right now I was not loving Katie because she was totally monopolizing all of Reneé's attention. She was like, "You have to sit with me Reneé because I'm the maid of honor!"

I wasn't jealous because Katie was the maid of honor. I knew Reneé would pick her sister, and besides, I didn't want to be maid of honor. I didn't want all the responsibilities.

On the plane, Reneé sat between me and Katie, while Chelsea and Margaret sat in the seat across from us. When the plane took off, Katie snatched up Reneé's hand. She was being so dramatic about the whole thing, cussing and freaking out, "What was that? OH MY GOD! We're not going to make it!"

"Katie!" I tried to grab her attention. "Have you never flown before?"

"Not since my first honeymoon! And I was taking Xanax back then." She studied me for a minute. "Oh. Do you have a Xanax? Or a gummy? I'd take a multivitamin if you told me it would help."

"Girl, you know drugs work backwards on me, because my—"

"Polarity is backwards," Katie finished my sentence for me. "Yes. I know all about your polarity problems. And none of that helps me right now."

One good thing about Katie is she is not afraid of being a little bitchy. Because I can be a little bitchy back and no one has hurt feelings. Is this what sisterhood is? Why aren't more women like Katie?

Reneé gripped Katie's hand, diverting her attention, "It's okay. They're professionals and soon they'll bring around the drink cart!"

Except they never did. We had turbulence the whole ride because of some storms. and as a result, all of us—including the flight attendants—made promises to Katie that she'd soon have one of those foot-long drinks in the shape of a penis in her hand.

Once we landed, we took turns watching each other's luggage outside the bathroom. It was crowded in the ladies' room and I just wanted to hide in the stall. The chatter around me was relentless—the white noise of people genuinely enjoying each other's company. I kept having to remind myself that I was there for Reneé.

When I finally walked out, Chelsea was complaining to Reneé about Katie. "It was so embarrassing. Everyone on the plane applauded when we landed because they were getting away from her."

"She's not a good flier, but now that we're on the ground, she'll be fine, right Gabbi?"

Look, I get it. Katie's loud and overbearing. I honestly couldn't imagine a better city to bring her to. But I was not in the mood to buck anyone up. So I gave them my most honest answer, "We should start drinking. Like, immediately."

I have discovered that the only way to survive on these girlfriend trips is to find someone to pair off with. Sadly, the only person I wanted to pair off with was Reneé, and it seemed like everyone else wanted the same thing. She was the bride, we were supposed to make a big deal over her, but she was my best friend and this whole group thing is bullshit.

I missed my friend. She was right here with me, but she

was *not* with me because she was with them. I didn't even know how to make this party perfect for her because I was too damn broken.

After we dropped our bags at the hotel—a nice place that Margaret selected on the recommendation of the many travel Facebook groups she was a member of—we got drinks, then food, then drinks again. Then we rode back to the hotel, changed into our party clothes and set out again. Margaret had put together a party game/scavenger hunt/truth-or-dare game where everyone was given initiatives for the night. We walked from bar to bar, drinks in hand—tiara and sash on Reneé—trying to complete our individual initiatives.

Bourbon Street was steamy and hazy. Every few feet a different bucket drummer or bucket drum circle was going to town on the lids for tips. Behind that, electronica beats drove from the clubs onto the streets. The smell of weed permeated every space. And nearly everyone carried glow in the dark cups with straws sticking out of the top.

Finally, Chelsea complained about her feet hurting and we found a bar with outdoor seating. But no matter where we went, we had to scream to carry on a conversation. The booze was not improving my mood. The second that Katie started to bitch about her ex, I pounced on the opportunity to jump on the men-are-garbage train.

"Did Reneé tell you about how he was cheating?" She barely paused for me to gasp. "Yeah. He was sexting this woman on Facebook. He didn't log out of his account and when I went to Facebook for my stuff, there it was. It just popped right up."

"What did you say when you confronted him?"

"I laid a trap for him. I printed out all the messages, so he couldn't delete them before the divorce. Then I picked the nastiest one and texted it to him right before he was supposed to walk in the door. He didn't even remember it. So he thought I was in the mood. Instead he found a suitcase full of his shit waiting on him."

I clapped. "Yes, girl! Yes!"

"And you are not even going to believe this shit. She wasn't even real! It was a total catfish situation." Katie started to laugh.

"No!" I pushed her on the shoulder.

"My cousin texted me as soon as she heard. He kept trying to video chat with this girl to set up a real date. She was supposed to be in Memphis, and he drove all the way there and she never showed. His brother did a reverse Google Image search and found this 'girl' had several other social media accounts under different names."

"Do you think it was really a man?"

"Yes," Katie said. "Because men are the worst."

"The absolute worst! Ugh. They ruin everything! The guy I was dating set up a Tinder account under my name to try to set up a threesome."

"I'd be okay with a threesome if it was two hot dudes."

"Yeah, that wasn't the plan," I said. "And I forgave him. Because I thought he was it. That we were it. Did Reneé tell you that he just ghosted me?"

"You're better off," Katie shook her head. "Because I'm telling ya, the last thing you want is to be married and realize what a dirtbag he is, because then you have to get the lawyers involved. I promise, will never get married again. I'm done. It's just all so fucked up anyway."

"Here, here sister." We sloppily clinked our plastic cups together and fell into giggles on top of each other.

"Hey. Y'all," Chelsea interrupted us. "Can we not

completely dump on the institution of marriage at Reneé's bachelorette party?"

Katie mouthed *Sorry*, but I kept giggling. I decided my new game tonight was to torture Chelsea.

Margaret clapped her hands together and asked, "What's next on the initiative? Who's winning so far?"

Reneé burped and said, "I think it's Katie!"

Katie cocked her hat and shot a finger gun across the table to her sister. So far Katie had sung a song at karaoke, chugged a hurricane, slapped the ass of a go-go dancer, surreptitiously untied a woman's halter top in the crowd, and asked a stranger if she could have their hat, which she was now wearing.

"I never win anything," Chelsea said, "And I'm so over this sticky-sweet mixed drink bullshit."

I was, too. But I wasn't going to say anything about it. I was barely drinking anyway. Mostly I was just carrying around a big, half-empty cup.

Margaret turned toward the bar, "They've got straight liquor."

"We should do shots!" Katie suggested.

Chelsea said, "Yes! I'm going to get us a round."

"No," Reneé adjusted her tiara and slumped on the table. "I can't. I'll be throwing up tomorrow."

We all said, "That's the point!"

"Reneé," I rubbed her back. "The only reason we came all this way is so you get knee-walking drunk and have a hot stranger rub his stuff all over you."

"I promised Robert no strippers."

Katie said, "Bullshit! You know he's having strippers."

"We made a deal!"

Chelsea returned with a tray of vodka shots for all of us.

We slammed our little plastic shot glasses on the table. Katie shouted, "WOO!" We didn't even toast. It tasted antiseptic.

Reneé immediately stood up and rushed inside to the back of the bar where the restrooms were located.

"Oh no. She's going to throw up," Margaret said. "I'll go check on her."

I took this opportunity to give Chelsea as much shit as possible. "Well, you've done it now Chelsea! You got the bride sick!"

"It's not my fault! I didn't make her take it!"

"It's not even midnight yet," Katie jumped in, as if she knew what my plan had been this whole time. "We're going to have to go back to the room now before we even see any penises!"

It felt devilish to torment Chelsea, like we were back in middle school being the mean-ass girls picking off the weak of the herd. Chelsea was a mean girl herself back in the day. She had to have been, because she wasn't taking the bait.

"I wouldn't be sad to go back to the room," Chelsea said. "Come on! Wouldn't you rather put on cozies and order McDonald's?"

"God, I love McDonald's," Katie had now shifted over to Team Chelsea.

Reneé rushed back to the table, fresh and revived. "Haaaaaaaa! Where's my drink?"

We all cheered as we watched her grab her cocktail from the table and teeter away into the street. She called for us. "Come on! This place is over!"

Katie rushed behind her and steadied her when she almost lost her balance.

As we gathered our things to follow, Margaret asked, "Who's ready for the midnight ghost tour?"

Chelsea walked behind her and shouted over the bucket drummers, "No one!"

The lure of McDonald's and cozies was too strong. Chelsea was getting her way. On the walk back to the hotel, we passed by a variety of sights. A woman held a huge snake like the one from the Britney Spears performance at the Video Music Awards. One of the club bouncers looked like Newman from *Seinfeld*. A woman twirled a baton of fire. In one area, a woman sat at a table under a lonely street lamp shuffling a deck of tarot cards.

We'd passed several of these women heading out, but this one caught my attention because I recognized the deck she was using. It was the same one I owned. The Goddess Tarot. My aunt had given me the deck. They had been hers that she'd bought back in the 90s. She said the reason she liked them was because there was no Death card to freak people out, and it celebrated women instead of the typical patriarchal set that everyone else used, *blah, blah, blah*. I thought they were pretty.

And I was a little drunk now, which was making me chatty. "Hey!" I beelined for her table. "I know those. I have those cards. They're cool right?"

"Do you want a reading?" she asked. She looked tired, like she couldn't even be bothered to put on the show any longer. She didn't wear a scarf or flowy skirt like many of the others, but jeans and a T-shirt with fringe sewn onto it. On the ends of the fringe she'd tied pony beads.

"Hey," I bumped her table, making everything on it wiggle. "Sorry. Hey. If you stood up and spun around, would those beads click together?"

"I want a reading!" Katie pushed past me and plopped her butt down on the padded folding chair. They negotiated the price.

Chelsea whispered to Margaret, "This is so corny. It's so NOLA, hokey-ass garbage: the mystics, the cemetery tours, the ghost tours."

"Oh my God, Chelsea!" I said when I returned to the group. "Why did you even come on this trip if you hate everything so much?"

"For the beignets, obviously."

Reneé removed her phone from her tiny crossbody purse, "Oh my God, I wonder if Café du Monde is open, because that would be so good right now." She thickly pressed into her phone screen.

Margaret leaned over to me, "I don't care if it is hokey. I'm going to do a reading. Are you doing a reading, Gabbi?"

"Yeah. I'm next." I was trying to listen to Katie's reading, but I couldn't hear anything because of everyone's chattering.

I think the woman told Katie, "You're in flux, like a cup on the edge of a table. You'll settle soon. I don't see a partner for you. This is your goddess card: Gwenhwyfar. She represents Judgment. No man could rule Wales without her by his side. She is the neck who holds up the head. Kings come and go, but you are the one who rules."

Katie thanked the woman and moved from the chair. She looked lost in thought as she rejoined the group. Reneé asked her in a too-loud voice, "Are you okay?"

I sat down at the table and handed over my money. The woman shuffled the cards. "You have this same deck?"

"Yes. But I haven't used it in a long time. I've been doing card pulls with an affirmation deck lately."

"What's that?"

"An affirmation deck? It's these cards that offer inspirational messages or mantras. The card you pull is the message you need to hear that day."

She rolled her eyes. "Millennials … Always looking inside. No concept of others."

She shuffled two separate decks. One she placed in the center of the purple-lined table. The other she placed next to a plastic tea light, with the little plastic flame to mimic a real fire. "Place your hand on the deck and ask a question."

"Aloud or silent?"

"Your choice."

I stayed silent, but anyone in my crew would have known what I was asking about. *Do Ethan and I have a future together?*

She arranged them in three rows. The first and third row each had two cards while the middle row had three. She flipped them over one at a time.

After a moment of reviewing the information, she said, "It doesn't look good for the two of you."

"Why?" I studied the spread. "All I'm seeing here are cups, coins, and staves. That's prosperity and magic."

"False prosperity. There is a deception. I see two faces. It would take time and patience for these two faces to become one. There's a lack of maturity," she tapped her finger against the Prince of Staves, a young man in red robes and jewels carrying a large stick. "There is also an outsider who could flip all of these cups over. That's beyond your control. But in the end, the transition will help you become the person you're trying to be. You will not like this transition, I'm sorry to say."

She flipped over a separate deck stack. It was two women sitting near a body of water. They were bare-breasted and held babies close to them. They gazed up at the sky in despair. "This is your goddess card. The Wawalak. They represent oppression. The Wawalak are aboriginal sister goddesses. They were swallowed by the Yurlunger, a great rainbow serpent. The sisters stuck together during the darkness in the belly of the beast until they were reborn back into the light. She is not alone. In partnership with her other goddess sister she is made powerful. Understand?"

I did not understand. "I think you read these wrong. The queen of cups, the three of coins, the two of cups," I tapped against the card of the couple standing together and holding a cup to the moon. I know that means marriage. "All of these are positive relationship cards."

"You don't read tarot cards like flash cards, memorizing meanings like some vocabulary test. *I* am reading these cards: the assignments, the multiple reverses here, but also the images on the card, the order in which they're laid, the story these cards tell. And I'm reading your energy."

"My energy? I am a goddamned ray of sunshine, so all you're getting from me is positivity and joy." I popped up from my chair.

Before Margaret could take my place I stopped her. "Don't bother. She's a crock."

I hustled everyone down the street. Chelsea was telling everyone how she told them so.

"Man, you should have gone first, Gabbi," Katie said. "Then I could have kept my money."

"What did she tell you?" Reneé asked.

"She was just doing it all wrong. Probably just makes up a bunch of stuff. I bet she's never even read the book that comes with the cards!" I was getting loud. I was just so mad. I grabbed my phone and tried to list the cards and the sequence she put them in before I forgot. I was going to do my own reading as soon as I got home to my own cards.

In partnership with my goddess sister. That bitch didn't know what she was talking about!

When I got home, I took out my own Goddess Tarot cards and arranged them in the exact same order. And I got out the tiny little book that came with those cards, which was difficult because it was crushed from being shoved in the box over and over again, the words faded. I was right; she was wrong. She had pulled the marriage card. And fine, the goddess card she pulled was about oppression, but that was just me and Ethan's relationship going through a rocky road. It didn't have anything to do with another woman or a "sister goddess." All this meant was Ethan and I were meant to be together, just like I thought.

We would be together. That's all there was to it.

I decided to give him space. He needed to miss me and realize how important I was to him. But that didn't mean it didn't suck. I still had to get up in the morning and go to work. I still had to go to the gym. I still had to not be with him.

It was the worst.

And while I kept telling myself, *You have to surrender to the process. You have to let him come back to you.* I was still in constant despair. I wanted to text him. I wanted to call him. And I had to stop myself every time.

Jack noticed. He caught me in one of my at-work pity parties, snooping online for whether Ethan was posting anything. Pointless. He never posted anything personal. He never even changed his status from being single to being in a relationship. And what a flimsy excuse: because people in his town would ask too many questions and that might affect his business. I guess that should have been a red freaking flag.

Jack came up to the desk and leaned on the counter. "What's up with you? You look so down."

"It's fine. It's just, Ethan … I'm giving him some space."

"Oh, no. Y'all break up?"

"He got all weird a while back, and he's not texting me back."

"I guess that's it then."

"That's not it. He's not ghosting me. He just needs to find his way back."

Jack popped candies into his mouth. "You're being optimistic. Usually when a guy stops texting you back, they're done."

"I have it on good authority that he will come to his senses soon and come back to me."

"Oh, do you now?" Jack always looked so self-satisfied when I told him it would all work out for me. Like he couldn't wait to catch me when I fell. Well, I hadn't fallen, so he could wipe that smug look off his face.

"Yes. When you think you have surrendered all, surrender more."

"Are you quoting your girl again?"

"Yes. I am quoting Celeste Sullivan. And I am surrendering to the process."

"Well, what do you think spooked him?"

I told him about the weekend, but skipped the part where I thought he was drinking bourbon on the drive. I was probably overthinking that anyway. And then I told him about the lunch with Joey.

Jack said, "Oh. That must have been it."

"What?"

"He's jealous. Of that Joey fella."

"Come on. That's his friend. And I was not flirting with him." I had seen jealous Ethan. Jealous Ethan was possessive, not distant.

"Or … he might have been thinking you were laying a man trap."

Man trap! I don't have to lay a trap to get a man. I am fighting off dicks on my walk to the mailbox. If I wanted to, I could have Jack wrapped around my finger, giving me a free condo and setting me up to a nice kept life. But that's not what I wanted.

Jack said, "Look, either way, that kid's an idiot if he's going to let someone fine like you get away."

"Thank you. But he's not letting me get away. I'm waiting him out."

He laughed then. "Because you don't chase deer. You just patiently sit in the stand until they wander by, and then BAM! You got them."

I thought, *It's not a hunt. Ethan is my soulmate. And when he recognizes that, he will be on my doorstep. It's as easy as that.*

Jack also added that it sounded like I didn't have my apartment situation worked out and to call him if I needed that space he had told me about. "We can't have you homeless, alright?"

I thanked him. But I wasn't ready for the strings that would inevitably go along with that one. Besides, when Ethan did come back, we would need to come to a solution together. Because he would come back.

I tried to keep that in mind. I kept telling myself, *It's all coming to you, you just have to be patient.* Which is one of the biggest challenges of keeping my vibe high. Being patient. While I was online, I searched to see if there were any Celeste Sullivan events nearby, but nothing. She was writing her new book. After that, she'd do another speaking tour. I thought about posting something to the Celeste Sullivan group, but I didn't want to hear from women like Ashley. And Reneé was in wedding mode. I didn't want to drag her into it. I legit didn't have anyone to talk to about this.

After work, I went to the gym. I sprinted for 10 minutes on the treadmill and then went to the plyometric area to do jump squats. I was on my second set when I spotted Joey chatting with someone in the weight room. I wondered if he knew that me and Ethan weren't speaking right now. He waved. I waved back and finished my set. I wanted him to see a strong woman who was not bothered by Ethan's absence. If Joey didn't know anything, it would stay that way. He walked across the gym to my section where I had moved onto box jumps. I was leaping onto a box, stepping down, then leaping again.

"Look at you, girl! You're getting it done."

"Like I always do. Every. Damn. Day."

"Every day!"

I was sloppy with my form. I was landing on my toes too hard instead of on the full foot. It was putting pressure on my knees. I knew better.

I stepped down and told Joey, "I'm going to hit up the free weights."

"Let me join you."

Joey's a chatty guy. Like, if he's not hearing the sound of his own voice, how does he even know he's alive? He chattered on about how the gym needed more hydration stations and less TV's, videos he'd been watching online, a cookout he went to over the weekend at his married friends' place out in the country. I nodded to all of it and did my reps, trying to concentrate on activating the correct muscles.

"What did you and Ethan get into this weekend?"

"Nothing much." There it was. He didn't know. Or he wanted me to tell him. "We didn't see each other really."

"Is something going on?"

"I don't know." I let the weight drop to the floor, which is one of the "no-no" rules of the gym. I didn't want to whine to Joey about Ethan, but I was also dying for information. "Has he said anything to you?"

"No. We've texted a little but nothing real. Do you think he's trying to ghost?"

"Is that his thing? Does he lovebomb and then ghost?"

"I have no idea what he does with girls." Then he laughed, "You make it sound like a hit and run."

"Well, it felt like it." I sounded bitter. I immediately wanted to take it back.

"You don't need someone who's going to treat you like that. I mean look at you," he pointed at the mirror. What I saw was a sweaty woman whose workout shorts were crawling up her crotch. My face was blotchy, not glowy. My legs were purple from the air conditioning. Sweat, legit sweat, was dripping from my ponytail. I looked disgusting.

Joey said, "You are crazy hot."

I knew what he was saying, but guys were always trying to butter me up that way. I was not feeling it. "I'm literally dripping sweat."

"Shut up. You got the whole package. C'mon. Let's get that open weight machine and do some lumberjack chops."

We did everything a person could do at the gym. We hit almost all the machines. We tried a bunch of different attachments. Joey showed me how fast he could jump rope. And for a little while, we laughed, and I forgot about Ethan. When we were finally done, he suggested we take a selfie together. I agreed as long as I could choose the filter we used. He said, "Fine. But nothing with eyelashes."

We placed our heads together and before the snap, Joey turned his head and kissed me on the cheek, except it wasn't a kiss as much as it was a raspberry. His lips buzzing against the side of my face tickled, and I squealed and laughed really loud. A few people turned and looked at us. We probably looked like a cute couple. And maybe Joey thought that, too.

"Look at us," he said when he showed me the photo. Not only did we look like a cute couple, but we also looked maybe a little in love with each other. A little voice in my head whispered, *Man trap*.

"Can you send that to me?" I asked, but he already had. It pinged as soon as the words were out of my mouth.

When I announced I was going to hit the showers and go home, he took my arm to stop me. "Hold up. Don't run off home. Let's go somewhere. We could go grab dinner. Have a few drinks—"

"You know I don't drink."

"Fine. We'll find a juice bar or something. This was fun. I don't want to stop the fun."

The best revenge would be to nail one of Ethan's friends. But I wasn't looking for revenge. And a part of me kind of wished I did feel at least a little something for Joey. He was a good guy. But I was in love with Ethan. But knowing Joey liked me like this could work to my benefit.

"You're right. It was fun. But I can't. Maybe some other … anyway. I need to go. But thanks. This made my day!"

I rushed to the ladies' locker room and sat down on a bench. I didn't want to wait. I cropped the photo of me and Joey and posted it with only a red heart emoji.

Fine. I set a trap. Now I just had to be patient and wait.

JENNA

So they were like … done. At least, according to Ethan. He told me about how he was at her place, and all of a sudden she started angling to move in with him, like in our town. Who does that? He said she was pushing real hard, telling him how mobile her business is and she could work from anywhere. It doesn't even make sense. Physical fitness is not something people prioritize around here. The only gym is on campus, and that's full of broke college kids. Ethan said he was so freaked out by her dropping hints that he had to get out of there immediately. I mean, they just started dating.

I thought she was fast before, but I had no idea.

He and I went to lunch one day. I was working my route, and he texted to say he wanted Mexican, so off we went. Ethan was one of those guys with a constant running metabolism. Like a seventeen-year-old football player, he just burns like a furnace.

It was one of those days where you knew a storm was brewing, but it hadn't quite culminated yet. In the distance, I could see dark clouds in the west moving our way. Could bring a tornado, could just be a storm. All we could do was wait and see.

After lunch, we were back in my truck, and he was in the passenger seat scrolling on his phone. I was talking about … something, probably one of my nurses who was giving me a little attitude when I came in. I think she was mad that we ran out of the good pens. And Ethan interrupted me, "What the hell?"

He flipped over his phone so I could see a photo of Gabbi cuddled up with one of his cronies … what's his name? Joey. That guy, Joey.

I mean, I wasn't too shocked. He said that Joey was making a move on Gabbi when they were all having coffee one day. Like, was flirting right in front of him. Ethan was seriously thinking they were hooking up when he wasn't around.

And even though after he showed me the photo he was like, "Whatever." I knew he was hurt over it. He got really quiet, and I could see him over there looking through her photos for other pieces of evidence that she was hooking up with Joey. Eventually he said, "What the hell does this little heart mean?"

"I don't speak thirst trap, so I cannot say. You were the one who broke it off. I mean, what did you even tell her?"

"Just that I had to go. And when she texted me, I blew her off. I mean she was just … it would never work."

"Were you really hoping it would? She's just so not your type."

"Jenna. I need you to just not be so superior right now."

"Me? You're the one who said she was a good time at the time." He did. He said that right after that brunch where we first met her. He said he wasn't serious and they were just having a good time. No big. And I was relieved, because it wasn't like it was a secret that she and I didn't jibe. But it's so typical Ethan. He puts people on a shelf and then gets mad when someone else comes along and wants to play with them.

"You can't have it both ways." I couldn't believe he was making me defend her. "You either need to be in with her all the way, or break it off and let Joey have your sloppy seconds."

"I'm texting Joey."

"Why?"

"Because it's not done this way. You wouldn't get it."

"Spare me," I took the phone from his hand and tossed it in my driver's side door bin. "You need to cool off before you text anything to anyone."

"Give me my phone."

"You can have it when I drop you at your job." Which was a futile gesture because we were already turning into the drive of his building. After I parked, he jumped out and stalked around the vehicle to the driver's side door. I rolled down the window and handed him his phone.

"You're not the boss of me, Jenna." He shoved the phone in his pocket.

"Keep telling yourself that."

The whole thing was so dumb. He didn't want her, but he also didn't want anyone else to have her. It's just such a cliché. I don't think Ross is like that at all. He doesn't feel like he owns me. In fact, I don't think I've ever had anyone feel about me that way. And at that moment, watching Ethan get so upset that even though he broke up with Gabbi, someone was waiting in the wings to swoop her up, I wondered if it was a good or bad thing that no one had ever wanted to fight for me.

Ethan was so annoyed with me that he refused to text me back all night. Ross and I had dinner, but he was distracted texting his brother all night. I sat on the couch with *Real House-wives* playing on the TV, fidgeting with my phone, waiting for Ethan to text me back.

I didn't hear back from Ethan right away. And for a little while, I wondered if I would hear from him at all. I kept myself busy. I made appointments and previewed a few apartments after work. I went alone, but I texted and sent photos to Reneé the whole time. She told me not to go alone because she's always worrying about whether I'm being safe. The apartment managers were cool about it, probably because they were also women and constantly assessed their own safety. One of them asked if I wanted to put Reneé on Facetime, and another asked, "So what does Reneé think?"

Moments like that made me wonder why I didn't have more women friends, but then I had to remind myself that those women are paid to be nice.

All the apartments were fine: sterile, basic boxes divided into smaller boxes. Every rental property with "character" had been commandeered by the fixers and the flippers. I either needed to invest, like Ethan suggested, which would mean taking out a loan that I couldn't be certain that I could afford—or even be approved for—or chose one of the basic boxes for a while. It was disheartening.

On the drive home, it had started to rain, sloppy, sloshing drops. I listened to one of my Celeste Sullivan lectures on finances.

"Financial institutions thrive on your fear because fear keeps you in a stagnant space, paralyzed. You either panic and keep feeding the machine of living paycheck to paycheck, or make a rash investment and then tell yourself you're not good at managing your finances. Remember your money mantra ..."

I repeated the words aloud along with the voice, "Money flows easily in and out, like water."

But my heart wasn't in it. You have to really believe in your mantras and surrender to the outcomes for it to work, but I was caught in this loop of negative thinking: *Why doesn't anyone love me? Why can't love ever stay?* I turned off Celeste for Taylor Swift.

I wasn't hungry, just defeated. I was going to have a yogurt and go to bed. Maybe do some resistance booty bands first.

When I pulled into my drive, my headlights cut through the rain, illuminating my front porch. Ethan was sitting there.

My stomach flopped completely over. *How was I going to handle this?*

He must have parked down the street because I didn't see his truck. He was still in his work clothes, tie loose around his neck.

The rain pounded my car. I turned off the lights and waited. Should I run to the door? But before I could decide, he jogged through the rain to my car. I unlocked the door so he could get in.

"Hey." He said the word so softly, it was like a sigh or a whisper. It ran through me.

"What are you doing here?" The rain and his cologne intermingled with a light sweat. His hair cowlicked on his head. *Dear God, he smelled amazing.*

"I don't know."

We didn't speak. I stared straight ahead at my door, wondering if I could just stay in my car—stay in my car, suspended in this moment, forever. His energy was orange and driving, churning toward me. He wanted to touch me but he was fighting it. The interior lights of my Prius illuminated our faces like soft candlelight. My dashboard suddenly looked like the command center for a spacecraft, and any second now we could lose our sense of gravity.

"So, are we done?" he blurted out.

I scoffed. Like, I never knew what that word meant until I felt this noise emerge from my throat and, like, some little ping in my brain connected the noise to the word. The question threw me off.

I said, "I don't know. Are we? You're the one who blew me off."

"I didn't blow you off."

"Yes, you did."

"No, I didn't."

"Stop acting defensive. Do you want to be right, or do you want to keep talking to me?" I had pulled that right from my Celeste Sullivan relationship archives, but I knew I botched the quote.

"I'm defending myself because you're throwing your new relationship in my face on social media. You posted that picture of you and Joey with a little heart on it. Are you fucking Joey now?"

The post worked. Maybe it worked a little too well.

"That's insulting on so many levels," I said.

"You aren't denying it."

"Because you aren't my boyfriend anymore. You ghosted me. You stopped coming around—"

"I'm here now aren't I?"

"—you never changed your relationship status—"

"You know my social media accounts are only for business."

"—you've never let me post a photo of us together on my accounts." I made my voice deeper to mimic him, *"I gotta keep a low profile online, babe* ... whatever. At least Joey isn't embarrassed to be seen with me."

"I can't fill my social media with partying and randos."

"Oh! ... Oh! ... And that's me, right? I'm just some rando!"

What was killing me was that I understand being private. I even get sneaking around. But I always knew where those guys stood: married guys, guys with serious girlfriends, the hookups and the secret spots. I've been in fights with girls who are ready to snatch every hair out of my head because I was trying to "take" their man. That's a legitimate reason to keep me hidden away. But none of those sneaky fuckers were embarrassed of me like Ethan was. I wasn't his sidepiece, but somehow he was treating me like one.

He said, "You are not a rando."

"I can't do this. I'm not going to—" but I cut myself off because I was overwhelmed with that smell of his soap. His whole body energy changed to red, radiating with this fury like he was going to burst from his skin. I demanded, "Get out of my car."

"No," he said. "We're not done talking about this."

I opened the door and walked into the rain. The downpour soaked my clothes instantly. I tried to get to the door before he did. I was powerless, and I knew if he got any closer I would be completely lost. Lost to him. He followed me, and when he reached the top step I told him, "I didn't say you could walk in my house."

"We're not done." He reached for me, holding me by the

arms. "I don't want any other guys on your social media." He was close enough to kiss me. "You're mine."

"Then start acting like it." I broke away from him. "Tell everyone that I'm your girlfriend. I am not your dirty little secret."

"You were never my dirty little secret."

We rushed together like a warm front and a cold front colliding. He pressed me up against the wall in my entryway, and then we were on the floor coming out of our clothes. Outside, the thunder boomed and rattled the walls.

When we had finished, we relocated to the shower. I had banged my arm against the wall, and it was starting to purple. I could see all the marks where he had gripped me. He kissed them all away.

I told him, "This means we're together now. It's real. No more ghosting me. If you want to leave me now, you have to be man enough to tell me to my face."

"I'm not leaving you. I promise."

And I believed him. I honestly believed we would stay together forever.

No, he never changed his Facebook status. We went to Reneé's wedding together, and he let me post photos of us together on my own social media. He never suggested we move in together. I never met his parents. Ethan told me not to worry about Jenna, but I knew that she was the one calling the shots.

It wasn't until much later that it dawned on me how weird that was.

CHAPTER 7

EIGHT DAYS AFTER THE MURDER

After many calls, Lindy finally got someone on the line—other than Joey—who had seen Gabbi and Ethan together. She and Boggs took the call in an interview room, Lindy's phone in the middle of the table, the speaker icon illuminated. It was one of Ethan's back-home buddies named JT. He was reluctant to say anything at all—country kids are taught early on that what happens out in the country is their own damn business. At times like this, Lindy leaned in a little to her own country-ass accent, which always came across more like she'd walked off the mountain than out of the tobacco fields. But she was a woman and she was not sweet, so it reminded them too much of their own mamas, and they reverted to the tendency to deny, deny, deny.

Boggs slid right into the right accent, the right vocal range, the casual intimacy of an old friend. "Look man, we're not trying to jam anybody up; we're just trying to figure out who killed your friend. Anything you tell me can help."

"I heard it was a robbery."

"It might be. Who would rob Ethan?"

"I don't know. I figured some of those asshole college kids down the road heard that Ethan kept a safe full of cash in his house."

"Ethan kept cash at home?"

"Stacks of it. Said he got it all on the Boat."

"So he showed it to you."

He confirmed and then added, "Ethan wasn't that good at keeping secrets." They had found the safe JT had mentioned and it was empty. No cash in the house.

"When was the last time you spent time with him?"

"It was probably when he brought his girl out to the shooting party."

He explained that every once in a while a group of them would gather in the woods with a bunch of coolers, build a fire, cook out, and shoot targets. JT had purchased a new gun and they all wanted to try it out. Ethan had, in JT's words, brought someone with him. "She was blonde. I think her name was Abby or something."

"What did you think about her?" Lindy asked. " What was your impression?"

"I don't know. They were kind of all over each other. She didn't shoot. Ethan tried to show her how to hold his—he's got this nice Glock with a texture grip—"

Boggs interrupted, "I saw it. That's a nice piece."

"I know," he said. "I was going to get me one of them…" while he lamented his yearning for the same weapon, Lindy shoved Boggs on the arm so he would focus up.

Boggs interrupted JT's diatribe. "But you were saying that Ethan tried to show her how to use the gun."

"Yeah, yeah, yeah, but she wiggled her way out of it. And he made this joke about how he shouldn't be showing her how to use it because one of these days he's going to do something dumb, and she's going to shoot his ass. And without missing a step, she giggles at him and tells him, 'Nah. I'd stab you.'"

Lindy's head snapped up and Boggs repeated back what he had said.

JT said, "That's weird right? Because isn't that how he was killed? I never put that together until now. I can't believe I forgot about that. I mean, like, that's something, right?"

"Yes," Lindy said. She bounced in her chair. "That is definitely something. Thank you, JT, please contact us if you think of anything else, okay?"

Boggs pressed the button, ending the call. Lindy said, "Well?"

"It's flimsy," Boggs said. "People say all kinds of crazy stuff. Do you know how many times my wife has told me that she would poison me with antifreeze in my Gatorade if I ever stepped out on her?"

"Yeah. You stopped drinking Gatorade, too."

He waved his hand at her, "It's too sweet."

They walked back to their desks and reviewed the information they had. They finally got the cell phone records: pages and pages of text exchanges. Not only exchanges with the people they had met, but also exchanges between Ethan and many, many other women. Flipping through them, Boggs said, "They nasty."

"He kept himself busy."

"But a lot of these stopped a few months ago. It's mostly him and Gabbi, and they nasty, too."

Lindy pointed out, "Yeah, but see here how she's telling him that she's driving in to see him on the night he died? And he just says, 'K'. After all that, the texts are one-sided unless she's sexting him. Then, all of a sudden, he's interested. Looks like we didn't get any of the photos."

"Yeah, I was disappointed, too. They're in another file. They're mostly nudes."

"Okay," Lindy said. "So he knew she was driving in to see him. And honestly, are these kids made out of gasoline? It's an hour drive back and forth just to have a conversation?"

"And we know he's romancing this Hillary girl. But those aren't nasty. It's a bunch of heart emojis and kissy faces."

They reviewed their theories. Gabbi drives into town, they may or may not have had sex, he goes to the shower, she snoops on his phone, snaps, and stabs him.

"But we can't prove it yet." Boggs said.

Lindy reached across his desk and snatched the tiny basketball. She pressed her palms into it. Around them in the room, the phones rang, uniformed officers passed through, and other detectives worked from their desks on their own calls and cases.

Lindy bounced the ball off her desk and back into her palm. "Why did this kid keep so much cash around?"

"I don't know. For someone who's so bad at keeping secrets, this kid had a lot of secrets."

Lindy flipped through a file. "He was definitely broke. All his accounts were overdrawn, his credit cards were maxed out, he was late on his mortgage. The only thing that was kept paid was his cell phone and … yep, it's because his parents were still paying for it."

They reviewed the timeline again. Ethan is at home. Jenna and Ross are in Metropolis for his brother's band's show. They have digital alibis. Gabbi is driving to Ethan's. Time of death is around 10-10:30 pm. If she left after she texted, that would be plenty of time for her to get to his house, have sex, stab him, and sloppily try to clean up.

Boggs said, "But other than that text, we can't even place

her in town. We don't even have camera footage of her on his street."

"Because she didn't park on his street," Lindy said. "What if she parked at Walmart and blended in with all the other yahoos heading down the street to the party?"

Boggs grabbed his phone. "Let's go get the tape."

While Boggs phoned Walmart, Lindy called the next name on her list, Gabbi's boss, Jack Plummer. She got him on the second ring. After she identified herself, she asked if he could answer a few questions.

"I don't know how I can help," Plummer said. "Did she get into something on her trip down in Mexico?"

"No, sir. Were you aware that her ex-boyfriend, Ethan Moll, was murdered in December?"

"No. I mean, yes, I heard that he had died, bless her heart."

"You saw them together? Did he come around the office to pick her up?"

"Yeah. I know she was real crazy about him."

"Crazy, like …"

"Like they were serious. She was going to uproot her whole life. She was all in. And they were together for a while. I didn't even know he was her ex. I know she was really frustrated with him whenever he would get into his whole nonsense."

"Nonsense?"

"He was being a boy. All hot and heavy and then he'd ice her … box her out. Then they'd be hot and heavy again."

"So she spoke with you about him."

"We worked together. She'd be over the moon giddy and then she'd get all moody. When she told me that she was leaving to go do that Yoga Teacher Training, I figured they were finally over."

"When did she tell you that?"

"Oh, she called me on the way to the airport. Said she'd

make up the hours, quoted a bunch of her self-help stuff, and then she was gone. We had to let her go. Chad was livid."

"Chad?"

"My brother. He runs the practice. And he said we can't have someone on our staff we can't rely on."

"So she is no longer employed at Berry Hill Chiropractic."

"Nah. And it's probably for the best, really. She got a job at LA Fitness doing personal training. I mean, that's what she wants to do anyway. At least she can poach some clients when she goes out on her own."

"Do y'all still talk?"

"Yeah. She's renting my condo. I'm heading over there later to check on some things."

"Let's go back to when she called you and said she was leaving for her trip. Did you notice if she seemed upset or was acting erratically?"

"She sounded tired, I guess. But she *was* tired, driving back and forth from his place to hers. I mean, that's why she was moving, so they could stop the back and forth."

"She told you she was planning to move to Pleasant Springs and live with Ethan?"

"She told me that he was talking about them moving somewhere else. Like these romantic notions of the two of them driving his boat down to Florida and sailing off into the sunset." He giggled when he said it.

"Do you think she was bullshitting you?"

"A little bit. I think sometimes he told her what she wanted to hear to keep her."

"It doesn't sound like you liked him very much."

"She's my friend. I just wanted her to be happy. He made her miserable sometimes. But I always figured it was all to be young and in love."

"When she left town, she was still referring to Ethan as her boyfriend?"

"Yeah. I mean, wasn't he?"

Lindy thanked him for his time and ended the call. Boggs had ended his call as well and waited for the update.

"It seems," Lindy said, "that she called her boss the morning after the murder to announce she was about to get on a plane to Mexico. It was not a pre-planned trip. It was a last-minute decision."

"We'll need to contact the airline to see when the ticket was purchased," Boggs said. "But if she was fleeing, why would she come back?"

"Maybe she chickened out," Lindy said. "But it looks bad."

"Real bad," Boggs said. "I cannot get a human on the line at Walmart. We're going to need to run out there and see if the manager will let us look."

They grabbed their coats and headed out the door.

Later, when they returned, Boggs was carrying a large box of Clif bars under his arm. At his desk, he opened the bottom drawer, ripped open the box, and let all the bars fall into it. Lt. Delphrain emerged from his office. "Y'all go Christmas shopping?"

"Shopping for evidence," Boggs said. "The manager at Walmart is emailing us the surveillance videos as we speak."

"Without a warrant?"

Lindy, who was checking her messages, said, "The manager is on Boggs's church league soccer team."

"Praise be," Delphrain said. "So what do we know?"

Boggs pitched a Clif bar across the desk to Lindy, who caught it, then flipped it on its side to view the nutritional content. "Goddamn, these have a lot of fat in them."

Delphrain took the bar from her hand and also viewed the content. He asked, "What do we know?"

Boggs said, "We know that someone entered the vic's residence sometime between 9 pm and midnight through the back door. We have no visuals."

"Did you check the neighbors?"

Lindy said, "One doesn't have a security system and the other gave us a 10 minute speech about how this is America, and he is protected from search and seizure."

"Right."

Boggs said, "Whoever did it took the vic's hunting knife and stabbed him with it. Then they drug the body into the shower and turned on the water. We have evidence that they sloppily tried to clean up, wiped down the knife, and placed it in the gun safe."

"They had to know him well enough to know the combination of the gun safe," Lindy said.

"Right," Boggs said. "The next morning, the friend, Jenna, enters the residence at 7 am and discovers the body."

"Who had the motive?" Delphrain asked.

"We still haven't determined that." Lindy said.

"What about the girlfriend?"

"Her alibi is shaky," Lindy said. "She said she was at home packing for her trip."

"Her last-minute trip," Boggs said.

"Yeah. She didn't tell her employer that she was leaving until the morning of her flight. She also has a wound on her hand. It looks like it could have been a knife. She said it came from running her hand along a broken tile in the pool at her yoga retreat in Mexico."

Delphrain opened the Clif bar that had been meant for Lindy and chewed on it, ruminating.

"He was talking to another girl," Boggs said. "The girlfriend didn't tell people about the break up. The best friend—that Jenna girl—accused her of being 'obsessed' with him."

"Looks bad for her," the lieutenant said.

"Right," Lindy said. "We're waiting for the DNA results on the weapon to see what's on it."

"Oh," Boggs said and flipped back his notepad. "The friends at the shooting party said—"

"Yeah, yeah," Lindy said. "Listen to this."

"According to one of the people at a shooting party, she had made a joke that if he ever pissed her off she wouldn't shoot him, she would stab him."

"Yeah, it's looking real bad for this girlfriend," Delphrain said. "But it's still circumstantial. It's not enough."

"Any defense attorney is going to point out he was living beyond his means and likely owed some bad guys some money."

"We need to put her at the scene," Delphrain said. "Talk to the judge and get a warrant for Captain America's backyard security camera.

Lindy spun in her chair and pulled up the form to start the paperwork for the warrant. Boggs's phone pinged. "Hey. We got the Walmart footage."

All three gathered around his computer screen. They waited for him to click on the email, click on the download, click through a pop-up that warned of an eventual system upgrade at midnight that night, and click on the play button.

The angle of the first video was of the entire parking lot, a wide shot of cars in spaces, cars coming and going, and the gleam of headlights. At the edge of the parking lot, cars parked and packs of young people tumbled out.

"And here are the yahoos," Lindy said. The college kids carried large cups, beer boxes, and paper bags with handles emerging from the top.

Delphrain asked, "Do we have an angle…yeah, that one."

Boggs clicked on another video in the file, which offered a closer look at the yahoo section. Through the trees, college students leapt over the drainage ditch or used the makeshift bridge the local residents kicked over every week. The cars were standard college cars—Hondas, Priuses, Corollas, a few 4-Runners and Ford F-150s. One really nice Lexus. The cars remained parked and more entered the scene. A glimmer of headlights and a blue Prius pulled into a space. The plates were obscured.

"Is that her?" Delphrain asked.

On the screen, a body exited the car. Their face was obscured by a hooded sweatshirt.

"That looks like her car."

They watched the hooded figure disappear into the woods, joining the other college kids. "She's walking into the trees with the other yahoos."

"If that's her," Delphrain said.

"If that's her," Boggs said.

Delphrain said, "Either go get your warrant or go redneck whisper that guy and get his backyard camera footage."

Lindy went back to her form and Boggs clicked through the videos to see if he could get a better angle on what could be the girlfriend's plates.

Boggs spoke better Spanish than Lindy, so he was the one to contact the resort where Gabbi claimed she stayed.

He didn't need it. The place where she allegedly stayed was not an exclusive five-star resort but was a mini resort for smaller groups and conferences, like the resort version of a Holiday Inn. After half an hour on the phone, Boggs flung his pen across the desk at Lindy, who was finding its location on Google maps and checking flight records.

"Here's what I now know," he announced. "One Gabbi Edwards stayed with them from December 15-17, but here's the thing—she was not there getting her Yoga Teacher Training certification because they were not hosting yogis that week, they were hosting Juice Plus+ downstream distributors. The yogi event was the week before. Edwards checked in, asked for extra towels, and complained about the state of their gym. Otherwise, she was quiet and calm and did yoga by the pool."

"Where she cut her hand?"

"Where she did not cut her hand. He said he has no paperwork on file for that type of injury, but they did have a guy crack open his head when he passed out drunk on the tile floor in his room."

"She said she cut her hand on a tile in the pool."

"Not only did he tell me they had no paperwork to that effect, but that he thinks he remembers that she had a bandaged hand when she got there."

"He noticed that?"

"He was concerned she would bleed on all their linens."

"So it was a bad cut."

"Enough for him to be worried."

"So she lied."

"Yep. I asked him if there had ever been an incident in that pool because of a broken tile. He said, 'No.' I asked if she could have cut herself on a glass in her room. He said they only offer their guests plastic cups. And then he went on a tear about drunk American tourists and why they can't have nice things."

"Sure, sure," Lindy said. "He's not wrong. Rednecks are usually why we can't have nice things."

"Rednecks also invented air travel. Nothing more redneck

than looking at your brother and saying, 'What if we built a flying machine in our yard?'"

"Whatever. Gabbi lied. Flat out lied to our faces."

"Yep."

"I'm going to try to get with Customs about her time of entry, see if they have her on camera with the bandage on her hand."

"Great. Tell me all about it in the morning."

"Wait. You're leaving?"

"I have dinner with my baby's daddy."

"Yikes."

"I'd rather be on hold with Customs, trust me." Lindy grabbed her jacket and headed to the door.

The plan was to have Jeff come over for dinner, but those knuckleheads had gotten together and had one of their, "You know what would be fun?"—offs and changed all the plans. Like they always did. April texted and explained they were all heading out for a nice dinner and they were going to look sharp.

Pleasant Springs only had a few fancier restaurants in town, something other than Applebee's and O'Charley's. The one April loved the most was the one with the absolute worst service. Proclaiming her undying love for their cheesy potato soup, she insisted they go there for every special occasion, despite the fact that the food always came out late and the waiters were careless and slow. It didn't matter. She'd texted that she'd saved up all her Weight Watchers points for the day, nibbling on carrots and celery, and eating straight from the tuna packet—she was going to splurge tonight.

April left Ella at her mother's and then tagged Lindy as designated driver. She wore a new dress and wiggled her way into her wedding Spanx. When Lindy pulled her in for a hug and told her how sexy she was, April called her a liar. "I have another twenty pounds to lose."

"Not lying." Lindy wasn't the liar. She kissed her and ran her hands down April's hips, cupping her, admittedly larger, rear. But Lindy was into her post-baby bubble butt.

"We're going to be late," April announced, while also placing her hand on Lindy's breast. As if coming to her senses, she pushed Lindy back. "You're tempting me and you have no concept of the time it took for me to get into this dress. Later you can cut me out of it. It'll be sexy."

"To be continued," Lindy said.

Eating anywhere without Ella was odd. Breaks from her were a pleasant change of pace, but Lindy often eyed the back-seat to see an empty car seat, would panic, and then relax knowing that Ella had not been carelessly left at home in her crib, but was instead being spoiled by April's mom, who would dutifully text photos and videos while they ate: baby sleeping on PopPop's chest in the recliner, baby playing on the floor, baby eating and smearing food on her face.

They also didn't need to worry about being late. Because Jeff was also late. Lindy didn't need another reason to be annoyed by this guy, but there they were. All he had to do was shower and throw on clothes. Lindy took the seat with the best view of the exits. She reached over to her left, where she always placed Ella. Instead that seat would be filled with Jeff. A server swung by with a water pitcher, then little saucers of olive oil and herbs. When April requested a glass of pinot noir, the server reported that she was not allowed to take orders for alcohol and a different server would stop by eventually.

The server disappeared before Lindy could ask for a Diet Coke. April took her hand, "I'm glad we can be out like grown-ups."

"Yeah," Lindy scanned the room. This was being a grown-up? Wearing uncomfortable clothes at a bougie restaurant waiting for the sperm donor when she could be in her cozies pouring her own wine and seducing her wife? "So nice." From Lindy's vantage point, she could see straight into the bar. Posted up on a stool, sucking down something from a tall glass, sat Ned Rockford. He was missing his signature polo shirt and was wearing a suit. A suit that stopped being crisp several hours ago.

"I'm going to go get your drink from the bar. And I'm going to ask for a country club pour. I want you sloppy tonight."

Inside the bar, the noise level rose about 10 percent. The music was a little louder, the conversations were a little more raucous, and the laughter a little more intense. Someone had hung little white twinkle lights and garland around the bar. Lindy sat on the stool near Rockford and ordered her drinks.

"Well, if it isn't Detective D'Arnaud."

"Rockford. How are you this evening?"

"Wyatt, I am rolling," he smirked, possibly waiting for her to catch his *Tombstone* reference. He was drunk.

Lindy nodded like they were now members of a mutual appreciation society. "Are we celebrating?"

Rockford sucked down the dregs, the straw signaling its cry for a refill. "Ah, no. Not exactly." He looked like a man exhausted from carrying it all around. "It's not the same without Ethan."

"Losing a partner can be hard."

"He was just so impatient. These kids all are. These idiots. It's all about now. They don't want to build anything. I'm trying to build something here."

"Were y'all arguing about that? Was he stepping over the line?"

He tutted his finger at Lindy. "Always working, aren't you?"

The bartender came by and dropped off Lindy's drinks. She dropped her card on the bar, but Rockford said, "You put Detective D'Arnaud's drinks on my tab and bring me another Tom Collins."

"I can't have you pay for my drinks."

"I insist, I insist. You're clearly off duty, are you not, officer?"

Each time he referred to Lindy as being law enforcement, the baby-faced bartender flenched. "Fine," Lindy said and shooed the bartender away. She took a sip from her drink. "So the kid, you told him he was going too fast—"

"He was out there working it like the rent was due. Where do they say that? Is it *Drag Race*? Do you watch that show?"

"I think you were a little closer with the *Tombstone* reference. So Ethan wanted to expand?"

"It was too many new people, too many young people. And those are the ones who don't want to do the work. They want everything to happen fast, fast, fast." He snapped his fingers to punctuate his words.

"And you two fought about it."

"He just didn't get that we were building a structure, a delicate ecosystem, and then to add all these new people, these young people, with all their questions and their nonsense."

"How did it even work? Ethan would bring someone in—"

"It's all about contacts. You can call it a 'good old boy' system if you want, but it works. People are always more comfortable working with people they know. You have to be able to trust people in business. And we were vouching for people. We established trust."

"C'mon. You're making it sound like a bank ad."

Rockford shrugged. "You're not from here. And you're not

in business. So you ain't gonna get it." He swayed a little on his stool. "Some of these people have been running businesses for generations. Ethan knew that. He was supposed to be next in line for his daddy's gas distribution company."

"If he was the sire of this huge company, then why was he working with you?"

"He was on borrowed time. His daddy was calling him back at the first of the year. He was on his way out and he kicked over a candle on the way out the door."

"How did he—"

"Where's my Tom Collins?" He pounded on the bar and sought the bartender, who was talking to a patron at the end of the bar. "Hello. Yes. You. Please. Can you please bring me another Tom Collins, please?"

The bartender nodded and started mixing a drink, but it was not a Tom Collins. It was likely time to cut Rockford off.

"I am trying to keep this town alive." Rockford stared ahead at his reflection in the mirror behind the bottles of liquor. "They can't even see it."

Lindy looked around and could see April standing in the doorway that separated the restaurant from the bar. April was waving to get her attention, then shrugged and mouthed, "What are you doing?"

Lindy waved her off, but April came over to the bar where they were sitting. "You never came back with my drink."

"April Robertson," Rockford bellowed. "How's your daddy, girl?"

"Hello, Mr. Rockford," April used her University Administrator voice, the same one she used with scholarship winners, reporters, and recruits. "He's good. But you know it's April D'Arnaud now."

"Yes. Because you are married. I just didn't know how y'all did names. I gotta tell ya, you two are a fine, fine lesbian couple," Rockford turned and placed his hands on April's shoulders. "I mean seriously."

Lindy stood, ready to step in, but April worked her way out of his grip. "Thank you, Mr. Rockford," she said. "Now, are you going to be okay getting home? Do you need me to order an Uber for you or call your wife?"

"I guess I can't say that I was going to take my own car, sitting here next to the law."

Somehow April took Rockford's phone, pointed it at his face for his Facelock, and then opened the app to order him a car that was ten minutes away with surge pricing. "Would you like to join us until your car gets here?"

"No. No, I couldn't do that."

"I'll tell you what, let's walk outside and get some fresh air together."

The bartender slid Rockford's card across the bar with the receipt for his multiple drinks. Rockford signed the slip but left no tip. Lindy pulled some bills from her wallet and threw them on the bar.

April held out her arm. "Lindy, please take my drink to the table. Jeff needs someone to talk to."

Rockford said, "Jeff Tankersley? I just had a meeting with his daddy."

"Yes, he's visiting from Lexington." April gestured for Lindy and together they pulled Rockford to his feet.

Once standing, Rockford chucked Lindy on the shoulder. "You got yourself a good woman, D'Arnaud."

Lindy knew that.

April and Rockford made their way through the bar. Rockford wished every table along the way a hearty "Merry Christmas!" Once they made it out the door, Lindy grabbed their drinks to transport to their table. Waiting for her were more drinks, a basket of bread, and Jeff.

He slipped out of his quilted barn coat and hung it on the back of his chair. Underneath, he wore a fleece quarter-zip with a checked button-up collar peeking out from it. He always dressed like he was ready to pose for one of those holiday family portraits in front of an old barn or perched on a bright patch of grass. Portraits for pretty families. Pretty, perfect families.

Jeff nodded when Lindy sat down at the table and asked, "Where'd April go?"

"She's escorting a drunk to his Uber."

"Isn't that your job, Officer?" Jeff lifted his phone from the table.

"I'm a detective. Not a bouncer."

They sat in silence. Lindy watched as Jeff smiled down at his phone and swiped up and down, as well as left and right. It looked like he was playing *Candy Crush*.

When April finally returned to the table, she placed the napkin in her lap and said, "I can't believe they didn't cut him off sooner. I was practically holding him up when the car arrived." She rubbed her arms over her cardigan. "I'm freezing."

"Here," Jeff removed his sportscoat and draped it over April's shoulders.

She said, "Thanks, hon."

They talked like that to each other. *Babe, hon, darling*, and *sug*. Lindy wasn't quick enough on the draw to offer her own coat. He could be as chivalrous as he wanted, in the end, it was Lindy taking April home.

"Who was it?" Jeff asked.

"Ned Rockford."

"That guy," Jeff chuckled.

"You have many dealings with Ned Rockford?" Lindy asked.

"No, but my daddy has. He's just one of those guys who always has his hand out. He's got a plan, he's got a scheme, he's got a deal. He's shady."

"Do you know shady dealings? Has he pulled your daddy into anything shady?" Lindy was recalling Rockford's exit line of how he'd just met with Jeff's daddy.

"I don't know anything for a fact, but there's a reason why he's no longer the president of the Pleasant Springs Chamber of Commerce."

"What was the reason?" Lindy pulled a piece of bread from the basket and opened it to see little specks of red.

"I don't know, but I remember there was a meeting before the meeting where Rockford entered his letter of resignation."

April rolled her eyes. "There's always a meeting before the meeting."

Lindy showed April the bread and asked, "What is this, red pepper flakes?"

"It's sun-dried tomatoes."

Lindy placed the bread onto April's plate and dug around in the basket. "The meeting before the meeting is how things stay covered up."

Jeff said, "It's been like that since the town was founded. It's our longest running tradition." Then he laughed, "Hey, I moved out of this town. Y'all are the ones who stayed. Y'all are the ones keeping it propped up."

Lindy bristled at his insinuation that part of her job was to keep the secrets of the movers and shakers of this town covered up.

April ran the sun-dried tomato bread through the olive oil drizzle and said, "But you're thinking about coming back. You said you were talking to your daddy about it."

"I am, and he wants me to, but I don't know. I've got real spoiled to city living."

"You were never really the country type," April said. "I remember we were once invited to a field party and you fretted over whether your Lexus could go off road."

"I loved that car."

"It was an SUV. And it was barely off road." April looked at her menu again. "Did I miss them taking our order?"

"You did not," Lindy looked around the room for a server. "They haven't looked our way at all." Finally catching one's eye, she waved them over. Except the server turned and hustled back into the kitchen.

April took a long sip from her wine. "That's good. That's real good. You know what, Jeff. You should look at those houses off Farm Town Road. New builds, high end. Not too far from our place."

"I think I'd be more interested in the condos they're renovating on the square."

"That would be cool," April said. "And maybe after you get settled, we can see about maybe starting a new family project."

Lindy placed her hand over April's. "I thought we decided we weren't going to bring that up tonight."

"Did we?"

"Yes."

"What family project?" Jeff asked.

"Hey," Lindy said. "Are y'all going to be able to have that meet-up with your parents and Ella?"

"Oh, yes!" April exclaimed. "Did you ask your daddy about that?"

"Not this trip. Coordinating both my parents' schedules has always been almost impossible, with my mom and her luncheons and Daddy and all his traveling. I have to go through both of their assistants. I know the only place I'll find both of them in the same room is Sunday at church."

"That's a shame, because Ella is doing the cutest things right now. Lindy, show him the video of Ella rubbing that cake on her face and cackling."

"Sure." Lindy whipped out her phone, cued up the video, and passed it over to April.

Finally, a member of the wait staff appeared, looking somewhat confused, "Has no one taken your order yet?"

"No," Lindy said. "Here's what I want—"

"Let me go get you a server."

When the server left, Lindy announced she would be at the bar until an actual waiter appeared.

A manager eventually emerged and offered the table a free round of drinks. And eventually the food arrived. But too late, because April did, in fact, get sloppy. Too sloppy. April passed out in the car on the way home. Ella was sleeping over at Grandma's house and Lindy couldn't even take advantage of having an empty house.

Lindy put her wife to bed and walked the perimeter, making sure all the windows and doors were locked. She checked the security system and scanned the cameras to see a deer on the far edge of their property near the tree line. It looked directly into the camera, its eyes glowing like ghost eyes from the night vision.

She texted Boggs, reminding him that they needed to get with Detective Rouse to see what he knew about Rockford. He was clocked out for the night, the little crescent moon indicating he'd silenced all his messages.

Later, April wandered into Ella's room where Lindy was sitting in the rocking chair, just like she did every other night.

"What are you doing in here?" April asked.

"The lights help me think." Lindy was holding a stuffed bear up to her chest, as if she were rocking it to sleep.

"Our baby's mobile helps you think?"

"Yeah. How about that," she set the bear down and pulled April into her lap. "Why are you up?"

"I was going to get some water. And some ibuprofen. What are you thinking about?"

"I'm thinking about the meeting before the meeting."

"What meeting?" April sounded groggy. She kissed Lindy on the nape of her neck.

"The meeting before Rockford was asked to step down as president of the Pleasant Springs Chamber of Commerce."

"It was because of what had happened on the plane."

"What plane?"

"He was on a private plane with this corporation he was trying to woo. I don't know, they make faucets or something. They were all drinking bourbon and doing God-knows-what else, and one of them got really handsy with the attendant, and even the pilot was saying they stepped over the line, so they were held at the airport…they weren't in Nashville, maybe in Louisville? Anyway, it barely had a write-up in the paper, but it was not good for the town's image, so he was asked to step down."

"How do you know all this if it was barely in the paper?"

"I don't know. It's just what I heard." April placed her hand on Lindy's shoulder. "Babe?"

"Yeah?"

"My head hurts."

"Let's go find you some ibuprofen." She eased her from her lap and took her by the hand. They walked out of the nursery together.

"Babe. I want McDonald's."

"I know. But you made me promise to not buy you any when you get like this."

. . .

The next morning, Lindy and Boggs debriefed about the dinner and then tried to track down Rouse. Rouse had the day off and was out hunting deer.

"If he wants deer, he can just check my backyard," Lindy said.

"That doesn't count," he said. "It's alright. I think I know where he goes."

It was still early, and Boggs explained that by the time they drove out there, Rouse would be heading back to his truck. And they were right. They found his truck parked in a field along the tree line of a stretch of woods. They sat on the tailgate and waited.

The sun looked like it might try to shine a little that day, but it was still frigid. The cold of the truck metal bore right through their clothes. Lindy put on her gloves and placed her hands under her butt. She relayed to him everything she had learned about Rockford and the plane. "Did you know about that story?"

"Yeah. I heard it was bourbon and men acting rowdy. But it wasn't because he was showing his ass, it was because he got caught. It made everybody look bad and ended up blowing the deal. If he'd been cool and gotten the company to relocate to our town, he could have kept his job."

"This place is something else."

"Yes, it is." Boggs pulled out the knife he kept on his belt and trimmed his nails with it.

"Do you like living here?"

"Yeah."

"Why?"

"Because I understand it."

"Even when it's wrong?"

"Did you ever hear the theory that the reason people self-sabotage is because then they can predict the outcome? They'd rather it be a disaster they're familiar with than anything new, even if something new equaled something good."

"That's not healthy." Lindy huddled and stared down between her dangling feet into the frosty grass.

"We always prefer the devil we know."

About that time, they saw a man emerge from the woods, head to toe in camouflage, a bright orange hat on his head and a rifle hanging from a strap on his arm. It was Rouse. Boggs gave a friendly wave.

Rouse locked his gun in his truck and retrieved a thermos from the toolbox. "Y'all want coffee?"

After they retrieved enough cups and she had taken her first sip from Rouse's thermos—surrounded by the camo, the guns, the coffee—Lindy smiled for the first time all morning.

"Is there whiskey in this?" she asked.

"Nah. It's a Jack Daniel's blend my wife bought me."

Boggs gave him a rundown of the case. Rouse explained that he'd been investigating Rockford for years. "But he's slippery. I got wind of that 'business' he's running out there. But it's not much of a business."

"Lay it on us," Lindy took another sip from her cup.

"A business offers a good or a service. They advertise a service that they never actually provide."

"They claim it's for marketing services, right?" Boggs asked.

"But they never execute it. Instead, they offer a networking opportunity."

Lindy asked, "Right. So, how's it different from other business fraternities?"

Rouse refilled his coffee cup, "One could argue it's a business fraternity. But a business fraternity has a variety of options for networking. They have luncheons. They have seminars. They have workshops. They have them at places where many people will feel comfortable joining. In places that are not casinos."

"So the casino is the linchpin," Boggs said. "Do you think it's because they have the hotel? Is it drugs and prostitutes?"

"Nah. Rockford's already gotten in trouble for Kentucky-boy shenanigans. And he was on the fringe of those characters who were involved in the Kentucky Chamber of Commerce hullabaloo years ago when they were recruiting new businesses into the state by taking them to the strip clubs. Rockford's old school, but he's watched all his boys get taken down because they—"

Lindy interrupted, "Because they had their dick out."

Boggs kicked her foot.

"Exactly. Sexual harassment. Strippers. Prostitutes. Rockford's a weasel. But a weasel will adapt."

"So if it's not hookers and blow, then what is it?"

"Are you familiar with the gifting tables?"

Boggs cocked his head. "Wasn't that what those women in Connecticut got busted for?"

"I don't know what that is," Lindy said. "What is it?"

"It's a pyramid scheme," Rouse sipped from his cup. "They like to say it's a circle, but it's a pyramid. New members come in at the bottom level with a cash 'gift' for the head of the table. People work their way up to the head of the table by bringing in new people. Except instead of allowing a random assortment of downstream distributors to recruit, he hires Ethan to pitch it as a networking group."

"So how does the casino fit into it?"

"People can walk in with cash. The head of the table can transfer the cash into chips or credits and then cash out at the end of the night. They have a reason for meeting in a location that's alluring and fun. It makes it look more official. But it's shady. The problem is, I can't prove that's what they're doing."

"So how'd you find out about it?" Lindy asked.

"A disgruntled member reached out to me, but they won't go on the record. No one will go on the record. I was keeping my eye on that kid's Facebook page whenever he posted photos from the events. All the big local families have a toe in this one: The Moores, The Tankersleys, the Chandlers."

Jeff was a Tankersley. So his daddy was all up on this one. Last night Jeff had all but called Rockford a weasel.

"The casino can always claim plausible deniability," Rouse continued. "They just allow a civic group to host an event there. What that group does when they're there is their business. So the casinos are no help. Wouldn't even see me. I reached out to some of the lower-level players. They all but accused me of being a conspiracy theorist ... except now. How hard are y'all looking at Rockford?"

Boggs said, "Rockford wouldn't have killed his golden goose."

"Are you sure about that?" Rouse propped his foot on the back bumper. "I also got another tip—a little Kentucky twist—new members were expected to arrive with a gift for the host."

Boggs scratched his forehead. "I guess we're not talking about a bottle of bourbon."

"Only if it retails for at least $1,000."

Lindy asked, "How many tables were they running?"

"At least twelve. Once a month, they were walking out with $12,000 in cash split between the two. I mean $6,000 a month isn't a lot, but that's the point, right? No one blinks an eye at, what, an extra $72,000? Keep it under that $100,000, stash it in a safe at home, pay cash, don't get too flashy."

Lindy said, "And anything this kid got that was flashy, people would assume his rich-ass parents bought it for him."

"If anything about this case can be tied to Rockford, people will turn on him," Rouse said. "I'll get enough people to testify about how the tables worked."

"Well, we appreciate the information," Boggs stood and held out his hand. "We'll check up on his alibi."

Rouse shook it. "You keep me updated on this."

"Rouse," Lindy stood and shoved her hands in her pockets. "You know if we bring him, we'll get the credit for your case."

"I don't give a shit about credit. Just bring him down."

They thanked Rouse for the coffee and information and Lindy and Boggs drove back to the station.

GABBI

Ethan didn't come out with it all at once. At first, he asked if I had a passport. I said no. So he pulled the application up on my laptop and told me to fill it out. He even made the appointment and drove me to the passport office. When I asked why he said, "Because an adult should have a passport."

Then later he asked me how I felt about boats. About Belize. If I had ever sailed.

I thought it was a game, so I played along.

Then he asked me if I trusted him. I told him yes. It was late one night at my place, one of those talks couples have in the moonlight, except it wasn't the moon but a security light on the end of my block. Our spring fling had developed into a strong relationship by fall.

He told me a story. He told me that when he was going to school at the University of Kentucky, he was called in to the police department for questioning about a girl who had been held against her will in one of the rooms in his fraternity house.

"I lied. I knew they were up to something, but I kept my

mouth shut. I have to live with that," he said. "And the reason I didn't say anything is because I knew that if they started investigating our fraternity house, they'd know I was dealing coke."

"Why are you telling me this?"

"Because I've done bad things. And I need to know if you can handle it."

"What happened to the girl?"

"What always happens. No one believed her. She eventually quit school."

"Wow." It was the only thing I could think to say. We were sitting across from each other in my bed. He was leaning against my headboard and I lay across the foot of the bed.

"Yeah. I got in a fight with one of the guys. He was being a smug dick bragging about—anyway, I knocked the shit out of him. I was so pissed. And I was going to tell the cops the truth, but he called in a tip about me selling cocaine, and that was it for me."

"Did you go to jail or anything?"

He shook his head. "My parents did their thing and moved me back home. And ever since then they've kept an eye on me, making sure I don't embarrass the family."

"Did you really know what those boys did to that girl?"

"Not until it was too late. But," he leaned forward and reached for my hand. I sat up across from him, both of us sitting in lotus position. We were connected in that moment, almost synchronous breathing together. He held both of my hands. "Listen to me... true, honest, right? I've done some shady things. I think back on some of the situations I've put people in. I know what I'm doing. I know how to work people. You've seen me do this. And I can't sit here and pretend my hands are completely clean. I'm flawed as fuck."

"But you don't ..."

"I was a kid who really liked cocaine and girls and had a problem taking no for an answer."

"And now?"

"I can now accept that no is a valid answer and can walk away. It turns out I have other vices, though. I'm not telling you this because I need forgiveness or because I want you to be afraid of me. If we're going to do this—if it's you and me forever—I need you to know all the parts of me."

"Okay."

"And if I say *Trust me,* I need you to do that. I need you to trust me."

"Okay."

"Because I love you." He said it. And I believed him. Not because I needed to believe him, but because it was true. I felt it was true.

I moved and curled up next to him. He leaned back against the headboard again and placed his hand on my head, brushing my hair with his fingers. The next thing I knew, it was morning.

I didn't like what I heard. I didn't know how to process any of it. He was a liar. He lacked integrity. He wasn't wrong; he was flawed as fuck. But so was I. I'd cheated. I'd lied. I'd lacked integrity. I let the information sit there in a neutral space. I wondered how many other people he'd told this to. It seemed like there was a lightness to him afterward, like he didn't have to carry something very heavy anymore.

But he was just easing me into it. Later he started talking about trust again.

Again, he tells me that I need to trust him.

"I'm serious," he said. "I need to know if you're in. That if we're together, we are each other's ride or die—like, not in just words, but for real."

We were, again, at my place. I'd made dinner for us. Now we were on my couch looking at my new passport that had arrived in the mail a few days before. I didn't like how I looked in my photo. It also felt official or something.

"I told you that I was dealing and got busted for it," he stood up and started talking with his hands like he was giving a presentation. "My parents hushed it up. The cops were only interested in who my dealer was. My parents made me go to school closer to home so they could keep an eye on me. I rolled right into the new chapter like nothing happened. That's when I met Jenna. You know, she knew what it was like to have everyone whisper about you. I didn't have to worry about her doing that. But I was still drinking a lot. I've taken all kinds of other drugs—as long as it wasn't coke. I've been wild in a lot of other ways, but it was all hidden, right? Like, I would be out with Joey and slip off to take a pill or a shot or something and come back like I hadn't done anything at all. And that's Joey, who I actually let me see cut loose. I have to make sure everyone sees me in a certain way…But I think what I'm figuring out is all this stuff I'm doing in secret is to escape my public life. You are my secret life."

"Ethan, I told you," I said. I slapped the passport shut and tossed it on my coffee table. "I don't want to be your secret." He pushed it out of the way and sat down on the table across from me.

"You're not getting it," he took my hands and kissed my knuckles, like he knew I wanted to punch him. "You're amazing. If I walked you into my mama's house, introduced you to my daddy, they'd accept you. But then you'd have to do what they said, too. You'd be the wife of their golden child. They'd be all over everything you did."

"I'm not ashamed of my life." I was getting really sick of how small he made me feel when he talked about his family.

"I'm not saying you should be. It's them. This isn't a group that will eventually accept though willful defiance. These people are masters of psychological warfare. They will pick you apart every second of every day through both passive aggression, then active hostility. And don't assume my sisters would be allies—well, except for maybe Aimee. You know how that woman in your Mastermind group is always picking you apart?"

I released his hands, "I can handle that. I am handling that."

"Yes. But this would be every day of our lives. And in addition to that, they would hold the money over our heads at every turn."

"I don't want their money."

"Because you've never had it," he said. "The Bank of Mom and Dad has some serious terms and conditions. Having my own money… That's freedom."

"Okay. So?"

"They told me it was about legacy and heritage. My dad flat-out said he would shut down the family business before he would pass it on to my sisters, only to see it mismanaged by one of their husbands. He said that's the whole reason to have a boy. I'm not exaggerating. This is what he told me. That's what they think of me. My dad gave me a timeline for getting mine and Rockford's business off the ground. That timeline is almost up."

"But your business is doing well."

"It's not. It's a scam," he said. "I knew it was a scam when I got in on it. Rockford is trying to pretend it's a business fraternity, but it's a pyramid scheme. I'm playing ignorant in case it goes south. My plan has always been to get in, stash as much cash as I can, and then just disappear. Not like, burn off your fingerprints disappear, but just be far away when it all crumbles around Rockford's ears."

"And then what?"

"And then rebuild. Start a new business. I can always make money. That's never been a problem for me. But it doesn't matter. I'll be gone. If I'm ever questioned, I'll tell them it felt too shady so I quit. I didn't realize I was doing anything wrong. Rockford will talk his way out of some white-collar sentence, and we'll be sipping Mai Tais someplace where no one can find us."

"That's why you keep talking about Belize."

"Why not? They speak English and there's no extradition."

"But we'd be fugitives."

"No. I earned all this money. Maybe by shady means, but I still had to work for it. And you haven't done anything wrong. Rockford will never come after me because he'd have to admit what he's been up to."

"This is a lot," I fell back into the couch cushions.

"Maybe this will change your mind." He stood and walked to the bedroom, then he returned with his gym bag. He placed it on the coffee table and opened it. Inside the bag was stacks and stacks of cash.

"Oh my God!"

He pulled out big wads of it. It was like something in a movie, the stacks with the money wrappers around them. He tossed a few of the stacks into my lap, and I ran my hands along the bills, flipping through them to make sure he wasn't putting me on. It was real. It was real cash.

And I could see my future. This was our money to build our business. Together we could build my brand. I could help people get fit. I could have my own coaching service for all facets of life. I could have my own Mastermind group. I could develop affiliation agreements for fitness equipment. I could be a cardboard cutout at Dick's Sporting Goods that teenage boys would try to steal.

We could build something amazing together.

And that's when we hatched our plan. He left the money with me and told me to hide it. He trusted me that much. We were each other's partners now.

But he told me we had to pretend to be broken up. When he gave the signal, we'd ride off together into the sunset. I couldn't tell my mom. I couldn't tell Reneé. He couldn't tell Jenna.

I just had to trust him and be ready to run.

CHAPTER 8

TWENTY-FIVE DAYS AFTER THE MURDER

People tend to scatter both before and after the holidays, which left Lindy leaving messages for people that went unreturned.

On Christmas Day, Lindy made the rounds at April's family homes. Ella wore a red velvet dress and white tights with ruffles on the bottom. Lindy watched April pass on her aunt's famous mac and cheese, which on the Weight Watchers app is called, "Wearing your holiday halo." Now Lindy waited to see if April would crack over New Year's.

April loved tradition, ritual, dressing up, and pageantry, but Lindy's favorite part of the holiday was sipping coffee while Ella tore through the Santa wrapping paper that morning, and polishing off the leftovers plate later that night.

When they got back to the station, Boggs checked on the status of the warrant for Integrated Business Solutions, but no dice yet. They drove out to the location. Rockford's white Cadillac Escalade was the only car in the lot. The area was quiet, only the sounds of the occasional car driving down the highway.

When Lindy pulled on the door handle of the business, it was locked. They looked and saw that the windows had been papered over so no one could see inside. For all intents and purposes, Integrated Business Solutions was no longer offering business solutions.

"Mr. Rockford!" Boggs called. "Sir, we know you're inside. We'll have to break down the door if we suspect you are in danger, sir!"

Rockford's voice came from the other side of the door. "No, no. Detectives, I appreciate what you're doing, but as you can see, we are closed."

"Are you permanently closed or just closed today?" Boggs asked.

"We are closed right now and, like I said before, my clients have private information that I am obligated to protect."

"Mr. Rockford, you are not an attorney, psychiatrist, or priest," Lindy called out. "You do not have an expectation of privacy."

"That remains to be seen. You must speak to my attorney. His name is Lemmy Lynn Rogers, and his office is on the square in Kanton."

"Yeah, we know all about Lemmy Lynn," Boggs said.

Lindy asked, "Who is he?"

"He's a family law attorney who handled both of Rockford's divorces." He directed his voice back to the door. "Sir, if Lemmy Lynn told you to barricade yourself in your office, then you are getting bad advice."

"We'll see. But I am not coming out of this office, and until you have a search warrant, you cannot come in."

"He and Captain America must be members of the same Facebook group," Lindy said.

Rockford's voice came from the other side of the door again. "You should know that I'm filming this in the event that you try to break down the door. Which you cannot do unless I am under arrest or under distress."

"I think I smell gas," Lindy said. "You could have a gas leak in there, Rockford."

"Nice try, D'Arnaud," Rockford said. "This whole complex is electric only."

"Mr. Rockford, can you tell us where you were the night of December 14?"

"I was at home with the current Mrs. Rockford. And I'm offended by the question."

"Fine, Rockford," Lindy tried again. "I know you're worried about your legacy. You told me how important this town is to you. And I hear you. April tells me all the time how much she loves this town and she's like you, she wants to make it better. If we catch who killed Ethan, we are making this town safer. Having an unsolved murder is not good for tourism."

He paused. Maybe she was getting through to him. Instead he said, "Detectives, I'm walking to the back of the building now. I expect you'll be gone soon."

They decided to try their luck next with the neighbor who didn't want to hand over his security footage. Immediately, they noticed the neighbor had multiple signs posted on his lawn and door: *ADT, No Solicitors, Beware of Dog, I Don't Call 911* with a rendering of a pistol.

"This guy seems social," Boggs said.

Lindy said, "Come on man, this is your moment. Now get out there and shine."

Boggs held up his badge so whoever opened the door could see it and not shoot. "Mr. ... crap, what's his name?"

Lindy flipped through her book looking for where she'd scribbled it down. "Watson. Anthony Watson."

"Mr. Watson. Sir. If you don't mind, we're detectives with the Pleasant Springs Police Department. We're investigating the murder of your next door neighbor, Ethan Mo—" and then the door swung open.

A middle-aged man, short, gray beard and short, gray crew cut, placed a rifle to the side of the door. "I don't know anything!"

"Okay. That's what our officers told us when they canvassed, but you see, sir, we noticed that you have an ADT system, and your camera—"

"Then you know that I told them that my camera is my business, and unless you have a warrant, I ain't gotta give you anything."

Lindy almost slid her hands into her pockets, but instead rubbed them together. Her hands needed to be visible with Captain America.

Boggs rubbed the back of his neck, "Yes, sir. You're right. We do have to get warrants for everything. And that some-times puts us in a situation where a murderer could slip into some other house—"

"Son, unless you got the paperwork, I ain't gotta give you nothing. Y'all have a nice day."

And with that, he slammed the door.

"You're losing your touch, Boggs."

"You were a lot of help."

"My plan was to not make any sudden movements."

They trotted to their car, but before they climbed in, Boggs said, "What was the problem with the other side neighbor?"

"According to this ..." she flipped open her notebook. "They don't have a camera."

"Then what's that?" he pointed at the neighbor's home where a camera sat in the corner.

They backed the car out of the drive, to make sure Captain America saw them leave his property, then pulled in at the other house. It didn't look like anyone was home. There was what looked like a camera in the corner of the garage. They crept around the side of the home and saw another that pointed right into Ethan's back yard.

A woman's voice called from the house, "Can I help y'all?"

The back of the house had a large, screened-in back porch, with matching furniture. A woman stood in the doorway to her house, with a hand behind the door. Another instance where they made their hands visible and announced themselves in case what she was holding was a petal pink-handled Glock.

Boggs smiled and introduced himself and Lindy. "We're investigating the homicide of your neighbor, Ethan Moll."

She stepped out of the door toward them, "Oh my gosh, yes. Here, please come in. I'm home for lunch."

In her hand, not a Glock, but a baby carrot. "Please sit down. Do y'all want some hummus or something? Y'all don't mind if I snack, do you?"

She grabbed the tub of hummus and the plastic bag of baby carrots and planted them on the table. Then she pulled out a green and gold pack of cigarettes and lit one up. She was in her 30s, but her skin was impacted by the smoking. "I told the officers I didn't see or hear anything, or at least I didn't hear anything unusual. I cannot wait for that damn fraternity house to relocate."

"Yes, ma'am," Lindy said. "We were actually wondering about your cameras. It looks like you have a few, but you told the officers that it was broken."

"It is. It was an old one my daddy got at Trade Day."

Lindy whispered to Boggs, "I don't know what Trade Day is."

"It's like a flea market but mostly old men and farming equipment."

The woman said, "Yeah. My daddy installed it because he was worried about all these college kids roaming around. We've never been able to get anything off of it. And then, you know, with the ice storm, the lights were flickering. So when the officers asked to see it, we saw that it had shorted out."

"Can we still see it?"

"Sure," she said. She walked back into the house. Boggs took one of the baby carrots and popped one in his mouth.

"If she's some anti-cop poisoner, I will tell everyone you lived a life of risks."

He crunched on the carrot. "Please stop predicting I'll die of poisoning."

The woman returned with a black box and a wad of cords wrapped around it. "I don't know what works or what doesn't, but it scorched the wall when it went. I'm surprised it didn't catch fire. I'm telling ya, this house has not been right since we moved in, but everyone on this block has told me that they have one thing or another that wasn't done right when these houses were built. But we're in it now. Couldn't move if we wanted to. Not even with a murder next door."

"Did y'all ever see anyone sneaking around? Maybe creeping around the back yards or tapping on back doors?"

"No. Nothing like that. And he was a real sweet boy. I didn't care much for his girlfriend."

"You met his girlfriend?"

"Yeah. That big, tall girl. She's the one who discovered the body, right? I felt so bad for her." Then her voice dropped. "I think he was cheating on her."

Boggs said, "You saw him with another girl?"

"Yeah, on and off I'd see two of them together. But you know, now that you say something, he started keeping his back porch light on. He didn't before, and all of a sudden he did."

"And you thought it was odd."

"I noticed it, but then I thought maybe he got some new lights from Sam's Club or something. When something's new, you use it, right?"

"Yes, ma'am," Boggs said. "Do you mind if we take down your cameras, in case it has a memory card or a backup system?"

"I never even thought of that. Let me get you a ladder."

After several minutes of finding a ladder, finding a screwdriver, then finding a Phillips head because that's what they actually needed, Lindy and Boggs returned to the station with a cardboard box full of a Trade Day security system.

"What do you bet that woman's heading to Tillman to buy a new security system from Sam's Club before she goes to bed tonight?" Lindy asked.

"I think she texted her daddy and he's already looking for one on eBay."

While Boggs drove, Lindy futzed with the camera and located a tiny ridge and pressed it. Out popped a tiny memory card. Lindy texted someone in IT to let them know what they had found.

CHAPTER 9

TWENTY-FIVE DAYS AFTER THE MURDER

Hillary Wilson was a teacher at Heritage Christian Academy, a county private school forty minutes outside of town. Hillary taught third grade.

When they set up the interview, she asked if they could meet with her in her classroom while she changed her homeroom decor. She escorted them through the building and babbled a little about how they could come back under more pleasant circumstances, like Career Day or Safety Day. The school smelled like industrial cleansers and the sawdust they sprinkle on vomit.

They'd already cleared Hillary's alibi—she'd been on a retreat with her church and had 15 other upstanding church members who were happy to alibi her.

Her classroom was warm, like her. She had many soft surfaces: pillows and beanbags. She had a carpeted area. On the walls hung the works of the students. Lindy squinted at one grouping of torn construction paper collages before it revealed itself to be the topography map of Western Kentucky. An ancient overhead projector was shining a light onto the class whiteboard, superimposing a silhouette of George Washington onto a piece of posterboard. She turned off the light and they could see she was halfway through tracing. She tossed her pen onto the cart holding the projector and waved them to sit at a wide table with a set of tiny, but sturdy, chairs.

"We needed to get some clarity about your relationship with Ethan."

"Okay. We were friends."

"We were told he was trying to be more than friends."

She shook her head like the line of questioning was typical. "I mean, he tried. I don't know what else to say about it."

"You two were going to attend a wedding together after the new year."

"Yes. We have mutual friends who wanted to have a winter wedding. It's this weekend, actually. It feels so weird to go now. But I'm a bridesmaid, so I gotta go."

"Were you under the impression that you two were going just as friends?"

She sighed. "I was not interested in pursuing a relationship with Ethan. He would call and text me, and I would tell him I just wanted to be friends. But he'd push back. He's very talkative, and if you let him talk long enough, you end up thinking … well, maybe? But then I'd come to my senses and know that it was a bad idea."

Boggs asked, "I gotta admit, I'm a little surprised you wouldn't be interested. I mean, isn't he the kind of guy some girls would want to lock down? Good family, good job, you two are old friends, he owns his own house … I don't see why you wouldn't be interested."

"It was more important to Jenna that he and I become a couple than it was to either one of us."

"You and Jenna are close?"

"Oh, yeah. When her mom went to jail, she practically lived at my house."

"Her mom went to jail?"

"For embezzlement. It was only 18 months, but it was a big deal in the town where we grew up. People still whisper about it. But her mom came out of prison, started over with a new career, and never not once touches anyone else's cash box. You know, people around here will forgive but they never really forget. Her and Jenna are, like, on some small-town watch list or something."

"But you trust her."

"I do. I saw what she went through. She's incredibly guarded over it. She assumes whenever she walks out of a room that everyone is talking about her. I think she had this romantic idea that if I got together with Ethan that we'd be couple-friends. And I think she wanted Ethan to settle down. I'm telling you, with both of them working on me ... well, they could convince the paint to come down off the wall."

"But even so. We saw how hard he was working to make it happen. You weren't at all interested?"

"I don't think he was really interested in me. I got the sense that he was still seeing someone else."

"Why did you get that sense?"

"Because she came to our church with him one day while he was texting me."

"You saw Gabbi Edwards at your church?"

"I think that was her name. She's not too tall. Blonde hair. Very pretty. Like Instagram pretty."

"And he introduced her to you?"

"No. I was talking to Jenna before church started, and she was trying to get everyone ... I mean my family, Ethan's family, her and Ross, to all go eat after church. There's this buffet off the interstate that everyone goes to after church."

"Hutchinson's?" Boggs said. "That place is good."

"I know. And you know it's big, and they have this extra

room they'll let you use if you come with a party of fourteen. She was coordinating this big group so she could get the private room, so I was like, fine. That day, I was supposed to sing a solo, which is why I didn't sit with them. And when I was in the middle of my song, I saw someone walk in late and sit down with Ethan."

"And that was Gabbi?"

"Yeah. You couldn't miss her. She wore a red dress. And she had this pretty fringed shawl with all this cool embroidery on it."

"You don't seem very threatened by her."

"If that's who he wants to be with, then he should be with her. I was just worried about Jenna."

"Why?"

"She was so mad that day. I know her. She was trying to keep a smile on her face, but she was fuming."

"But did Jenna say anything?"

"I know she was having a really bad day. She was mad that her plan fell apart. I think she and Ross were fighting …"

"Why would she and her fiancé be fighting?"

"I don't know that they were. Jenna made a remark that Ross was sulking in the car and she had to handle that, too," she said. She took a sip from a white water bottle covered in pink and white heart stickers, some that had dissolved from the dishwasher. "I don't know what to make of this, but I'm going to tell y'all anyway."

Lindy looked at Boggs and flipped to a fresh piece of paper.

"Okay, so after the service, I had to pee. And I always use the upstairs one by the office to avoid the crowd. I ran up the back steps, and I heard Ethan and that woman having a conversation."

"Were they yelling?" Lindy asked.

"They weren't shouting. But it was intense."

"What were they saying?" Boggs asked.

"Things like, 'You know you're not supposed to be here,' and 'You're not responding to my texts,' and 'You said you trusted me.'"

"So it was a fight?"

"It may have started out as a fight, but it became something else." Hillary rubbed her hand against her forehead and ran it down her face and over her mouth. "I think they were having sex in one of the Sunday School rooms."

"You do?" Boggs said.

"I do. And that's when I ran downstairs to use that bathroom instead."

"Did you see them come out of that room?" Lindy asked.

"No. I did see them walk out of the church, but only him. I don't know if she snuck out the back or what."

"Did you speak to him or mention you heard him?" Boggs asked.

"No." She added a few o's for emphasis. "I tried to get out of there as quickly as possible. I told Jenna I couldn't do Hutchenson's and told my parents that we'd called it off."

"Did you tell Jenna?"

"Anything I would have told her would have been gossip, and I try very hard not to gossip. In fact, telling y'all makes me feel uncomfortable."

They confirmed a few of her statements and closed out the interview. Hillary escorted them out of the school and warned that she would be contacting one of them for Career Day.

When they started the car, the radio automatically played ESPN talk radio. Lindy turned it off and quietly looked through her notes. They were left with only the sound of the roar of the engine and the car wheels on the road. Eventually Lindy said, "You know what I'm thinking?"

"Are you thinking, why didn't we know Jenna's mom went to jail for embezzlement?"

"Yep," she said. "Are we bad at our job?"

"We might be."

"You know what else I'm thinking?"

"Why aren't we looking closer at Jenna?"

"Bingo."

When they walked in the door, Delphrain called them to his office for an update. They updated him on the conversation with Captain America and how they'd be filing a warrant. They updated him on the other neighbor's camera system, which was currently with forensics. They updated him on the interview with Hillary at the school. They updated him on the information about Jenna's mother's jail time, bracing themselves for the cussing about due diligence, which never came.

Before they walked out, Delphrain updated them on the Rockford warrant.

"It's not going to happen. Not enough probable cause."

"Same problem Rouse was up against."

"I'll tell you the same thing I told Rouse—the only way you're ever going to get someone like Rockford is to catch him red-handed. I told him that if he notified the FBI, they could at least set up a sting."

"They're not going to touch anything under a million."

"That's what those women in Connecticut thought," he said. "Look, take your eye off Rockford, because I am elbow deep in calls from everyone in town who's telling me that they heard from one cousin who heard from another cousin that it was the jealous girlfriend."

"I'm not convinced," Lindy said. "And I'm not convinced we've got the right jealous girlfriend."

"Then get some proof. Do your job," he said. "But remember, don't go out there chasing zebras when what you got is a bunch of horses."

Lindy said, "I hate that expression."

A knock on the door frame got all of their attention. A uniformed officer announced that Jenna was waiting in the bullpen. She wanted to speak to the detectives.

Jenna and Ross sat in the waiting area on a bench. Jenna kept her boxy tote bag on her lap, and Ross stared off into the distance.

When the detectives approached, Jenna stood and removed a binder from the tote bag. It was thick with paper, and glimpses of blue indicated she'd divided it into tabs. Ross stood behind her and shoved his hands in his pockets. His hair had been styled before, but now it looked like he had cut it short, practically bald. Jenna held out her hand to shake. "Detectives. I was hoping to speak with you about the progress of the case, if you'll allow me some time."

"Sure. We can do that," Boggs said and pointed toward the interview rooms.

Jenna charged forward, throwing her tote over her shoulder.

Lindy hung back when she saw Ross sit back down on the bench. She nodded to Boggs, and he nodded back before jogging to show Jenna which room she would be sitting in.

Lindy also placed her hands in her pockets and said, "You want a Dr. Pepper?"

Ross shrugged noncommittally.

"Come on. Let's get you a Dr. Pepper."

He followed her and she dug around for her wallet. "So how are you holding up these days?"

"Fine."

"You cut your hair." The last time she'd seen Ross, he was polished, with nice hands and an asymmetrical haircut with pomade. He still had thick lashes and eyebrows, but they didn't look as manicured anymore. He looked worn down.

"Yeah, I just got sick of styling it all the time. My brother's the rock star. I don't have to be."

At the machine, Lindy tapped the side of the machine with her credit card, knowing that with the stupid surcharges, this soda would cost almost ten bucks. He better have something good. The drink made the clunking sound when it fell in the bin. Ross retrieved it and popped it open.

"I guess this has been hard on both of you," she offered.

"Yeah. Me and Ethan lived together once."

"So you two were close?"

"I guess. You know, you live with someone, you know them different than everyone else. One time I lived with these two howlers that didn't do laundry, they just bought new underwear."

"Some people might call that smart."

They walked together toward a different interview room, but he took a left to the entryway bench.

"It's quieter back here." Lindy pointed toward the room.

"I don't want to miss Jenna when she's done."

"Okay."

He sat down on the bench. He was being chatty. "That's how I met Jenna. She was just there, like part of the package. She'd show up in the mornings, and they'd head off to classes, and then they'd come back together. At night she would pack it in and head home, or sometimes she'd crash on the couch."

"It didn't bother Ethan when you two started going out?"

"No. He encouraged it. We were always doing everything together anyway," he said. "Ethan looked put-together. But he couldn't take care of himself. That's what Jenna did. She made sure he got places on time. Made sure he got the best deals on his car and his cell service. She set up a Google Calendar for him so she could send him reminders of his appointments."

"That's…"

"Nuts, right? I know. It's weird. But it's just Jenna. She tries to do all those things to me, too, but I've told her I don't need it and I don't like it. I'm a grown-ass man who can make his own dentist appointments, and I don't care if she gets a better deal with AT&T; I like Verizon."

"Do y'all fight over it?"

"Not anymore," he said. "But she can't help it. Jenna has to control the chaos, even when there's no chaos to control. She likes to drive, you know what I mean?"

"So what happens when she doesn't get her way?"

"That's the thing. When I stood my ground and told her that if me and her were going to work out, she needed to back off and let me make my own decisions, she respected that. I think that's why we work. Ethan let her be in charge because he couldn't be bothered to do those things himself. He liked being managed."

"But didn't he present himself as …?" Lindy asked.

"It was all bullshit. He knew how to look put-together, but he also knew that, without Jenna, it would all fall apart."

"So if Jenna didn't like the girl he was dating, would he break up with her?"

Ross lowered his voice, "Look. Ethan kept a lot of secrets from Jenna. He and Gabbi were still together, and I don't know if he knew how to get out of it. They were supposed to be broken up. He told me that she was texting him all the time and she was still coming over to his house. She'd just let herself in. He said no matter what he told her, she just kept coming back."

"And he was also going out with Hillary?"

"Tried to. He and Jenna worked on Hillary like it was a project."

"Why?"

"Because Ethan wanted to make Jenna happy, and getting Ethan to settle down was going to make Jenna happy."

"No offense," Lindy said, "but did Jenna have some idea in her head that the four of you would live together in a house together somewhere?"

"Not the same house, but maybe the same cul-de-sac. Back-yards that butt up against each other. Sunday dinners. I figured she would grow out of it. But when they started working on Hillary together, I thought it would just blow up in their faces. I'm shocked Hillary ever agreed to go with us to the wedding."

Lindy leaned back on the bench. "What did you think about Gabbi?"

"She was obviously crazy. Why would she keep coming to town after he broke up with her?"

"Are you sure he wasn't just keeping her on the line?"

"Maybe. I don't know. I don't know anything anymore."

He finished his drink. Lindy took the can from him. She told him she'd throw it away, but instead she walked to the cabinet where they kept evidence bags and dropped it in one. Better to have DNA and not need it than need DNA and not have it.

Once she'd logged it, she found the room where Boggs and Jenna were chatting. Jenna was going through her binder, which was printed pages of Facebook, screenshots of text messages, and typed pages.

"Good," she said when Lindy entered the room. "Perhaps *you* will take me more seriously."

Before Lindy could sit down, Jenna asked, "Why have you not arrested Gabbi for Ethan's murder?"

"Obviously we cannot disclose any information about a case as long as it's still under investigation."

"Yes. That's what he's just told me, but what I don't understand is how she can walk around free and still post on Facebook about her empowerment group, and her new direction in life, and how much she appreciates everyone's sympathy after her boyfriend died. I mean, didn't she tell y'all that they were broken up? Now he's her boyfriend."

Lindy glanced down at the printout that Jenna was laying her finger against. "Let's slow down a minute," Lindy said. "We've talked to many people and they've all told us how close you and Ethan were."

"Yes, we were close."

"Many people we've spoken to were under the impression that you and Ethan were a couple."

"It is possible for men and women to be friends without being romantically involved."

"Sure, sure. You're saying people misunderstood."

"Yes. We were always just friends. We looked out for each other."

"Like who you two dated?"

"Sure. He would let me know if I was talking to a guy who was a player, and I would tell him if he was talking to someone who was crazy. Except he didn't trust me about Gabbi. When I said she was crazy, and then when they broke up, he started to see it."

"Crazy like what?"

"She wouldn't let him go. Always texting him and trying to get him to be with her. I haven't even gotten to the part where I saw her at Kohl's. I mean, what is she even doing in our town if not trying to be closer to him?"

"You saw her at Kohl's?"

"I was shopping for work clothes. And she was in athletics by the door. And I asked her what she was doing in my town."

"You confronted her?"

"Someone had to! I reminded her that Ethan had broken up with her and she needed to move on. I told her that her fixation wasn't healthy. And she said, 'You don't understand,' and, like, threw her sports bras at me and ran out the store."

"And that's it?"

"No. Obviously I went after her."

"You chased after her?"

"Chased," Jenna rolled her eyes. "I walked swiftly through a parking lot, and when I got to her car, she told me it was none of my business and for me to stay out of it. And I told her it was my business. Anyway, she got in her car, and I yelled after her that if I ever saw her car on Ethan's street, then I was going to have her arrested. And I wish I had seen it because then she *would* have been arrested for stalking and Ethan would still be alive."

"Did you ever wonder why Ethan never called it off?"

"I think he did call it off! But Ethan never liked being the bad guy. I told him he needed to get over that, but it was against his nature. I told him he had to be firm and maybe a little mean."

"Did she exhibit any violent behavior?"

"Not that I saw. But she was obviously obsessed with him."

"Obsessed is an interesting word, Jenna," Lindy said. "We've been talking to a lot of people who think that applies to you."

"You're not paying attention."

"What was the plan that night at the bar?" Boggs said.

"I don't hang out in bars."

"But Ethan did," Lindy said. "And one night you got all dolled up and met him and his friend Joey—"

"Oh," Jenna said, leaning back in the chair. "That was nothing."

"You walk into the room and suddenly Ethan is sending the party down the street," Lindy said. "Didn't you tell Ethan you were coming?"

"I felt like going out and I knew he would be there."

"Because you kept tabs on all his comings and goings."

"That was our way," Jenna sat back up in her seat. "He gave me his schedule. It's not like I hacked into his calendar."

"It makes sense," Boggs said. "It makes sense if you were taking an opportunity to change your relationship status from friends to more than friends. People would understand."

Jenna crossed her arms and shook her head. "No. No. No."

"Jenna, here's what I'm seeing," Lindy said. "You're describing a woman who inserts herself into a man's life, texts him constantly, calls him late at night, makes unexpected visits to town, enters his residence when he isn't home—"

"I have a key! That gave me permission to be there."

"Look at your notes, Jenna. You have pages and pages here on Gabbi. Who's obsessed? You didn't like your friend's girlfriend, a girlfriend you encouraged him to break up with, to the point where you pressured another friend Hillary to—"

"I thought they would make a good couple." And like a light came on in her face, she said, "I'm on the suspect list?"

"We're looking at every angle here."

"Y'all are unbelievable! What do you want? You want me to take a polygraph? You want me to ..." she fumbled and slammed the binder closed. "You want fingerprints? DNA?

You want to dig through my car?" She tried to shove the binder in her bag, and after only a second of struggling with it, tossed it on the table again. "I didn't kill Ethan. I lo— he was my friend. Forget this. I'm getting a lawyer."

She scooped her handbag onto her arm and stood to leave. Boggs blocked the door and she stood as tall as possible. And Lindy marveled at how tall she really was. A height that seemed supernatural and intimidating. "Unless you plan to arrest me, you better stand aside."

Boggs paused and Lindy nodded for him to move.

Once she left, Lindy said, "She grew three more feet just now. Holy sh—"

"I know, right?" he said. "Do you think her little boyfriend's into that?"

"Yes, I do. I think he is super into it. Damn, Jenna."

"You know what else I'm thinking?"

"If I were Gabbi and saw that coming toward me in the Kohl's parking lot, I'd be scared right out of town."

JENNA

Fine. I went to the bar looking for Ethan.

I don't really know why. I wasn't unhappy with Ross. We were fine. And Ethan and I were the same as we always were —just friends.

But after years of listening to him laugh in that mischievous way with his fraternity brothers, or seeing that smile he would get when reading an incoming text—usually from a girl and after every time Ethan would make some snide remark about how I needed to cut loose and let go, I decided to do it.

I live everyday so on-guard, so in control, so protected behind the many walls I have built around myself. Every decision, every day, is designed to keep me out of trouble, out of the mouths of the gossips, out of being confronted with any decision that might lead me to making a horrible choice and ruining my life.

So just for once, I wanted to be a little bad.

I did the best I could with what I had in my closet. Jeans that were too tight paired with a blouse that showed too much cleavage. I used makeup that I found in the back of my drawer, some stuff I'd forgotten I had and was sure would give me an eye infection. I even tried to follow one of those Youtube videos for creating the perfect smoky eye, but only ended up looking like a panda.

And after all that work and making that long drive … it was just awful.

The bar was loud and it smelled gamey. People gathered in different pockets, some playing pool, some gathered around a dart board, some crowded onto couches and around tables.

All the women in the room moved with a loose fluidity, and the guys were square-chested and long-armed, as if ready to scoop up handfuls of ass cheeks.

I was so out of place.

When I found Ethan, he was facing the other way. I tapped him on the shoulder, and when he spun around, all I could think to say was, "Surprise!"

His face went absolutely white. Just drained of all color, like I was a ghost or something. And finally I saw what everyone else alluded to and made veiled, sly remarks about. In Ethan's eyes, I was not a friend or even a woman. I was a mom. I might as well have been standing there in a housecoat with curlers in my hair. He loved me. He needed me. But I was not on his level.

He said, "What are you doing here?

"I came out. You always tell me to come out." I thought maybe it didn't have to be that way. I could prove to him that I could be fun.

He looked around, as if expecting his real parents to walk in any moment. "Okay. Okay. Let's get you a drink. Head up to the bar and order something and I'll be right behind you."

I looked over his shoulder. I could see his little crony, Joey, taking a shot from a tray of drinks. "Or I could just grab one of those."

"You don't want those. They're gross. Just go to the bar and I will be right there. I promise."

I did what I was told. When I looked back, I could see Ethan talking to Joey, looking like he was handing out instructions. I ordered a rum and Diet Coke. Eventually, Ethan joined me at the bar. All the spots were taken, so he just stood next to where I was sitting. It was too loud, so we had to shout a little.

"What are you doing here?" He signaled to the bartender and made a writing motion.

"I told you that I came out. You're always telling me to cut loose, so I'm cutting loose."

"What about Ross?"

"What about him?" I said. "I'm just having a drink."

He said, "What did you think was going to happen tonight?"

"I thought I was going to have a drink with my friend. Why are you being so weird about it? Have a drink with me!"

The stool next to me opened up and Ethan took it. He said, "This isn't you."

"Why not? I just wanted to have a little fun. Why can you do this and I can't? Because you're a boy?"

"Because I know how to play the game. Don't try to be two people, Jenna. It's exhausting." The bartender handed him a little plastic tray. Ethan glanced at it and pulled out his wallet.

"I'm not being two people. You just don't like that I can be more … that I can be … I don't know. Different sometimes, I guess." I knocked the side of my drink, spilling some of it on the counter. I grabbed a cocktail napkin and dabbed it up. I balled it up and flicked it onto the bar. I was getting a headache. I was nowhere near buzzed, and the noise of the bar was making my head throb. This place was gross and the people were crowding me. I didn't like it.

He said, "You should go home, Jenna."

"But I want to have an adventure!"

"So go skydiving. Don't do this." He threw some bills into the little plastic tray. "I'm heading out. Call Ross. Do something with him."

And he left. I didn't call Ross. I finished my drink and I drove home alone.

When I left the station, I was so freaking mad I couldn't even stand it. Ross was no help at all. He was quiet the whole drive back to my place, and then he excused himself saying he needed to clock some hours today. I hated his haircut. Just looking at him pissed me off.

I plopped down on my couch and propped my feet up on my coffee table. I was searching for my stupid, tiny remote when my phone buzzed. It was a text from Ethan's sister, Chrissy.

> Jenna, we know you mean well, but would you please stop posting memorial tributes about Ethan on Facebook? Also, can you please stop starting and egging on discussions about how the police are not doing their job? Our mother is very upset and none of these posts are helping her heal from her tragedy. We know you cared for Ethan, but this is a family issue, and we need to heal as a family.

I couldn't even live. The cops weren't listening. Ethan's family wasn't listening. Ross was shutting me out. I could feel the cry coming on, but it was stuck somewhere in my chest. I was so pathetic. I was half in and half out of my nice suit. I was supposed to be on my route right now, but I couldn't find the energy to put on my sales smile, so instead I was wrapped in a blanket on my couch, staring at a blank TV, because I couldn't find the stupid remote!

Why does no one care? Why am I the only one who cares? I stood up and started stalking around my house. I couldn't even sit down. I changed into an old T-shirt and some sweatpants. I grabbed a pack of makeup remover wipes and cleaned my face. Back in the living room, I found the remote on the floor. I turned on the TV, then turned it right back off. I walked to the kitchen, opening the fridge and looking in kitchen cabinets. I wanted nothing. I hated everything. I cleaned, scrubbing my counters with a spray cleanser and the rough side of the sponge. But it wasn't enough. I stripped off the gloves and decided I couldn't be inside anymore. I grabbed my keys and left.

I walked around my neighborhood. I was cold at first, but I warmed up as I moved. The sun was shining on me through some hazy clouds.

I know Gabbi did it. I know it. Flashes of Ethan's smiling face. Then flashes of his body in the shower. Why didn't he listen to me? I wanted to smack him. I imagined hitting him in the face with my palm. *Smack*. His handsome, all-American, only-good-things-happen-to-me-face. *Smack*. I could almost feel the sting on my palms.

I walked faster. My neighborhood wasn't good for walking. There were no sidewalks, and it was close to a main highway. But the strides kept my blood pumping. Blood pumping felt good.

I realized my fists were clenched. My nails had dug into my palms. I once took a self-defense class where they warned us all not to tuck your thumb in your fist, or you risk breaking it.

Keep it straight, the guy had said. Keep your wrist straight.

Carry the power through your arm. Imagine you're punching *through* the assailant instead of hitting him.

When everyone took turns punching and kicking the padded attacker, I couldn't do it. I couldn't bring myself to do it. Instead, I made jokes about it.

I didn't want anyone in the class to see me hit anything. I've been called boxy, stout, and sturdy my whole life. Being teased as a kid when my height came in. Mean boys called me butch. Another called me a "big bitch."

So I didn't punch. I had to make myself shorter and smaller. Instead, I asked the instructor, "Isn't this the moment when I douse you with pepper spray?"

The women in the class laughed, but some of them grumbled how I wasn't taking it very seriously. The instructor warned how women were always at risk of violence. I knew that. But I deflected anyway. "Why do I need to know this? Who gets murdered around here?"

Ethan did.

I churned on, exiting my neighborhood and marching down the highway, staying in the emergency lane. A few cars honked.

I couldn't believe I chickened out when I could have punched a guy! Why? Because I was worried that a bunch of women who had never liked me anyway would tease me like we were in grade school? Standing up to that cop today felt really good.

I wanted to punch that lady cop in the face.

I walked on and realized I was on the edge of campus. I could see the rec center inside. A row of ellipticals lined the windows to the outside, and inside, young women pumped away on those machines like a flock of multi-colored gazelles. I could never be a gazelle. But I didn't want to be a gazelle. I wanted to be a bull: angry, powerful, terrifying.

I walked inside, right past the desk where people scanned their cards for entry. The teen at the desk called after me, but I thought, *Come and get me. Ask me to leave. I wish someone would.*

I checked a few rooms until I found one where they must hold kickboxing classes. There were gloves and dummies stashed in a curtain-covered storage area. I tugged at a foam "man." The weighted base swiveled but I couldn't get it to move. While I was trying to drag this heavy man, a young woman walked in. She had a short, black, pixie cut and tattoos on her incredibly cut arms. I stopped what I was doing and took in her black joggers and black tank over a black sports bra. She looked tough.

She said, "We don't have a class scheduled for another hour. And we don't let people hang out in here when there isn't a class."

"I don't want to hang. I want to punch something." I pulled at the foam man, again.

"Right. Except our boxing class isn't on Mondays, it's on Thursday—"

"Look, you're very nice. And normally I wouldn't be caught dead in a gym. And you could probably haul me out of here if you wanted to because you are clearly jacked. But my best friend was murdered. I am dealing with a lot of shit right now, and I can either hit one of these dumb pretend men, or I can punch out all the walls in my house."

"Are you a member here?"

"No. But I'll pay for it. Here," I pulled my keys with my ID and extra cards from my pocket. "I'll pay for a class or whatever, but…just…Can you help me out here, okay?"

I watched her take me in. The fitness music outside the room was slightly muted, but I could still hear the thump, thump, thump of the bass on the high energy song. She scanned me, holding her hands in front of her stomach, like she was in first position, or some pre-fight stance. Then she lifted the bottom of the free-standing punching bag, and I caught the head as it tilted. We carried it to the middle of the room.

"I'll let you hit this thing for fifteen minutes, will that be enough?"

"I will leave after fifteen minutes."

"What's your name?"

"Jenna." I shook out of my sweatshirt. "What's yours?"

"Amanda. And don't post a five-star review or anything telling people that I let you do this."

"I promise."

Amanda ran and grabbed some boxing gloves. She talked me through warming up first. While I bounced for jumping jacks and mountain climbers, Amanda turned on the music for the "class." It was speed metal. I was into it. She showed me some punches. Jab, jab, uppercut.

Amanda didn't make conversation, only encouraged. "Good. Now jab. Jab. Back. Now bounce back on your heels. Good." I felt the contact with the bag, the resistance against my glove. I punched and punched. My heart pounded. My brain said, *You should stop because you're being stupid and this is pointless. You're making a fool out of yourself. This girl pities you. She's going to tell everyone about the gross girl that demanded to hit something.*

When the fifteen minutes was up, I held out my hands so Amanda could remove the gloves. I was sweating. My ponytail had fallen over to the side, practically all the way out. But I saw myself in the mirror, and I didn't look like a gross blob, but like something feral and wild. I liked it.

"Do you feel better?"

"I feel different."

She shrugged. "You got some power there. You should

come back on Thursday. Add a little strength training, a little cardio, a little pop, pop, pop." She punched her hand against her palm to punctuate her words. "I can help you."

"Maybe. This whole thing isn't really me."

"It could be," she said. "It could be the new you."

"Right," I said. "Thank you. It was nice to meet you Amanda."

"See ya soon, Xena Warrior Princess."

"Who's that?"

"Google her. She's pretty badass."

When I got home, I looked up Xena Warrior Princess, but all I saw was some chatter about queer representations on television, with a picture of the character screaming and wearing chainmail. I was like, *Did she think I was gay? Is that why she called me that?* And then I was like, *I can't ever go back to that gym again.*

Later that day, I could feel soreness in my arms. I told Ross about what I did. He told me I should keep going back. "It was just a one time thing."

But later, I thought about the feeling of hitting that dummy, the weight of my hands in the gloves, the exhilarating feeling that washed over me when I stopped. I didn't care if Amanda might have been hitting on me. I wanted to hit something again.

GABBI

I might not have noticed it at all, except for how much more attuned I am when I enter spaces these days. I assess everything when I walk through a door now. What is the vibe? I tune into my intuition. Celeste Sullivan says to listen to your gut, and if it's telling you to run, you need to listen to that queen and haul ass out of there. I might be paraphrasing.

I was still getting used to the vibe at Jack's condo. I'd already burned sage, rearranged the furniture, and placed quartz crystals in essential spots in the new place, but I still hadn't gotten the energy right.

I entered the condo door and climbed the staircase entryway that led upstairs to the open-floor-plan living space. But on this day, after I tossed my keys into the bowl at the top of the landing, I could tell something was off about the vibe. My jasmine incense scent had been clouded with something musty, something sweaty, something desperate.

I ran out of there. I grabbed my keys and ran right back down the steps.

I'd only lived there for a few weeks, but my downstairs neighbor, Ed, had already made his presence known. He ran a cobbler shop downstairs, and Jack had hired him to keep things working smoothly at his other rental properties. I wondered if it had been him. He could have gone in and repaired something, that was part of the deal when I signed the lease. But nothing was broken. And Ed was always supposed to text me beforehand.

Once outside, I stood on the street corner and looked up and down the busy road. Ed had hung a *Be Back in Five Minutes* sign in his window. Cars sped past and I spotted several cars parallel-parked down the street and in the public lot across the way. When the delivery truck for the pizza place on the corner moved, I could see a black Chevy Tahoe just like Ethan's. And as irrational as it was, for a second I thought maybe it was him. That same flip over in the stomach as that night when I came home and found him waiting for me. That rush of relief and excitement. He's here!

But he wasn't. Ethan was gone.

I walked closer to the truck. Lately, I'd been trying to tune into his spirit, hopeful that he was still with me somehow. But the only time I ever felt his presence was when I masturbated. Typical Ethan. Always liked to watch.

Over my shoulder, I heard a smack, like my front door had been swung open and slammed closed. I ran back to the condo. My front door bounced against the latch without catching, and I could hear the tap, tap, tap of metal settling. I ran around the corner, but no one was there.

I turned around and ran back down the street toward where I had seen the black Tahoe, but it was already speeding around the block, too far away for me to catch anything that would identify it—no license plate number, no bumper sticker, nothing.

Seriously, like, was someone really in my house? Was I being robbed?

I grabbed my phone from my pocket and called Ed to see where he was. He was repairing a clogged drain in the neighborhood and said he'd be back in a few minutes. I waited inside my car.

He walked through my apartment with me when he got there. He always wore a pair of Rustler jeans from Walmart and a white T-shirt. He wore a Carhartt jacket over it to ward off the chill. He kept his hands in his pockets as he checked behind all the doors and closets. I leaned into the damsel in distress routine while I followed him around: wringing my hands, crying, playing up the astonishment and the creepiness of it all. I mean, obviously, I was scared. Since Ethan's murder, I've felt a ferocious need to protect myself. But I always caught myself and remembered that violence is not good for my spirit work.

On the walkthrough, we didn't see where anything was missing. My laptop and tablet were on the floor where I'd left them. My jewelry was untouched. My stash of secret cash was undiscovered. All that remained was the stench of the home invader.

"Gabbi, hon. Are you sure someone was here?"

I smiled. If I pushed it, he would say I was making it up. So I played the embarrassed woman who overreacted. "I'm so sorry, Ed. You know, I think I'm just more suspicious since my ex-boyfriend was killed."

"That makes sense," he said. "But it looks like everything's okay now."

"Thank you for helping me check." I placed my hand on his arm to show a level of intimacy, but then I told him, "I never had brothers or uncles to protect me, and it's nice to know I kind of have one with you, Ed," to make sure he didn't think it was going to get sexual.

"Do you want to borrow my gun?"

A laugh had burst out of my mouth before I could stop myself. "Oh no. I don't like guns, but thank you."

It took a while before I could get him to leave. Eventually, I had to tell him that I was expected at the gym to get him out of my place.

Ed watched while I checked the locks on the doors and all the windows. One of them had been open, and the screen had been popped out. I looked out the window and saw a simple drop to the roof of the building next door. There was a fire escape ladder that anyone could have climbed to reach that window. *Was that how they got in?*

I locked it and asked Ed if we could fix it so it won't open any more. He said he would find me something.

After I escorted Ed out, I was left wondering who'd driven off in that black Yukon. It hadn't been Ethan's truck. But I knew someone who had one just like it.

JENNA

I went to the boxing class after all. Turns out, I liked it a lot.

When I left, I was sweaty and tired, and absolutely starving. I called Ross to see if he'd eaten yet but he didn't answer. I'd texted him all afternoon but no response. Now, he wasn't answering the phone at all. It went to his voicemail immediately, like his phone was turned off or something.

I walked through the door of my house and flipped on the light, and there in my chair—my chair—sat that bitch, Gabbi.

I jumped in shock, fumbling my phone. When I caught it before it hit the floor, I accidentally pressed the side button, which caused the swipe for SOS screen to light up.

Before I could say anything, Gabbi said, "We need to talk."

"You need to get the hell out of my house!"

"I said we need to talk."

And what happened next still makes no sense to me. I've never been in a fight before in my life, and somehow taking two short boxing classes made me think I was some MMA fighter. I rushed her and yanked her by the hair from my chair. She snatched my hair, and I lost my balance. We fell to the floor, kicking and clawing each other. And I was just screaming at her, "You bitch! You took everything from me!" and she was shrieking, "Jenna! Stop it! Stop it! I have to tell you about Ethan!"

And then she somehow flipped me over, rolled on top of me, and pinned my shoulders down with her knees. She said, "Jenna! Stop it! I've done yoga every day for five years. I strength train at the gym three days a week, and I have whooped girls bigger than you at the bar. If I wanted to hurt you, I would have done that already. I need you to listen to me."

"I don't want to talk to you!"

"I won't let you up until you calm down and listen to me."

I was stuck. Her knees pressed into my shoulders, and I couldn't throw her off of me, no matter how hard I tried. I didn't have a choice. "Fine. Just let me up."

"You won't call the cops?"

"I'll give you ten minutes before I call the cops."

"If, when I'm done talking, you still want to call the cops, then you can call the cops." She rolled off me and stood up.

I sat up from the floor. I was scanning the room for where my phone fell. Gabbi picked it up from the floor and handed it to me. "Set your timer."

I swiped the phone to life. "Get on with it."

Gabbi sat down on my couch, turning to the side to face me while she talked. "First, tell me: Why was your truck at the end of my block today?"

"What are you even talking about? My car was being serviced all day, and as soon as I got it back, I went to the gym."

"You went to the gym?" Her voice raised at the end like she was talking to a child who drew an adorable unicorn picture at preschool. I could have snatched her hair again.

"Shut up! We're not friends. Now get on with it so I can call the cops."

"You're telling me you were nowhere near Tillman today? And you were definitely not on my street?"

"I don't even know where you live! I try not to think about you at all. And your ten minutes is gonna be up soon."

She said, "I didn't kill Ethan."

I straightened my shirt, which had gotten twisted in the melee. "Well, I don't believe you."

"I figured that. But I need you to think back. Ethan was in trouble. He was acting weird. I know you saw it. He was selling his things. He was sneaking around."

"People sell their things. He was sneaking around to keep away from you."

"Did he tell you that?" she asked. "Did he tell you I was stalking him? Did he ever tell you that he didn't want me around anymore?"

The truth was: I didn't know why he was doing anything. Because I was keeping my distance. I'd neglected him, and now he was dead. He had sold some of his things. He had ignored the few texts I had sent him. I thought it was because he was mad at me. He never said she was stalking him. But I wouldn't give her the satisfaction of admitting that.

Gabbi said, "He was about to disappear. We were going together."

I snorted, "You're delusional. You two were done."

"We weren't done. He wanted us to pretend we were done."

I swiped my phone alive again. I thought, *Just call the cops already*. "That's so dumb. Why would he want to do that?"

"It was all Ethan's idea. He said if everything went sideways, no one would even know to look for me because we were done."

"What went sideways?"

"His job. Did he tell you anything about what he did for a living?"

"Ethan consulted for marketing small businesses. He sold memberships to their networking program. It's not complicated!"

"It was a scam, Jenna. I don't know how it worked, but it had something to do with those nights at the casino. He said eventually the whole thing would collapse, and he didn't want to be anywhere near it when that happened."

"You're making that up. Ethan wouldn't do anything illegal." But even then I didn't really buy it. Ethan's ethics were loose at best.

"But you know he would do something illegal because you know what happened in Lexington."

"He didn't tell you about that." I was surprised. That was Ethan's dark truth. I didn't like how I was sitting on the floor, but I didn't want to move. I didn't want to give her the satisfaction of knowing that I was uncomfortable.

"He did. And his daddy kept him on a short leash after that. If Ethan embarrassed the family again, his daddy was going to cut him off from everything. But you know what he was more afraid of—that his daddy was going to call him back to the family business."

I watched her for signs, something that I could call her out on, something that told me for sure she was a liar. But I couldn't tell. Ethan must have told her these things. Not even Ross knew about Ethan and his daddy's deal. I didn't trust Gabbi, but I had nothing to prove she was lying either.

"Ethan had to get this whole thing wrapped up before New Year's."

I knew that. I knew that Ethan hadn't convinced his daddy that he had "made it" on his own. His daddy wanted him home, to take his place leading the family business. He would train and eventually Ethan's daddy would retire—but Ethan said his daddy would never retire, so he would forever be in his shadow. Lexington was his opportunity to break out, but he botched it. He had to prove himself fast, and I can imagine him trying to fast-track it, knowing his time was limited.

"Celeste Sullivan says that dysfunctional families are institutions, and when you leave the center of that institution, you don't even realize you have the freedom to just walk away. You've been institutionalized. You don't know who you are without the institution. Ethan was making a break for it. He said he'd always be in his daddy's shadow, and his sister Chrissy is better suited for it anyway, but his daddy was always worried her—"

I finished it for her. "Her husband's name would be the company name, and they would lose their legacy."

"Archaic, right?" Gabbi giggled. That obnoxious giggle.

"Why are you telling me all this?" I asked.

She buzzed her lips. "Because you loved him, too. My friends—well, Reneé—like, they would get it in theory. But they didn't know him, didn't love him. They don't know what it was like to get swept up in his ideas and plans, and you just ride that wave of fun, but then he gets into his planning phase and is completely untouchable. Like you just orbit around him."

I knew what she was saying. I loved those times when he and I would put our heads together and put things into motion. The day we descended on the dealership and bought our trucks together, making those salesmen run around in circles. In college when we coordinated which one of us would attend classes and take notes to share with the other one.

Gabbi kept talking, "He had no problem putting me on a shelf, and then there I was, waiting for him to pick me up again. And when I would tell him I was sick of it, he'd smile and tell me to 'trust' him. I wasn't stalking him, Jenna. But when he asked me to just hang on and lie low with him, I couldn't stay away."

I had been on that same shelf before. And I did know. I learned how to make myself essential by clearing the decks for him so he could work uninterrupted. It didn't all start at once, but a little piece at a time.

"You're also one of the few people in his life that even know I exist, like I'm a real person, not just 'the ex.' Even your hate for me makes me more real than the image everyone else has because he kept me hidden so well. And if I don't talk about all this, I'm actually going to go crazy."

I stood from the floor. I walked into the kitchen and pulled a bottle of tequila from the top cabinet. I grabbed two novelty neon shot glasses that had "Panama City Beach" written across the side. Gabbi watched me from the couch.

I poured a shot and downed it. No lemon. No chaser. Just the warm tequila working its way down my gullet, opening my sinuses and wrapping a blanket around my brain. I watched Gabbi approach the bar, take the other glass, and tip it, indicating she wanted one, too.

"I thought you didn't drink."

"Tequila's okay," she said. "It's agave instead of sugar, which means your body metab—"

"I swear to God, I know we're having a moment, and I allowed your guru-talk for a little while, but if you start preaching to me about your fitness nonsense, I'm getting the box of cheese puffs from my cabinet and shoving them all down your throat."

The obnoxious giggle came out of her stupid mouth again. Then she said, "You need to work on your anger issues."

"Why didn't you go to the cops with any of this?"

"Same reason you don't believe me. All of this makes me look like a liar and even more guilty."

I leaned against the counter. "If Ethan was selling all his stuff to get out of town with you, then where's the money? The cops said his safe was empty and he was totally broke."

"I had it. I was supposed to drive it to a port in Miami. We were going to take a boat and live on it for a while, sailing around—he said he taught himself to do that—but he was so 'fake it until you make it' I figured we'd end up hanging out in some coastal town because he couldn't figure it out. He talked a lot about Belize."

"So where's the money now?"

"I hid it. When I came to his house that night, I came in the back like he told me to. I was there to tell him bye, and we wouldn't talk or text until we saw each other in a few days. But when I walked in, I could tell something was wrong. I could hear the water running, but the TV wasn't on, and you know he liked for it to be on in the background when he took a shower."

I knew this feeling. It was like when I walked in and found him that morning. The sound of water running and knowing it wasn't like Ethan.

"When I got back to where he was, I found him in the shower. The knife was still in his chest. I pulled it out and cut the fuck out of my hand. I thought maybe I could put pressure on it and call an ambulance, but he was already gone." She was crying while she spoke, but it was a steady stream of tears running down her face, and the gurgle of phlegm gathering in her throat. She cleared it and wiped her nose. "And then I heard someone in the house, shoes on the hardwood floors. I think only one person. And they were out the back door. I dropped the knife and ran, and realized that … I panicked, too. Ethan was gone. No one knew I was supposed to be there.

And I had the knife in my hand. No one was going to believe I didn't do it."

"Did you see who it was?"

She shook her head. "I don't know who it was."

"How do you know I didn't kill him?"

Gabbi laughed, hard. Perhaps it was the tequila kicking in, but she was practically wheezing over the idea.

"This feels insulting."

"C'mon, girl! You are a stone-cold bitch, but you're not a killer. Also, what's wrong with you? … Asking that question … Why would you want anyone to think you're a murderer? Like … seek therapy."

"You're telling me that you didn't go around telling those cops that I was some crazy-jealous, lovelorn, rejected woman, obsessed with Ethan, who just loses it and stabs him?"

"I didn't. But I know you definitely told the cops that I was some crazy stalker. And everyone on Facebook."

I was quiet for a moment and poured myself another shot. "You don't need me to believe you. You need the cops to believe you. Take all this to them, take the money to them—"

"Oh, hell no! I'm sorry, but the last thing Ethan would want would be for the cops to have this money. Otherwise, what was it all for? Fine. Ned Rockford started the scheme, but Ethan promoted it. He worked for every dime of that money. And if the scheme collapsed, the cops would have taken it. Why do you think we were running off?"

"And you're the only one who knows where this money is? Show me. Show me where you hid it, and I'll believe you."

She twirled the empty shot glass on its side. It was on its third spin before she spoke. "You have to leave everything here. No phone, no bag, no wallet."

"Can I at least wear shoes?"

"Yeah, you'll need those."

I walked back to my bedroom to look for a sweatshirt. Gabbi asked if she could fill her water bottle from my Brita pitcher, and then she made snide comments about all the food in my fridge. "If you're going to strength train, you need more protein in here."

"Shut up!" I yelled from the bedroom. "We're not friends."

I loaded her up in my truck and she directed me. We drove out of town, past Bell Eagle gas station, all the way out of civilization. I paid attention. She pointed to a field drive. "Pull off here." Then she directed me to drive along the edge of the field to the wood line. We parked my truck and walked into the dark with our flashlights lighting the way. We paused at a gnarled tree, then kept going until we reached a tree stump.

Gabbi pulled out a little gardening spade from her hemp tote. She handed me her bag and flashlight. "Make sure I can see."

She got on her knees and started digging. The hole got wider and she went deeper. "Isn't the ground hard?"

"It rained, so that helps. This isn't easy. You want a turn?"

"Nope."

She continued to dig and eventually said, "Here it is."

I looked down at what felt like some archaeological dig, but instead of a skeleton, it was a black duffle bag. It was Ethan's bag. I was with him when he bought it. Gabbi unzipped the duffle and I could see inside. It was stacks of cash. I dropped to my knees and reached inside. "Whoa!"

"I know, right?"

I pulled out bundles. One of the wrappers slid from a stack and flew into the dirt hole. Individual bills scattered across the top of the bag. I was giggling over it, and Gabbi was giggling with me, scooping up the bills.

"Do you believe me, now? Do you believe that this was Ethan's money?"

"I believe it's Ethan's money." I said.

"Good. Because I think someone else is looking for it. Someone broke into my place and I think this is why."

"Who?"

"I don't know. Rockford, maybe?"

"You think he killed Ethan?"

"I don't know."

Gabbi took the money from my hand. "We need to bury this and get out of here."

After we reburied the money, we stepped out of the woods together and drove back to town in mostly silence. Gabbi scanned my satellite radio until she was satisfied with a song that was more bass than lyrics. She said, "You should add this to your playlist for when you go to the gym."

"Once again … shut up!"

I dropped Gabbi at the spot down my block where she had parked her car. I asked before she got out, "Hey. Why did you bury it? You could have just taken this money and run off with it."

"Where would I go without Ethan?"

"Well then, why are you telling me? Why are you showing me?"

"Because you're the only other person Ethan trusted."

If he had trusted me, then he would have told me, wouldn't he?

"Now I'm trusting you. You cannot tell anyone about this."

"Okay," I said.

"Not even Ross."

"O-kay!"

"Can you stop the internet smear campaign?"

"No promises there."

"I guess you wouldn't be you unless you hated me." Gabbi

climbed from the truck. "Besides, even if you're a bitch, you're my bitch now."

She slammed the door, and I drove off.

When I got back to my house, I showered off all the dirt and put on some pajamas. I had a little more tequila and then laid down to go to bed.

I was drifting off when I heard my phone buzz. It was a message from Ross.

U up?

Not really. About to go to bed. You coming over?

I'm probably going to crash here. Been a long day.

OK. See ya tomorrow.

My brain spun. Honestly, I was glad Ross wasn't here, because I was worried I would tell him about going off into the woods with Gabbi. I didn't know how I felt about any of it, and until I did, I wasn't saying anything to anyone.

CHAPTER 11

TWENTY-NINE DAYS AFTER THE MURDER

That morning, Lindy got a text that said:

You're going to like what I found.

Great! Bring it on!

Within minutes, one of the forensics nerds came to Lindy's desk carrying the cardboard box full of the security camera parts. "Where'd that lady say she got this?"

Both Lindy and Boggs said together, "Trade Day."

"Figures," he said. "Okay, well let me educate you on this relic. You know those new systems, like the Ring system, are a camera that will live-stream and record to the owner's phone or laptop, right? This device predates live-streaming. It's a motion-activated system that snaps rapid succession photos. Except it's glitchy, so you might get one photo, you might get 100 when it's activated."

He held up the scorched black box. "This thing is useless now. It acted mostly as a power source. It stopped downloading images a long time ago, but the backup memory card provided a few images. I just sent them to you."

Lindy asked, "So what am I going to like about them?"

"There are images on different dates of a young woman in the vic's backyard going in the back door."

Boggs and Lindy wheeled their chairs closer together at Lindy's laptop. They clicked through on the images.

Boggs said, "Some of these go back at least a month." It was Gabbi. Blonde hair. Blue hoodie. Yoga pants. The outfits changed, but it was Gabbi.

"I also got a bunch that must have been triggered by a squirrel or a stray cat, nothing on those. But keep clicking because right before the system died ..." they clicked to the end and he said, "Boom."

Through the sleety rain, the camera caught an image of a small hooded figure entering through the back door.

"We can't see her face in this one," Boggs said.

"But that is the same hoodie she's wearing in this image," Lindy clicked to a previous photo.

"This is it. We have to bring her in, right?"

"Here's what we have," Boggs said. "We have her on tape at Walmart getting out of her car and crossing the tree line into his neighborhood with the party kids."

"Yep."

"We now have her on tape entering the house."

"Yep."

"We have a cut. Which she lied about. When the DNA eventually comes back, it could be hers."

"This is it. It's her. We have to bring her in."

CHAPTER 12

ONE MONTH AFTER THE MURDER

Gabbi's law of authenticity made her difficult to read. When your life is a lie, even the truth seems false. They let her stew in the interview room, but she didn't stew. Other people will sit in the corner and ruminate. Gabbi refused to sit still. She paced. She hummed. She stretched. At one point, she threw herself into a headstand. She eventually sang Taylor Swift's "Blank Space" to herself. She didn't ask for a lawyer. Instead, she requested a green tea.

"We can get you coffee or water."

"I can't have coffee. My polarity is backwards, so caffeine actually makes me sleepy. Alcohol makes me uptight. I can't wear watches because they always—" on and on it went. Lindy was reminded of how much attention April's gluten-free aunt received at Christmas dinner, explaining why everything they were eating was poison.

Outside the room, Lindy watched the live feed of Gabbi from Boggs's computer. Boggs, leading the search of Gabbi's condo, was on the other end of the line.

"I think she might need a mental health screening," Lindy said.

"I think you should be here sorting through all this junk."

"We wouldn't get anywhere. All she does is flirt with you."

"It doesn't sound like you're getting anywhere."

"Shut up." On the screen, Gabbi windmilled her arms down until she was in downward dog, then threw one of her legs into the air and arched it over her head. "I can't keep watching her like this."

"All we've got is a journal and a book with a bunch of these little flags marking it up next to her bed."

"Unless there's a confession letter or blood evidence, that doesn't help us."

"We've got the cut, which didn't happen in Mexico like she said. We've got her car, and we've got her entering his home through the back door at the time of death."

"No face on that tape."

His voice muffled, like he had let his phone hand drop and was speaking to someone else in the room. "Oh ho!" he said. "We got something!"

"You got something!"

"We got something! I'm heading back!"

When he finally entered the interview room, Gabbi was meditating—cross legged in the middle of the table, her back pressed against the wall. So performative. Lindy thought, *Even Tony Robbins meditates sitting in a chair. She didn't have to climb on the table.*

"Get down, for God's sake," Lindy commanded, and Gabbi slid herself to where she could place her feet on the chair, holding her hand out for Boggs to help her. And, being the typical Kentucky boy, he did.

Being around Gabbi turned Lindy into someone's old grandma. Lindy found herself tutting, picking, and directing, almost always a step away from telling her, "Act like someone raised you." It was the worst part of her.

How could she flip it on Gabbi? What did she have to do to get Gabbi to show her worst side? The girl who was raised in Kanton with all the other country-as-corn kids, who still attended high school basketball games, cruised around town square, and hid out in the country building bonfires, shooting off guns, and going mudding on ATVs. The one who maybe started school, but didn't finish because she didn't know what she was going for. The one who probably thought she had scored getting into Ethan's family, and maybe worried what she was going to do with her redneck relatives at their high-class wedding. What did Lindy need to do to get this girl to unleash that Kanton native who was ready to take a bitch down and then sashay away?

Gabbi slid into a chair. "Can I leave now?"

"No," Lindy snapped. "But we are going to offer you an opportunity to tell us what happened the night Ethan died."

"I was at home packing for my trip."

Boggs stepped in with his gentler tone. "We know that's not true, Gabbi. We know that you came to see Ethan that night."

She shook her head.

Lindy placed the photo from the Walmart surveillance tape on the table. "This is your car parked on the other side of Ethan's house. We have you on tape getting out of your car and following the party kids across the ditch." Lindy placed a photo from the neighbor's surveillance tape showing a hooded figure going into Ethan's back door. "You enter the premises here."

Gabbi shook her head.

"We also know the cut on your hand didn't happen in Mexico."

"It did happen in Mexico."

"No," Lindy snapped again. "That's a lie. And we know

it's a lie because we talked to the concierge at the resort. He remembered you arriving to the property with the cut. There is not one piece of paperwork from where you cut your hand at the resort."

She smiled a terse, tight-lipped smile, like a stress response. "So I cut it before. Who cares?"

"We care. Because it's exactly the kind of cut that happens when you remove a bloody knife from a body."

"Y'all are sick and gross."

Boggs asked, "What happened when you went into Ethan's house?"

"I didn't kill Ethan."

"We didn't ask that. We asked what happened when you went into the house."

She looked around, catching a glimpse of herself in the glass. She moved a lock of her hair that was out of place, and tucked it under her ear. She smoothed it down. Then, as if on cue, she sparkled, as if suddenly aware that she could be on camera. "I was at Ethan's house. I walked in, just like I always do. He had asked me not to park in his driveway. He had told Jenna we broke up. That was a lie. So when I came to see him, I parked at Walmart and walked across the ditch... like the party kids. He asked me to do that."

"Why would Ethan lie about the breakup to Jenna?"

"Because she hated me. And it was mutual."

"Okay," Lindy said. Jenna was what brought out the worst in her. "So you're in the house. Then what?"

"I walked inside and took off my shoes. Ethan had this thing about shoes in his house."

When Lindy and Boggs walked the scene, they noted how there were mats with shoes on them next to all the vic's doors: the garage door mat had his hunting boots, the door behind his back door had slide-on house shoes and sandals, the front door had no shoes. It had been stiff when they entered, as if no one had ever used it. Back door guests are best.

"Something wasn't right. I can do that, you know? I can walk into a room and feel the vibe. I absorb the energy of a room. I can feel people's feelings sometimes. I took a quiz online that said I was an empath and it was like—"

Lindy interrupted her. "Can you focus, please?"

"Like I was saying…something was off. I could hear the shower. I called out to him that I was there, but I didn't hear anything back. But I heard something else. Like someone moving around in his bedroom. I mean, he could have been warming the shower up before getting in. But he didn't answer me back. I took off my jacket and threw it on the couch. I thought maybe he wanted me to join him in the shower. But when I got back there, he was … he was crumpled, like in the corner." She cleared her throat. "He was dead."

With the exception of the throat clearing, she was perfectly composed, as if she had practiced saying this to them.

"I panicked. He had a knife in his chest. Like right in his heart. So, I pulled it out. It was hard to do. I was trying to put pressure on his chest, like maybe save him or something." Here, her voice wavered again, but she cleared it. "It was too late. It was all too late. He was gone. I didn't even realize I had cut myself until later."

She swallowed and composed herself again. "I heard something. I heard someone running down the hall and out of the house."

It was the some-other-dude-did-it defense.

Lindy asked, "And then what?"

"I didn't kill him."

"So you said. And then what?"

"I had the knife in my hand. I had my fingerprints and

blood all over it. So, I wiped it down and put it in his gun safe."

"And then you tried to clean up the blood?"

"No. I didn't try to clean. That was all there when I got there."

Lindy said, "Super. But the problem is we don't have anyone but you on tape entering that house. You and your electric blue hoodie."

"It wasn't me."

"It was you," Lindy pushed.

"I can feel your frustration."

"Can you? What else am I feeling right now?"

"When we judge others, we're really only judging ourselves." Her quotes had a sing-song quality to them, like little rhymes they teach kids in Vacation Bible School.

Boggs said, "We can't help you unless you're not honest with us."

"I'm telling you the truth."

"Really?" Lindy asked. "You're telling me that you walked into your boyfriend's shower and pulled a knife from his chest, and you're not even shedding a tear over it? Did you practice this for your followers?"

She laughed, a throaty, *ha* sound. "You already think I'm fake. If I was crying, you would have called that fake, too."

"I mean, you perform everything else. I don't see why this should be different. People who loved him have done nothing but cry over him. Jenna was just here, and she was a wreck over losing Ethan. I mean did you even really love him, Gabbi?"

"You are not listening, bitch. I loved Ethan more than I have loved anyone. We had plans and some fucker, some asshole, ruined everything, and I'm not going to take the fall for it! That's some bullshit! Someone else was in that house!"

And there it was. All that earth-goddess, manifesting, garbage had been shed. She was that Kanton girl chugging Natty Lights from the bed of a pick-up truck. And she killed her boyfriend.

"Okay, let's calm down." Boggs reached across but never touched either of the women, instead placing a hand on the table in their path. "Gabbi. Gabbi. Look at me. Here's what we have. We have you on tape. We have you entering the premises. We have the cut on your hand. We have your DNA on the murder weapon. You just told us it was you who wiped it down and placed it in the gun case. We know he was talking to other girls. We know you went there to confront him about the texts between him and Hillary. And you stabbed him."

"No. That's not what happened. Hillary? Who is ... Oh!," she laughed again. "Are you kidding me with this school teacher bullshit?"

"And now we have this," Lindy said, and placed another photo on the table. It was an image of an electric blue hoodie stretched onto a silver table. On the hoodie were splotches of dried blood. "This is your hoodie. We found it in your closet. And it's being examined by our technicians right now to determine if that's Ethan's blood. But you and I know it is."

"That's not mine."

"You were wearing this hoodie when you got out of the car at Walmart."

"But that one is not mine."

"Then why did we find it at your house?"

It was like all the air had been sucked out of the room with a vacuum. Gabbi was stunned. She'd lost that meanness from before and it had been replaced with utter shock. She croaked, "Lawyer."

"What?"

"Lawyer. Lawyer. Lawyer," repeating the word like a siren.

"I'm being set up, and I'm not saying another word without my lawyer."

They left her alone to stew further. Another officer would eventually escort her to the phone. Lindy walked to the other side of the window and observed Gabbi's newfound panic.

Boggs asked, "What are you thinking?"

"I don't know. But something isn't right."

Boggs left to notify the Assistant District Attorney they were arresting Gabbi Edwards for the murder of Ethan Moll.

CHAPTER 13

FIVE WEEKS AFTER THE MURDER

On the screen where the producer watched the film, a blonde woman with a power bob said, "I must be honest. It all sounds a little far-fetched."

"I know, but it's the truth. Someone else was in that house when I got there, and they killed Ethan. Not me. I loved him. I wanted to marry him."

They'd set up a filming area in the visitation room. It had been set up with mostly extension cords, clamp lights, and duct tape. Gabbi sat for her interview in her striped prison pants and a thermal shirt. She'd swiped some of that duct tape and taped up her boobs like a beauty queen contestant, and cuffed the sleeves of the shirt.

"And you claim he felt the same way toward you. That he was serious about you. Even though he never proposed, he told everyone in his life that you two broke up, he never introduced you to his parents."

"I met his parents. I met them at church."

"A church service that you crashed."

"How can someone crash a church service? Isn't the point that it's open to anyone?"

"But were you invited? Did Ethan ask you to attend with him that day?"

Andrea! The sound from her mouthpiece was set too loud. She reached for it and called, "Monica! It's still too loud. Can we not turn it down?"

A woman approached and disconnected Andrea from her microphone and earpiece. "We're going to need to reset. Let's take five, everyone!"

Andrea continued to bicker with the woman about how the technical difficulties were stepping on the flow of the interview. Monica apologized and they speculated on what might be causing the problem. Andrea then apologized for snapping.

While they went back and forth, Gabbi slipped away from the scene. She walked toward a mirror that someone had erected and placed clamp lights on the end of. She stood in front of the mirror and checked her reflection. She checked her angles, futzed with a blemish, then centered herself, took a deep breath and said to her reflection, "I swear, I did not kill Ethan … I swear … swear … SWEAR … no, too much. I swear, I did not kill my fiancé … can't say fiancé without a ring. It will make you sound crazy. Ethan. I did not say Ethan. Say his name so they know you haven't dehumanized him. Ethan, Ethan, Ethan. I did not kill Ethan."

She buzzed her lips and placed her hands to the sides of her face and tugged her skin back, a child's attempt at a temporary face lift. "I did NOT kill Ethan. That's better. I did NOT kill Ethan."

The makeup person approached, "I'm going to give you a little touch up."

Gabbi sat back in the chair with her hands on her lap. "Can you give me a little eyeliner wing?"

"They don't like it when I do that. I can only take the shine off your face so it doesn't interfere with the lighting."

"I like yours. What kind do you use? Is it Makeup Forever?"

This was the footage that all the news outlets fell in love with. All of her efforts to make the interview look like she was not in prison, yet here she is in her striped pants, practicing what she's going to say and asking someone to make her eyes more prominent.

The TV news commentators mocked her. Influencers on social media remixed her old videos. Teens and true crime junkies filmed reaction videos to the footage.

JENNA

Once Gabbi was arrested, it was like she was everywhere. She was interviewed from jail. There was even footage of her before it began, showing the tech how she wanted her eyes lined. Because when you're being accused of murdering your boyfriend, it's essential to make sure your eyeliner wings are sharp. And somehow Gabbi made prison pants and thermals look chic. I wondered if she found a clip to pin the back together like the girls on *America's Next Top Model*.

I watched it, her pleading about how she was being framed, and how she and Ethan were soul mates and were planning to be married.

She killed him. Maybe it was for the money. But why didn't she just run off with it?

And then, she kept calling me. My screen would light up with a number I didn't recognize, and then I'd get a voicemail that informed me that I was getting a collect call from an inmate at the Newburn County Jail.

I hadn't told anyone about the money. I wasn't even sure why. I knew I should tell the cops, right? Didn't it make Gabbi look more guilty? I didn't tell Ross either.

But I kept thinking about the money. All that money out there.

When I made coffee in the mornings, the pop and hiss of my Keurig would get me thinking about the money.

On the way to work, if I saw signs for Land Between the Lakes, I would think about the money buried in the dirt. And also think that I hoped to God that some rando wouldn't find it.

I'd even think about the money when I was standing by my microwave heating up leftover lo mein. Although, me and takeout had been on a break. I'd been reading about how protein helps build muscle, and that's what I wanted.

Gabbi was right. I wanted to be strong.

I wanted to be able to knock someone on their ass if they stepped to me.

I'd become that bitch who takes up all the room in front of the grocery store cold case, reading the nutrition labels on all the yogurts, which is where Hillary found me.

"Jenna? Oh my, you look so different."

I gave her a hug. "Different good?"

"Yes. I was just surprised. Did you get taller? You look taller."

We shopped together—pushing our mini carts through the store, pointing out BOGO offers, talking about our jobs and, eventually, Ethan.

Once the door was open to talking about Ethan, I fell back into my old habits of shit-talking Gabbi.

"I guess you saw her interview," Hillary said.

"I couldn't miss it," I said. "Three different people texted me the link. Ross told me not to watch it, but it was unavoidable."

"I would just ignore it and ignore everyone who's out stirring up a bunch of stuff."

"Stirring up what? I mean, what else?"

Hillary sighed, like she realized that she'd messed up. "You haven't seen any of the comments."

"Like on social media? I deleted a bunch of those apps." After I'd received the message to stop posting Ethan memorials, I'd been avoiding all social media.

"For the best. People are … you know … people."

We'd made our way to the self-check register and took turns at the same machine. I botched the scan and had to flag down an attendant to correct my mistake. "So what are they saying?"

"I wouldn't worry about it."

"Tell me."

"Well," she fiddled with the items in her reusable shopper. "Ethan didn't have the best reputation, and some people are taking this as an opportunity to talk about it."

"What about his reputation?" We pushed our carts out into the parking lot, and unloaded my things into my truck.

Hillary suggested we drive to Sonic together to talk.

"We can't. I got a truck full of yogurt now!"

"Fine," she said. "You know everything that happened at UK that got him kicked out. I think you need to ignore it and remember the Ethan that you knew."

"Why do people want to tarnish his memory?"

"I don't know. I guess people need to dissect things. It's not like any of it is new information."

It was late in the evening and the parking lot was mostly empty. My face was hot despite the crisp air. "That doesn't mean people need to keep digging."

"He did tell you the reason he was kicked out of UK, right?" Hillary asked, as if maybe Ethan had fudged the facts. "About the investigation over what happened? The judge who wrote a character letter on his behalf that almost literally said, 'Boys will be boys'?"

"That was his fraternity brothers. He was kicked out for selling drugs."

"Which also isn't great, Jenna!"

"Hillary. Where is your loyalty? Why aren't you sticking up for him? You were his friend."

"No, Jenna," she said. "We knew each other. We weren't friends."

None of anything she was saying made sense. Everyone loved Ethan.

"I'm not arrogant enough to say that I knew everything about him. What happened at UK was bad, and I know his family wanted to keep it all hushed up. And maybe he learned something from it. Maybe he asked to be forgiven. I don't think it's helpful to dwell on any of these things."

"Hillary, you were going out with Ethan, and now—"

"I was going to sit next to him at a wedding. That was all. I never got the impression that he was interested in me in a real way."

"Why would you agree to go if you didn't want to?"

She took me by the hand and said, "Because you're my friend and you asked me to."

"You did all that for me?"

"Of course."

And this almost knocked me back. As weird as it sounds, it was like this little voice inside was saying, *You mean you actually like me?* I just always assumed the only reason anyone liked me was because I knew Ethan. And here Hillary was, loving me for just who I was, to the point of putting up with a guy that she didn't really like that much. "I have to go."

"Okay," Hillary said. "Can I give you a hug before you go?"

I nodded. I might have cried a little on her cardigan. "Damn it, Hillary. You're out here being amazing and making the rest of us look like assholes."

I left Kroger and went home. I unpacked all my yogurt and other deals. Nothing made sense to me. It was like I knew Ethan, but didn't know him at all.

A couple of nights later, I came home from the gym feeling enthusiastic. Amanda had taken me through several leg-strengthening exercises, and when I had complained that I didn't want to punch with my legs, she said, "You want that punch to come from your full body, girl. Never skip leg day."

"You're a sadist."

"You love it."

I did. I never thought I'd ever say this, but, it was fun.

I had texted Ross before I left the gym, but he never responded. I called him when I put the key in the door. I preferred to be on the phone when I walked into my place alone, so that, in case someone was waiting to ambush me on the other side, someone would hear it and call the cops. You know, like when Gabbi had.

When Ross answered the phone, I asked, "Hey. Why aren't you here already?" but I could hear him speaking while I spoke, "Oh … I lost track of time."

"Okay. I'm going to hop in the shower, or should I wait for you to join me?"

"I can't come over."

"Seriously? I've barely seen you all week." I walked to my kitchen and refilled my water bottle from my Brita pitcher in the fridge.

"I've just been occupied with these projects I've been working on."

"That's great. I'm glad you've got all this new business coming in."

"It's not new … it's just—" he cut himself off. "Why don't you come over here?"

"Your neighbors creep me out."

"For God's sake, Jenna, they're not drug dealers."

Ross lived in a duplex, and I didn't care what he said, his neighbors were sketchy. "People are in and out of that place day and night. No one ever stays long."

The thing about living in a college town is you can keep living in your college apartment much longer than is appropriate. Ross moved in there after he and Ethan lived together, and the place just kind of stuck. It wasn't always a problem, because he was usually with me.

"I can't come over there," he said. "I'm working late. You can come over, and we can have sex, and I'll keep working after you go to sleep."

"Wow." He didn't talk like that. "What's going on? This isn't you."

"Nothing's wrong. I'm just working."

"And I don't work?"

"Yeah. You run your route and that's enough for you because I'm not asking you to buy the Hope-freaking-Diamond before I'll marry you."

"You don't talk to me like that, Ross. That's not what we do. And I never asked for the Hope Diamond."

"Did you or did you not send me the link to the Tiffany's website with a two carat ring?"

"That was just for the shape!" I wasn't going to turn down a two carat diamond from Tiffany's. "And I don't want to fight. I miss you. I want to see you. I'll come to you. Damn. Let me pack a bag."

"Fine." He hung up and I was left with my phone in my hand wondering what the hell his problem was.

And then I was stumped. I had never once packed a bag to stay with a boyfriend. What would I even need? I grabbed an old travel bag, a duffle that had a toiletry bag with some tiny Bath and Body Works bottles in it. I opened one, wondering when was the last time I had used anything with a peony smell. I sniffed it and wondered if I even liked that smell anymore.

I grabbed some pajamas and some underwear and threw them in the bag. This was work. It was 100 times easier for him to come here. And how did girls who get around do it? Did they just keep a bag in their car? Did Gabbi pack a bag every time she snuck down here to hook up with Ethan? It had never occurred to me before how the logistics worked. And apparently, she was staying with him every weekend. Well, that's what she said. She was a liar. I couldn't believe anything she said anyway.

But the money wasn't a lie. I saw the money. I touched the money. It was just out there with no one claiming it now. Unless Gabbi had told someone else.

If what she had said was true, and she didn't kill Ethan, then someone else did. And they might be looking for that money.

I should tell Ross. Or the cops. Whose money was it now? Out there resting in the field was a bag of untraceable and spendable cash. I liked cash.

I drove to Ross's, thinking how easy it would be to drive out to the spot where Gabbi had buried the cash and start digging.

When I got to Ross's place, he walked outside in his pajama pants and T-shirt. He had his "thinking robe" on, the one he wore when he was working because he got cold so often. He once had a "thinking hoodie," but I hadn't seen it in a while. He pulled me into a hug. I kissed him and allowed him to carry my bag inside where I flopped on his couch.

"I thought you needed to shower."

"In a minute. Do you want to show me what you're working on?"

He sat on the edge of the chair next to the couch, like he was placating me until I took my shower or gave up on him and walked out. I sat up and sat on the edge of the couch to mirror his energy. I sat up tall so my boobs were thrust out. I felt powerful and sexy. But instead of taking me by the hand, he rubbed his face with his hands.

"I'm not working on a project, I'm applying for jobs."

"Okay, I'm going to get—Wait, what? What are you doing?"

"I'm applying for jobs. I'm looking for a position for a designer at a marketing firm."

"But then you won't be your own boss."

"I know."

"I thought that was the problem with your last job. You wanted the freedom to call your own shots."

"It's incredibly hard to be your own boss, Jenna. You don't know. You work for a company. You get your leads from them."

"Yeah, because I wasn't like you and Ethan, preaching about entrepreneurship and mobile offices and digital nomadism."

"It's more than I can take on. If we're going to get married, I need something more steady."

"Okay, well let's get you some more contracts. We can sign clients up for annual programs. Longer terms. Raise your rates. I can help you work on your bids."

"I'm broke, Jenna. I'm flat broke, and I'm going to have a

nervous breakdown if I have to send out another solicitation email or make another cold call. I can't do it."

"Okay." I reached out and took his hands in mine, his so cold while mine were so warm. My blood was still surging from my workout. "I don't want you to have a nervous breakdown. It'll be okay. And I can always help. You can cut expenses on this apartment if you move in with me."

Honestly, I wasn't really surprised, because I had never gotten into Ethan's whole entrepreneurship nonsense. I wanted to know I had insurance, a steady check, co-workers, and directives. "Where are you applying? Maybe I can help."

"There's a place out in Dearborn who scheduled a virtual interview with me next week, but I'm applying everywhere, really."

"Deer Born." I fumbled over what backwater Kentucky town was named Deer Born, when it hit me. "You mean Michigan!"

He nodded.

"Are you freaking kidding me?"

"It's a good job."

"I don't want to go to Dearborn. I don't want to move to Dearborn. I don't want to tell people where I live by pointing at my mitten-shaped hand!" I held up my palm and dug into a spot with my index finger.

"They want me, Jenna," he said. "I can't ignore that. Right now I'm saying yes to everything."

"But you never said anything. You never mentioned you were even thinking about this."

"I didn't want to say anything until I knew I was sure."

"Like after they offered you the job."

He sat there. Passively. Meekly. Like it was all out of his control. I took a deep breath and exhaled, loudly.

"Is it at all possible that maybe you're doing something rash because you're grieving your best friend who just died?"

"No."

His voice was so sharp, so clear, so empty. First Hillary and now Ross. Gabbi was right. We were the only two who really loved Ethan. I couldn't accept that. "Give it a minute's thought."

"Ethan was not my best friend. He was your best friend. He was some guy I once roomed with in college, and if it hadn't been for you, he and I would have lost touch years ago."

He stood and took a step to the hallway. I guess we were done talking about it. "Are you staying?"

"No. I'm not staying." I was floored. I'd never heard him speak that way. It was so cold. Like Ethan had been nothing to him. I stormed from the duplex. One of the neighbors shouted from inside their place, "Keep it down!"

I pulled out of the driveway so quickly, I almost backed into the neighbor's friends, who had pulled in for what I could only assume was another drug purchase.

I just drove. I wasn't sure where I was going. I was just mad. I wanted to go back to the gym, but I knew Amanda was home by now. And I thought about calling her, but how do you explain to a new friend that your boyfriend just told you that your best friend who died was not his friend? And your boyfriend is taking a job in another city without talking to you about it first? Is this what girlfriends confide in each other? Wouldn't she be terrified that I was oversharing? Should I call Hillary?

I wanted to talk to Ethan. But he was gone.

The one time I would have answered one of Gabbi's jail calls and my phone was silent.

Before I knew it, I was barreling down 94 looking for the spot Gabbi took me to that night.

I was going to get that money. If that's what the problem was, if money was the reason Ross needed to leave, then I would get him some money. This was ridiculous. It had been Ethan's, and from what I could tell, I was the only one who really loved him. That money was going to be mine.

Ross wasn't my partner. I wasn't the one he turned to when he was in trouble. If he had told me about the money, I would have helped him. I could have supported him. But he shut me out. Ross shut me out. Ethan shut me out.

This was going to be my money. I would hide it until I knew what I wanted to do with it.

I found the pull-off where Gabbi had taken me. I took the flashlight from my glove box and the tire iron from the back. I followed the path to the gnarled tree. I spotted the stump. I set down the flashlight to illuminate where I dug as best as I could with the tire iron. I dug and dug, but nothing was there. I was sweaty and dirty. But no money. I found one of the bill wrappers, dirty and faded from its burial. It was gone.

The money was gone.

Lindy wasn't satisfied with the case. Something about it was off. She'd already been assigned new cases, but the Moll murder still bothered her. It nagged at her.

She came home from work and spotted April and Jeff were sitting on the back steps. It was cold outside, but Kentucky cold, so it was in the 50s. The sun was shining on a patch of grass in the backyard. April had assembled a blanket and toys for Ella who was dressed in a hat, coat, and little baby shoes. She played with her toys while the adults chatted.

Lindy asked, "Why are y'all outside?"

"Ella needs the Vitamin D."

Lindy stepped down around them onto the grass. Ella, seeing her, toddled her way. Lindy scooped her up, causing the baby to squeal with delight. She then placed her back on the ground on her feet. Ella made her way over to Jeff, who patted her on the head, but drew his attention right back to April, who was telling them about an article she read about kids lacking Vitamin D.

Lindy asked, "Jeff. How's your family?"

"Good. They're good." he said. "They really like the idea of me moving back home."

"Me, too." April said. "You can be here for all Ella's holidays. You can come over for Halloween and Christmas morning. We can do a huge Thanksgiving."

"Sure," Jeff said. "We could do it all."

There had been times when Lindy would have loved to have hauled Jeff into an interrogation room and hooked him up to a polygraph machine, but at that moment she didn't need it. He would tell April whatever she wanted to hear as long as she kept talking to him. Ella was the price of admission to keep April in his life.

"Your parents would be welcome, too," Lindy said.

"Right. I'll let them know."

"Maybe we can bring it up when we all get together this week," April suggested.

"I don't think we need to nail down next Thanksgiving's plans already, April."

"You know, Jeff," Lindy suggested. "We planned to put up a playset when it warms up. One of those big ones from Sam's Club with the slide and everything. I'm going to need help putting that together. You can come over and give me a hand."

"We'll see. I would need tools and work boots or something, right?"

"You can wear mine!" April said.

"Shut up!" he pushed her foot from the step. April laughed and told Lindy a story she'd already heard about how, when April and Jeff dated, she wore a pair of Jeff's shoes for a Halloween costume and they fit so well, she would steal his shoes everyday, just to annoy him.

"Look," he defended. "I don't have small feet. You have large feet."

Except April didn't have large feet. She had average-sized feet.

Lindy asked, "You wear a seven, right?"

"I like to think I wear a 40 in European sizes," he said.

"I bet y'all shared all kinds of clothes." Lindy proposed. "If y'all were the same size."

"We weren't the same size," he said.

April said, "I'm a little shorter than him. I couldn't wear his jeans or anything."

"But y'all shared sweatshirts, right?"

"Everyone shares sweatshirts," Jeff said.

Under a hood from behind, Gabbi might could be mistaken for a man. A short man. A short man who styled his hair to make him look taller next to an incredibly tall girlfriend.

"I'll be right back," Lindy said. She pulled out her phone and excused herself. Ella had climbed the steps and called for her in baby language.

Lindy pulled out her phone and disappeared around the corner. She called Boggs, "Hey. I have a new theory." Outside she could hear April trying to distract Ella, who had now worked her way to the porch and slapped her hand against the glass. "Can you meet me back at the house?"

At the station, Lindy and Boggs sifted through the social media posts from the night of Ethan's murder. She then went back and studied all of Ross's posts of the band from that night. Jenna had complained to them that every show was exactly the same: the same songs, the same moves, the same poses.

However, from looking at the photos, it seemed one of the band members wore a different scarf over his deep V. It was a slight alteration that one would only be able to see if they looked at all the images the fans posted that night as well. The red scarf was now purple.

Lindy and Boggs dug around on the back end and found the date the photo from that night was originally taken, and then found where it had originally been posted a year before. The data showed that Ross had set the photos to post several hours before the show even started.

He had latergrammed his alibi.

Boggs cursed, "We gotta go back and talk to Captain America."

"We don't have a warrant."

"We have to get one."

After multiple phone calls and annoying many judges, they finally pinned one down outside the ladies' room of the courthouse.

"Y'all know how improper this is."

Boggs said, "We admit that it's tacky, but that's the level of desperation we are at this afternoon, ma'am."

"Follow me to my chambers."

With the warrant fresh in their hand, they were finally able to get the neighbor to release the surveillance video from that night.

At the station, they watched the video. Captain America's system was good. Even through the sleeting rain at night, they were getting a full color video. A hooded figure entered Ethan's back door. The light on the back porch showed that the figure wore a bright blue hoodie, black pants, white sneakers. Then twenty minutes later, they saw Gabbi. Her bright blue hoodie slipped off her head as she sprinted through the freezing rain to his back door. She was smiling and smoothed her hair down, sweeping it over her shoulder, before sliding the door open.

Soon after, the hooded figure ran out, the blue hoodie now

splotched with blood. Later, Gabbi also ran out the back door, bloodstains on her camisole and yoga pants.

"She's not wearing a hoodie."

"How did a bloody hoodie end up in her closet when she wasn't even wearing one when she left?"

Lindy stood up and started digging around on her desk and picked up a stapled printout of a spreadsheet. "Because we have it! Look!"

She tossed the papers over to Boggs, who scanned the spreadsheet down to line 28—one blue, hooded sweatshirt on the couch.

"She said she walked into the house, took off her hoodie," Lindy said.

"And we have her hoodie, so that means someone planted a hoodie in her closet for us to find."

"We can test the hoodies for Ross's DNA," Lindy said. "I saved a soda can he drank out of when he came in with Jenna."

They marched into evidence and located the items they'd retrieved from the victim's home. They located the hoodie in its bag; it was clean. Through the evidence bag, Boggs flipped the label over and showed Lindy the GE initials written in sharpie pen.

He said, "She lives her life at the gym; it's like camp, you have to write your name on everything."

Lindy said, "We are so about to get cussed over this."

"Come on. Let's go get him."

They picked up Ross at his house. He lived in a duplex off 12th Street. When he opened the door, he was wearing pajama pants, a T-shirt, and a hoodie that looked brand new. He didn't have any product in his hair. He was holding a bowl of cereal in his hand.

"Detectives?"

"We'd like for you to ride with us. We have a few more questions."

"Can I stop by later? I just got up and need to shower."

"No. We need you to come now." Lindy handed him a folded piece of paper. "We also have a warrant to search the premises."

"A warrant?"

"Yes. This warrant states we can look inside your home, in your garage, and in your vehicle. We're also seizing your devices."

When someone knows they're busted, they have a few tells. Career criminals are stone-faced liars. It's not what the cops know, but what they can prove. They will deny all the way through the trial and the conviction, and then after. But civilians, the ones who've probably never done anything before, those are the ones who give up. Because they can see the inevitable, can see that the cops have figured it out. The pale face, the darting eyes—it's like all the moisture is depleted from their skin, and their eyes turn inward, like they're searching their brains for the moment they messed up and if there's a possible escape from the situation.

Lindy gently took the bowl from his hand while Boggs walked him to the car.

A crew of uniformed officers had already surrounded the house, waiting for her to serve the warrant. Lindy walked the bowl to the sink in the kitchen and looked out the back window to the officers opening a shed in the backyard. She took out her phone and called Jenna.

JENNA

Detective D'Arnaud is the one who told me. She'd called me and asked me to come to the police station. It was weird. When I followed Detective D'Arnaud down the hall, my new heels clicked on the linoleum.

"Can we get you a coffee or something?"

"No," I said. "I'm fine, thank you."

"You look good." Detective D'Arnaud opened the door and moved back to allow me to enter.

"Oh." I'd tried out one of my new ensembles that day. I'd tucked a silky blouse into a pair of slacks and adorned it with a chunky belt with a huge gold buckle. Everything I had on was new, purchased at a store I normally walked past. It was a store for tough girls, sexy girls, or ball-busters. I thanked the detective. "I joined a new gym—"

But I stopped talking because I realized I was in a strange room. It was darker and missing the usual table and chairs.

I realized I was standing on the other side of the mirror of an interrogation room. And through the frame, I saw Ross. He looked worn, like he hadn't slept in days. Since the last time I'd spoken with him, when we'd fought about Dearborn. He hadn't responded to my text messages, and for the first time since we got together, I let him ignore me.

Under the harsh lights of the interrogation room, he looked hollow and sick. He was gnawing on his nails.

Detective D'Arnaud said, "Did you have any reason to think Ross and Ethan were mad at each other about anything?"

"No. Why?"

"We've just arrested Ross in connection with Ethan's murder."

I felt my tote bag slip from my arm and hit the ground. "No. That's not right. Gabbi killed Ethan."

"Ross confessed," she said. "He snuck out of his brother's show and drove back to Pleasant Springs. He snuck into Ethan's house and confronted him."

"No. No. That's wrong. You're wrong." I reached down and snatched up the handle of my bag. I stepped toward the door, but Detective D'Arnaud blocked the door from me.

"Jenna, you can't speak to him right now."

I stepped back. I felt like a trapped animal. I turned back and looked through the mirror at Ross again. Detective D'Arnaud stepped closer, and I bristled at her like a pissed-off cat. I might have even hissed.

She backed off. "Did he give any clues or indication that he did this?"

"No. This is ridiculous...Ross didn't—" When they'd fought, he'd said, *Ethan was someone I lived with in college, and if it hadn't been for you we would have lost touch years ago.* "We were with his brother in Tillman that night. He had an alibi. His Instagram proves it."

"It was a fabricated alibi. He set up the posts in advance from old pictures of the band. We also tracked his cell phone and it pinged on the towers by Ethan's house."

"But the blood. The blood on Gabbi's hoodie."

"Gabbi left her hoodie at Ethan's. It didn't have blood on it. The hoodie we found at her residence was Ross's."

That's why Gabbi had asked why my truck was on her street that day. Ross had taken my truck that day and then dropped it off without a word.

"No. None of that's right. Y'all are bad cops. You don't know how to do anything." On the other side of the glass, Ross looked up. Detective Boggs entered the frame along with a man in a suit who sat next to Ross and whispered in his ear. Detective Boggs slid a piece of paper across the table and Ross signed it.

Detective D'Arnaud asked, "Did you know that Ross bought a membership to Ethan's company?"

"I think so. Yeah. Maybe. I think I heard them talking about it."

"The membership program was a pyramid scheme. When he brought Ross in, Ross invested all his money."

The money in the bag. Ross couldn't have invested that much.

"It was all a scam, and he never recouped any of the money he'd invested. Ross was mad because he couldn't buy you a ring because Ethan blew all the money."

Who cared about a ring? I felt like some greedy little bitch for bringing that ring up over and over again. I was a spoiled princess, just like the rest of them. I could just vomit.

Detective D'Arnaud stood next to me, watching through the window with me. I got the feeling she wanted to reach out and touch me on the arm or something, but didn't. I was glad for that.

Detective D'Arnaud explained, "Ross was freelancing in a small town, and Ethan promised him that this network would get him more clients, but it never happened because it wasn't a real network. It was just a bunch of guys laundering money through the casino. It would have taken years for Ross to have worked his way up to recoup his initial investment."

"So he stabbed him? How does anyone make that leap? He was always so peaceful and nonviolent. He won't even kill the ants in his apartment."

"He told us," Detective D'Arnaud said, "that the knife was already in the room. They were arguing over the money, and he said he grabbed it off the bedside table and charged him. He said he was angry, and Ethan was always greedy, just taking anything he wanted. We think he could have been motivated to eliminate the competition for your affection."

"There was never any competition," I said. "No one ever believed me."

It always came down to that. Like when my mother told me that even sister wives get jealous, no one could understand that, for me, it wasn't about choosing, it was about having them both in my life for different purposes. They were my team. I thought Ross understood that. "Can I see him now? Now that he's signed your confession."

Detective D'Arnaud left and entered the room on the other side of the glass. Through the speaker Jenna could hear her tell him, "Ross, Jenna's here."

"No." He wiped his face with his T-shirt. "I can't. I've ruined everything. I can't—"

Detective D'Arnaud looked back through the mirror. He followed her gaze. "Jenna!" he shouted. "Jenna!" his voice broke almost to a blubber. "I'm sorry! I'm sorry. I'm...I'm sorry."

I had to get out of there. My heel wobbled when I made that first lunge to exit the room. I steadied myself, stood tall, and stomped out the door: through the bullpen, out the door, only to run into Ross's family waiting outside.

It was Ross's mother, father, and brother outside. The father was smoking, or it seemed that way. It had grown dark outside and everyone's breath made plumes of mist from their lips as they spoke. Everyone had on heavy coats and a few wore toboggans on their heads. They turned to me and asked, "What's happening, Jenna?"

I walked directly to his brother and got in his face. "What did you do?"

"I didn't do anything!'"

"But you knew?" I shoved him, hoping to knock him right on his ass, but he was just thrown backwards a little. "You knew this whole time!"

"I didn't know what he was going to do! I thought he was going to knock the snot out of him. I never thought he'd kill him."

I growled, "Idiots!" and stormed away. Ross's mother called after me, but I didn't look back. I couldn't look back.

I finally broke down when I reached the parking lot of my apartment. I howled and bawled, gripping the steering wheel and slapping my palm against it. Eventually, I heard a tap on my window. It was my neighbor. He asked, "Are you okay?"

"No," I was still screaming, crying. "My boyfriend killed my best friend!"

CHAPTER 15

NINETY-FIVE DAYS AFTER THE MURDER

The day Ned Rockford was arrested was probably the greatest day of Rouse's life. Boggs and Lindy rode out to see the bust, but hung back while Rouse made the approach to the house. Boggs packed a thermos of Jack Daniels-blend coffee to commemorate the occasion.

Many were probably hoping to have him outside in his boxers or robe—something humiliating—but in smooth, Rockford fashion, he was ready for them in a golf polo and pressed slacks. He opened the door, turned to be cuffed, and allowed himself to be escorted out. He only said, "My attorney will meet us at the station."

Back at the house, sitting in Delphrain's office, Boggs asked, "Do you think Rockford will ever feel responsible for that kid's death?"

"Nah," Delphrain said. "That kid roped in his friend who killed him out of jealousy. That's how Rockford will justify it."

Lindy asked, "Won't the FBI just come in and swoop it up because it was across state lines?"

"Probably. But Rouse got his perp walk. He's been dying to nail Rockford for years."

Lindy passed her phone over to Delphrain so he could see the screen. They'd taken photos of Rouse placing his hand on Rockford's head and guiding him into the patrol car. Earlier Boggs had shown Lindy how to crop the image and put a dramatic filter on it. Rouse was stern but at the corners of his mouth, a self-satisfied smile struggled to break free.

Lindy asked, "Should I send this to Rouse so he can make sure it goes in the file? You know, for his notes."

"That's so tacky," Delphrain said, passing the phone back to her. "So, yes. Obviously."

CHAPTER 16

105 DAYS AFTER THE MURDER

April wasn't supposed to be home, but her car was in the drive when Lindy pulled in. April should have been with Jeff at the Tankersley home, a tea for the family to meet Ella. Perhaps Jeff drove them all. For all Lindy knew, he could have a car seat in the back of his bougie Range Rover.

Lindy keyed into the house and heard the ting of the unarmed security system. Ella was on the floor slapping together wooden puzzle pieces. She made little blubbery toddler sounds as she worked. She was wearing a frilly, red dress, with little white hearts printed on it. Drool accumulated on the front, making the red look darker. April was lying on the couch near her, wearing sweats. The TV in the background played an old Thanksgiving episode of *Friends*. The one with Brad Pitt.

Lindy armed the system back and stripped out of her gear, locking her service revolver in the gun safe. Normally, she would have showered, but instead she joined April on the couch.

"What are y'all doing here?" Lindy lifted April's legs into her lap.

"Jeff canceled."

"Oh. Did he say why?"

"He was vague about it. Said he needed to go alone and now wasn't the right time to present Ella to his parents. Something about easing them into the idea." April wouldn't look at Lindy, just kept her eyes in the direction of Ella and the TV.

"Okay," Lindy said. "It sounds like she'll just meet them later."

"Not if I have anything to say about it."

Lindy had never heard April ever say anything hateful, but right now she sounded absolutely spiteful. Lindy said, "I'm the last person to defend Jeff—"

"No. You were right. You're always right. If they had really wanted to know Ella, to meet her, they would have come to me. I'm not some stranger. My parents and I have gone to their Christmas parties every year. I have sat with them at church. And since Ella has been alive, they've treated me and her like we were invisible. They have a grandchild that they are actively ignoring, which makes them non-grandparents. They're nobodies."

"Come here." Lindy readjusted April like some doll so she was now resting her head in Lindy's lap. She reached down and stroked her hair.

April said, "We don't need them."

"We don't."

"We are enough."

"This is what I've been saying."

Ella brought herself to her feet and toddled over to them. She slapped her tiny hands against April's belly and cackled, like she knew she used to live there. April scooped her into a big hug.

Lindy suggested, "Let's take a photo."

"No. I'm all puffy faced and—"

"Stop it. You know you're so pretty." Lindy pulled her phone from her pocket. "And we're going to take a photo of our family."

They all gathered on the couch and placed their heads together. Ella tugged on the collar of Lindy's shirt and April smoothed the flyaways on Ella's head.

Later, Lindy asked April to print a copy of the photo for her. She stopped by Kohls and picked up a rustic wooden frame for it. It sits on her desk at work, and when anyone says, "That's a nice photo." she tells them, "I know. It's my family."

JENNA

The last I heard from Gabbi?

She actually called me. I was surprised.

I was changing into a pair of leggings and a sports bra to head to the gym when she called. I'd joined a women's boxing group with my new friend Amanda. She'd been sparring with me and teaching me how to braid my hair so it won't get in my face when I get all sweaty. I like how I look now—strong. I changed everything after Ross's arrest: my clothes, my friends, my job. All that remained the same was my house. I'd thought about moving away, but I've been through people looking at me before and I know it will pass.

Punching things helps.

I didn't recognize the number, but my phone suggested it "might" be Gabbi Edwards. I considered letting it go to voicemail. I watched it ring while placing things in my duffle bag: my gloves, my towel, another set of clothes to wear out, a bag of toiletries. The phone kept ringing; I got curious.

"What?"

"The way you answer the phone is reflective of your energy," Gabbi said. "You're in sales. You should know that."

"What do you want, Gabbi?"

She paused. It sounded like she was sipping something through a straw. "Did you see me on the *Today* show?"

"No," I lied. The clip appeared on my feed. I had watched Gabbi help one of the B-squad hosts of the show onto a pilates machine. Gabbi was endorsing it. It even had her name on it. The host, probably for comedic relief, climbed onto the device in his suit and sock feet. In typical Gabbi fashion, she played to the audience, "Ladies, look at what it's already doing for his glutes!"

"Jenna, why do you lie?" Gabbi said. "My publicist reported to me that most of my returning viewers came from western Kentucky, so I know someone showed it to you."

"It's a big region. I'm not the only one who lives here." I had carried my gym bag to the living room. The TV was still on from earlier. I'd left it on Bravo because they were running *Real Housewives of Beverly Hills* episodes one after another. It was the one where they were having dinner in Amsterdam and Kim was drunk or high or something. I told Gabbi, "I guess being falsely accused makes someone popular."

"According to my publicist, if we play this right, I could become a full-fledged lifestyle brand. I am more than just my tragedy, you know. She's getting someone to ghostwrite a book for me!"

"Right," Jenna said. Gabbi had parlayed her tragedy into a multi-tiered brand. She called her brand *Pretty is as Pretty Does*, and had proceeded to monetize the fuck out of it: website, newsletter, Youtube channel, online chat spaces, fitness and life coaching. I was waiting to hear she was about to launch an app. "I guess the Ethan money is helping pay for that."

She giggled. "Ethan money. I don't know what you're talking about. You're so funny, Jenna."

"I need to go, Gabbi."

"Wait. No. Don't hang up. I called ... I jus t..." she cleared her throat. "No one else gets it. No one else knew him. Not like we did. He would have been so proud of all this. He would have loved this!"

"I can't say. Turns out I didn't know him at all," I said. I felt compelled to hang up on her then, like, that would have been a great exit line before *click*. But I kept talking. "I mean, that's why you really called, right? To rub it in. So you can feel superior."

"Honey, if I wanted to feel superior to people, I'd go online and see what my high school friends are doing," she said. "And you did know him. Of his two personalities, you knew the other one best. Can we stop competing and just acknowledge that? I think it would be good for both of our spirit work."

I wondered if she could hear my eye roll on the other end of the phone. "I gotta go, Gabbi."

"Okay, but can I at least add you to my *Pretty Is* membership group? You might get some benefit from it."

"I'm not concerned with what pretty is anymore," and I hung up. I needed to hit something.

You know, Gabbi's always in my feed, and at this point I can kind of see what she was saying. I did know at least one side of Ethan. And she got the other, like some weird timeshare situation, where one week it's family-friendly and the next is hedonism. I just wish he'd realized I could have handled that other side of him. I could have loved him anyway.

After I got off the phone with Gabbi that day, I left to meet my friend. I walked toward my car, but I stopped when I spotted a tiny vodka bottle in my yard. Since all the fraternities were relocated, it seemed they were walking past my house now for their events, leaving me to clean up empties. Occasionally I found a bra or a shoe. I must have missed one that morning. I crouched down to pick up the tiny, empty plastic bottle and when I stood, I saw a Crown Vic was driving down my street. It looked like Detective D'Arnaud was behind the wheel. She raised her hand to wave and I stood to my full height and waved back.

I suspect the detective sees a different person when she looks at me now.

ACKNOWLEDGMENTS

This novel would not have been possible if not for the support of my team.

Thank you to Jody Gerbig for her story guidance. Thank you to Madelyn Fox-Defago for her amazing copyediting skills. And thank you to Greg Stark for his awesome cover designs.

But thanks most of all to my husband Christopher Bradley, my first reader, my support system, and the person who reminds me to stay hydrated and get some rest.

ABOUT THE AUTHOR

Brandi Bradley is an emerging author in the southern crime and mystery genre. She writes short stories and novels about crime, family drama, flea markets, cowboys, rowdy girls, and gossip.

This is Brandi Bradley's second book.

Brandi Bradley's essays and short stories have been published in *Juked*, *Louisiana Literature*, *Carve*, and *Nashville Review*.

Visit brandibradley.com for information regarding upcoming projects.